# Ford County

Also by John Grisham

A Time to Kill
The Firm
The Pelican Brief
The Client
The Chamber
The Rainmaker
The Runaway Jury
The Partner
The Street Lawyer
The Testament
The Brethren
A Painted House
Skipping Christmas
The Summons
The King of Torts
Bleachers
The Last Juror
The Broker
The Innocent Man
Playing for Pizza
The Appeal
The Associate

# Ford County

*Stories*

## John Grisham

DOUBLEDAY
New York · London · Toronto · Sydney · Auckland

**DD**
DOUBLEDAY

All rights reserved. Published in the United States by Doubleday, a division of Random House, Inc., New York, and in Canada by Random House of Canada Limited, Toronto.

www.doubleday.com

DOUBLEDAY and the DD colophon are registered trademarks of Random House, Inc.

Book design by Maria Carella
Title page illustration by Louis Jones

Library of Congress Cataloging-in-Publication Data
Grisham, John.
Ford County : stories / John Grisham. — 1st ed.
p. cm.
1. Mississippi—Fiction.   I. Title.
PS3557.R5355F67  2009
813'.54—dc22          2009032845

ISBN 978-0-385-53245-7

PRINTED IN THE UNITED STATES OF AMERICA

1   3   5   7   9   10   8   6   4   2

First Edition

To Bobby Moak

When *A Time to Kill* was published twenty years ago,
I soon learned the painful lesson that selling books was far
more difficult than writing them. I bought a thousand
copies and had trouble giving them away. I hauled them in
the trunk of my car and peddled them at libraries, garden
clubs, grocery stores, coffee shops, and a handful
of bookstores. Often, I was assisted by my dear friend
Bobby Moak.

There are stories we will never tell.

# Contents

————•••••••••••••••••••••————

# Ford County

# Blood Drive

⊷ · · · · · · · · · · · · · · · · · · · · ⊷

By the time the news of Bailey's accident spread through the rural settlement of Box Hill, there were several versions of how it happened. Someone from the construction company called his mother and reported that he had been injured when some scaffolding collapsed at a building site in downtown Memphis, that he was undergoing surgery, was stable, and was expected to survive. His mother, an invalid who weighed over four hundred pounds and was known to be excitable, missed some of the facts as she began to scream and carry on. She called friends and neighbors, and with each replaying of the tragic news various details were altered and enlarged. She neglected to write down the phone number of the person from the company, so there was no one to call to verify or discount the rumors that were multiplying by the minute.

One of Bailey's co-workers, another boy from Ford County, called his girlfriend in Box Hill and gave an account that varied somewhat: Bailey had been run over by a bulldozer, which was next to the scaffolding, and he was practically dead. The surgeons were working on him, but things were grim.

Then an administrator from a hospital in Memphis called Bailey's home, asked to speak to his mother, and was told that she was laid up in bed, too upset to talk, and unable to come to the phone. The neighbor who answered the phone pumped the administrator for details, but didn't get much. Something collapsed at a construction site, maybe a ditch in which the young man was working, or some such variation. Yes, he was in surgery, and the hospital needed basic information.

Bailey's mother's small brick home quickly became a busy place. Visitors had begun arriving by late afternoon: friends, relatives, and several pastors from the tiny churches scattered around Box Hill. The women gathered in the kitchen and den and gossiped nonstop while the phone rang constantly. The men huddled outside and smoked cigarettes. Casseroles and cakes began to appear.

With little to do, and with scant information about Bailey's injuries, the visitors seized upon every tiny fact, analyzed it, dissected it, then passed it along to the women inside, or to the men outside. A leg was mangled and would probably be amputated. There was a severe brain injury. Bailey fell four floors with the scaffolding, or maybe it was eight. His chest was crushed. A few of the facts and theories were simply created on the spot. There were even a few somber inquiries about funeral arrangements.

Bailey was nineteen years old and in his short life had never had so many friends and admirers. The entire community loved him more and more as the hours passed. He was a good boy, raised right, a much better person than his sorry father, a man no one had seen in years.

Bailey's ex-girlfriend showed up and was soon the center of attention. She was distraught and overwhelmed and cried easily, especially when talking about her beloved Bailey. However, when word filtered back to the bedroom and his mother heard the little slut was in the house, she ordered her out. The little slut then hung around with the men outside, flirting and smoking. She finally left, vowing to drive to Memphis right then and see her Bailey.

A neighbor's cousin lived in Memphis, and this cousin reluctantly agreed to go to the hospital and monitor things. His first call brought the news that the young man was indeed undergoing surgery for multiple injuries, but he appeared to be stable. He'd lost a lot of blood. In the second call, the cousin straightened out a few of the facts. He'd talked to the job foreman, and Bailey had been injured when a bulldozer struck the scaffolding, collapsing it and sending the poor boy crashing down fifteen feet into a pit of some sort. They were putting the brick on a six-story office building in Memphis, and Bailey was working as a mason's helper. The hospital would not allow visitors for at least twenty-four hours, but blood donations were needed.

A mason's helper? His mother had bragged that Bailey had been promoted rapidly through the company and was now an assistant job foreman. However, in the spirit of the moment, no one questioned her about this discrepancy.

After dark, a man in a suit appeared and explained that he was an investigator of some sort. He was passed along to an uncle, Bailey's mother's youngest brother, and in a private conversation in the backyard he handed over a business card for a lawyer in Clanton. "Best lawyer in the county," he said. "And we're already working on the case."

The uncle was impressed and promised to shun other lawyers—"just a bunch of ambulance chasers"—and to curse any insurance adjuster who came slithering onto the scene.

Eventually, there was talk of a trip to Memphis. Though it was only two hours away by car, it may as well have been five. In Box Hill, going to the big city meant driving an hour to Tupelo, population fifty thousand. Memphis was in another state, another world, and, besides, crime was rampant. The murder rate was right up there with Detroit. They watched the carnage every night on Channel 5.

Bailey's mother was growing more incapacitated by the moment and was clearly unable to travel, let alone give blood. His sister lived in Clanton, but she could not leave her children. Tomorrow was Friday, a workday, and there was a general belief that such a trip to Memphis and back, plus the blood thing, would take many hours and, well, who knew when the donors might get back to Ford County.

Another call from Memphis brought the news that the boy was out of surgery, clinging to life, and still in desperate need of blood. By the time this reached the group of men loitering out in the driveway, it sounded as though poor Bailey might die any minute unless his loved ones hustled to the hospital and opened their veins.

A hero quickly emerged. His name was Wayne Agnor, an alleged close friend of Bailey's who since birth had been known as Aggie. He ran a body shop with his father, and thus had hours flexible enough for a quick trip to Memphis. He also had his own pickup, a late-model Dodge, and he claimed to know Memphis like the back of his hand.

"I can leave right now," Aggie said proudly to the group, and word spread through the house that a trip was materializing. One of the women calmed things down when she explained that several volunteers were needed since the hospital would extract only one pint from each donor. "You can't give a gallon," she explained. Very few had actually given blood, and the thought of needles and tubes frightened many. The house and front yard became very quiet. Concerned neighbors who had been so close to Bailey just moments earlier began looking for distance.

"I'll go too," another young man finally said, and he was immediately congratulated. His name was Calvin Marr, and his hours were also flexible but for different reasons—Calvin had been laid off from the shoe factory in Clanton and was drawing unemployment. He was terrified of needles but intrigued by the romance of seeing Memphis for the first time. He would be honored to be a donor.

The idea of a fellow traveler emboldened Aggie, and he laid down the challenge. "Anybody else?"

There was mumbling in general while most of the men studied their boots.

"We'll take my truck and I'll pay for the gas," Aggie continued.

"When are we leavin'?" Calvin asked.

"Right now," said Aggie. "It's an emergency."

"That's right," someone added.

"I'll send Roger," an older gentleman offered, and this was met with silent skepticism. Roger, who wasn't present, had no job to worry about because he couldn't keep one. He had dropped out of high school and had a colorful history with alcohol and drugs. Needles certainly wouldn't intimidate him.

Though the men in general had little knowledge of transfusions, the very idea of a victim injured so gravely as to need blood from Roger was hard to imagine. "You tryin' to kill Bailey?" one of them mumbled.

"Roger'll do it," his father said with pride.

The great question was, Is he sober? Roger's battles with his demons were widely known and discussed in Box Hill. Most folks generally knew when he was off the hooch, or on it.

"He's in good shape these days," his father went on, though with a noticeable lack of conviction. But the urgency of the moment overcame all doubt, and Aggie finally said, "Where is he?"

"He's home."

Of course he was home. Roger never left home. Where would he go?

Within minutes, the ladies had put together a large box of sandwiches and other food. Aggie and Calvin were hugged and congratulated and fussed over as if they were marching off to defend the country. When they sped away, off to save Bailey's life, everyone was in the driveway, waving farewell to the brave young men.

Roger was waiting by the mailbox, and when the pickup came to a stop, he leaned through the passenger's window and said, "We gonna spend the night?"

"Ain't plannin' on it," Aggie said.

"Good."

After a discussion, it was finally agreed that Roger, who was of a slender build, would sit in the middle between Aggie and Calvin, who were much larger and thicker. They placed the box of food in his lap, and before they were a mile outside of Box Hill, Roger was unwrapping a turkey sandwich. At twenty-seven, he was the oldest of the three, but the years had not been kind. He'd been through two divorces and numerous unsuccessful efforts to rid him of his addictions. He was wiry and hyper, and as soon as he finished the first sandwich, he unwrapped the second. Aggie, at 250 pounds, and Calvin, at 270, both declined. They had been eating casseroles for the past two hours at Bailey's mother's.

The first conversation was about Bailey, a man Roger hardly knew, but both Aggie and Calvin had attended school with him. Since all three men were single, the chatter soon drifted away from their fallen neighbor and found its way to the subject of sex. Aggie had a girlfriend and claimed to be enjoying the full benefits of a good romance. Roger had slept with everything and was always on the prowl. Calvin, the shy one, was still a virgin at twenty-one, though he would never admit this. He lied about a couple of conquests, without much detail, and this kept him in the game. All three were exaggerating and all three knew it.

When they crossed into Polk County, Roger said, "Pull in up there at the Blue Dot. I need to take a leak." Aggie stopped at the pumps in front of a country store, and Roger ran inside.

"You reckon he's drinkin'?" Calvin asked as they waited.

"His daddy said he's not."

"His daddy lies, too."

Sure enough, Roger emerged minutes later with a six-pack of beer.

"Oh boy," Aggie said.

When they were situated again, the truck left the gravel lot and sped away.

Roger pulled off a can and offered it to Aggie, who declined. "No, thanks, I'm drivin'."

"You can't drink and drive?"

"Not tonight."

"How 'bout you?" he said, offering the can to Calvin.

"No, thanks."

"You boys in rehab or something?" Roger asked as he popped the top, then gulped down half the can.

"I thought you'd quit," Aggie said.

"I did. I quit all the time. Quittin's easy."

Calvin was now holding the box of food and out of boredom began munching on a large oatmeal cookie. Roger drained the first can, then handed it to Calvin and said, "Toss it, would you?"

Calvin lowered the window and flung the empty can back into the bed of the pickup. By the time he raised the window,

Roger was popping the top of another. Aggie and Calvin exchanged nervous glances.

"Can you give blood if you've been drinkin'?" Aggie asked.

"Of course you can," Roger said. "I've done it many times. You boys ever give blood?"

Aggie and Calvin reluctantly admitted that they had never done so, and this inspired Roger to describe the procedure. "They make you lay down because most people pass out. The damned needle is so big that a lot of folks faint when they see it. They tie a thick rubber cord around your bicep, then the nurse'll poke around your upper forearm looking for a big, fat blood vein. It's best to look the other way. Nine times out of ten, she'll jab the needle in and miss the vein—hurts like hell—then she'll apologize while you cuss her under your breath. If you're lucky, she'll hit the vein the second time, and when she does, the blood spurts out through a tube that runs to a little bag. Everything's clear, so you can see your own blood. It's amazing how dark it is, sort of a dark maroon color. It takes forever for a pint to flow out, and the whole time she's holdin' the needle in your vein." He chugged the beer, satisfied with his terrifying account of what awaited them.

They rode in silence for several miles.

When the second can was empty, Calvin tossed it back, and Roger popped the third top. "Beer actually helps," Roger said as he smacked his lips. "It thins the blood and makes the whole thing go faster."

It was becoming apparent that he planned to demolish the entire six-pack as quickly as possible. Aggie was thinking that it might be wise to dilute some of the alcohol. He'd heard stories of Roger's horrific binges.

"I'll take one of those," he said, and Roger quickly handed him a beer.

"Me too, I guess," Calvin said.

"Now we're talkin'," Roger said. "I never like to drink alone. That's the first sign of a true drunk."

Aggie and Calvin drank responsibly while Roger continued to gulp away. When the first six-pack was gone, he announced, with perfect timing, "I need to take a leak. Pull over up there at Cully's Barbecue." They were on the edge of the small town of New Grove, and Aggie was beginning to wonder how long the trip might take. Roger disappeared behind the store and relieved himself, then ducked inside and bought two more six-packs. When New Grove was behind them, they popped the tops and sped along a dark, narrow highway.

"Ya'll ever been to the strip clubs in Memphis?" Roger asked.

"Never been to Memphis," Calvin admitted.

"You gotta be kiddin'."

"Nope."

"How 'bout you?"

"Yeah, I've been to a strip club," Aggie said proudly.

"Which one?"

"Can't remember the name. They're all the same."

"You're wrong about that," Roger corrected him sharply, then practically gargled on another slosh of beer. "Some have these gorgeous babes with great bodies; others got regular road whores who can't dance a lick."

And this led to a long discussion of the history of legalized stripping in Memphis, or at least Roger's version of it. Back in the early days the girls could peel off everything, every stitch, then hop on your table for a pulsating, gyrating, thrusting dance to loud music and strobe lights and raucous applause from the boys. Then the laws were changed and G-strings were mandated, but they were ignored by certain clubs. Table dancing had given way to lap dancing, which created a new set of laws about physical contact with the girls. When he was finished with the history, Roger rattled off the names of a half-dozen clubs he claimed to know well, then offered an impressive summary of their strippers. His language was detailed and quite descriptive, and when he finally finished, the other two needed fresh beers.

Calvin, who'd touched precious little female flesh, was captivated by the conversation. He was also counting the cans of beer Roger was draining, and when the number reached six—in about an hour—Calvin wanted to say something. Instead, he listened to his far more worldly sidekick, a man who seemed to have an inexhaustible appetite for beer and could gulp it while describing naked girls with astonishing detail.

Eventually, the conversation returned to where it was originally headed. Roger said, "We'll probably have time to run by the Desperado after we get finished at the hospital, you know, just for a couple of drinks and maybe a table dance or two."

Aggie drove with his limp right wrist draped over the steering wheel and a beer in his left hand. He studied the road ahead and didn't respond to the suggestion. His girlfriend would scream and throw things if she heard he'd spent money in a club gawking

at strippers. Calvin, though, was suddenly nervous with antici-
pation. "Sounds good to me," he said.

"Sure," added Aggie, but only because he had to.

A car approached from the other direction, and just before it
passed them, Aggie inadvertently allowed the truck's left front
wheel to touch the yellow center line. Then he yanked it back.
The other car swerved sharply.

"That was a cop!" Aggie yelled. He and Roger snapped their
heads around for a fleeting look. The other car was stopping
abruptly, its brake lights fully applied.

"Damned sure is," Roger said. "A county boy. Go!"

"He's comin' after us," Calvin said in a panic.

"Blue lights! Blue lights!" Roger squawked. "Oh shit!"

Aggie instinctively gunned his engine, and the big Dodge
roared over a hill. "Are you sure this is a good idea?" he said.

"Just go, dammit," Roger yelled.

"We got beer cans ever'where," Calvin added.

"But I'm not drunk," Aggie insisted. "Runnin' just makes
things worse."

"We're already runnin'," Roger said. "Now the important
thing is to not get caught." And with that, he drained another
can as if it might be his last.

The pickup hit eighty miles per hour, then ninety, as it flew
over a long stretch of flat highway. "He's comin' fast," Aggie said,
glancing at the mirror, then back at the highway ahead. "Blue
lights to hell and back."

Calvin rolled down his window and said, "Let's toss the
beer!"

"No!" Roger squawked. "Are you crazy? He can't catch us. Faster, faster!"

The pickup flew over a small hill and almost left the pavement, then it screeched around a tight curve and fishtailed slightly, enough for Calvin to say, "We're gonna kill ourselves."

"Shut up," Roger barked. "Look for a driveway. We'll duck in."

"There's a mailbox," Aggie said and hit the brakes. The deputy was seconds behind them, but out of sight. They turned sharply to the right, and the truck's lights swept across a small farmhouse tucked low under huge oak trees.

"Cut your lights," Roger snapped, as if he'd been in this situation many times. Aggie killed the engine, switched off the lights, and the truck rolled quietly along the short dirt drive and came to rest next to a Ford pickup owned by Mr. Buford M. Gates, of Route 5, Owensville, Mississippi.

The patrol car flew by them without slowing, its blue lights ablaze but its siren still off. The three donors sat low in the seat, and when the blue lights were long gone, they slowly raised their heads.

The house they had chosen was dark and silent. Evidently, it was not protected by dogs. Even the front porch light was off.

"Nice work," Roger said softly as they began to breathe again.

"We got lucky," Aggie whispered.

They watched the house and listened to the highway, and after a few minutes of wonderful silence agreed that they had indeed been very lucky.

"How long we gonna sit here?" Calvin finally asked.

"Not long," Aggie said as he stared at the windows of the house.

"I hear a car," Calvin said, and the three heads ducked again. Seconds passed, and the deputy flew by from the other direction, lights flashing but still no siren. "Sumbitch is lookin' for us," Roger mumbled.

"Of course he is," Aggie said.

When the sound of the patrol car faded in the distance, the three heads slowly rose in the Dodge, then Roger said, "I need to pee."

"Not here," Calvin said.

"Open the door," Roger insisted.

"Can't you wait?"

"No."

Calvin slowly opened the passenger's door, stepped out, then watched as Roger tiptoed to the side of Mr. Gates's Ford truck and began urinating on the right front wheel.

Unlike her husband, Mrs. Gates was a light sleeper. She was certain she had heard something out there, and when she was fully awake, she became even more convinced of it. Buford had been snoring for an hour, but she finally managed to interrupt his slumber. He reached under the bed and grabbed his shotgun.

Roger was still urinating when a small light came on in the kitchen. All three saw it immediately. "Run!" Aggie hissed through his window, then grabbed the key and turned the ignition. Calvin jumped back into the truck while grunting, "Go, go, go!" as Aggie slammed the transmission in reverse and hit the gas. Roger yanked his pants up while scrambling toward the Dodge.

He flung himself over the side and landed hard in the bed, among the empty beer cans, then held on as the truck flew back down the driveway toward the road. It was at the mailbox when the front porch light popped on. It slid to a stop on the asphalt as the front door slowly opened and an old man pushed back the screen. "He's got a gun!" Calvin said.

"Too bad," said Aggie as he slammed the stick into drive and peeled rubber for fifty feet as they made a clean escape. A mile down the highway, Aggie turned onto a narrow country lane and stopped the engine. All three got out and stretched their muscles and had a good laugh at the close call. They laughed nervously and worked hard to believe that they had not been frightened at all. They speculated about where the deputy might be at that moment. They cleaned out the bed of the truck and left their empty cans in a ditch. Ten minutes passed and there was no sign of the deputy.

Aggie finally addressed the obvious. "We gotta get to Memphis, fellas."

Calvin, more intrigued by the Desperado than by the hospital, added, "You bet. It's gettin' late."

Roger froze in the center of the road and said, "I dropped my wallet."

"You what?"

"I dropped my wallet."

"Where?"

"Back there. Must've fell out when I was takin' a leak."

There was an excellent chance that Roger's wallet contained nothing of value—no money, driver's license, credit cards, membership cards of any kind, nothing more useful than perhaps an old condom. And Aggie almost asked, "What's in it?" But he did not, because he knew that Roger would claim that his wallet was loaded with valuables.

"I gotta go get it," he said.

"Are you sure?" Calvin asked.

"It's got my money, license, credit cards, everything."

"But the old man had a gun."

"And when the sun comes up, the old man will find my wallet, call the sheriff, who'll call the sheriff in Ford County, and we'll be screwed. You're pretty stupid, you know."

"At least I didn't lose my wallet."

"He's right," Aggie said. "He's gotta go get it." It was noted by the other two that Aggie emphasized the "he" and said nothing about "we."

"You're not scared, are you, big boy?" Roger said to Calvin.

"I ain't scared, 'cause I ain't goin' back."

"I think you're scared."

"Knock it off," Aggie said. "Here's what we'll do. We'll wait until the old man has time to get back in bed, then we'll ease down the road, get close to the house but not too close, stop the truck, then you can sneak down the driveway, find the wallet, and we'll haul ass."

"I'll bet there's nothin' in the wallet," Calvin said.

"And I'll bet it's got more cash than your wallet," Roger shot back as he reached into the truck for another beer.

"Knock it off," Aggie said again.

They stood beside the truck, sipping beer and watching the

deserted highway in the distance, and after fifteen minutes that seemed like an hour they loaded up, with Roger in the back. A quarter of a mile from the house, Aggie stopped the truck on a flat section of highway. He killed the engine so they could hear any approaching vehicle.

"Can't you get closer?" Roger asked as he stood by the driver's door.

"It's just around that bend up there," Aggie said. "Any closer, and he might hear us."

The three stared at the dark highway. A half-moon came and went with the clouds. "You gotta gun?" Roger asked.

"I gotta gun," Aggie said, "But you ain't gettin' it. Just sneak up to the house, and sneak back. No big deal. The old man's asleep already."

"You're not scared, are you?" Calvin added helpfully.

"Hell no." And with that, Roger disappeared into the darkness. Aggie restarted the truck and, with the lights off, quietly turned it around so that it was headed in the general direction of Memphis. He killed the engine again, and with both windows down they began their waiting.

"He's had eight beers," Calvin said softly. "Drunk as a skunk."

"But he can hold his booze."

"He's had a lot of practice. Maybe the old man'll get him this time."

"That wouldn't really bother me, but then we'd get caught."

"Why, exactly, was he invited in the first place?"

"Shut up. We need to listen for traffic."

Roger left the road when the mailbox was in sight. He jumped a ditch, then ducked low through a bean field next to the house. If the old man was still watching, his eyes would be on the driveway, right? Roger shrewdly decided he would sneak in from the rear. All lights were off. The little house was still and quiet. Not a creature was stirring. Through the shadows of the oak trees, Roger crept over the wet grass until he could see the Ford pickup. He paused behind a toolshed, caught his breath, and realized he needed to pee again. No, he said to himself, it had to wait. He was proud—he'd made it this far without a sound. Then he was terrified again—what the hell was he doing? He took a deep breath, then crouched low and continued on his mission. When the Ford was between him and the house, he fell to his hands and knees and began feeling his way through the pea gravel at the end of the driveway.

Roger moved slowly as the gravel crunched under him. He cursed when his hands became wet near the right front tire. When he touched his wallet, he smiled, then quickly stuck it in the right rear pocket of his jeans. He paused, breathed deeply, then began his silent retreat.

In the stillness, Mr. Buford Gates heard all sorts of noises, some real, some conjured up by the circumstances. The deer had the run of the place, and he thought that perhaps they were moving around again, looking for grass and berries. Then he heard something different. He slowly stood from his hiding place on the side porch, raised his shotgun to the sky, and fired two shots at the moon just for the hell of it.

In the perfect calm of the late evening, the shots boomed through the air like howitzers, deadly blasts that echoed for miles.

Down the highway, not too far away, the sudden squealing of tires followed the gunfire, and to Buford, at least, the burning of rubber sounded precisely as it had just twenty minutes earlier directly in front of his house.

They're still around here, he said to himself.

Mrs. Gates opened the side door and said, "Buford!"

"I think they're still here," he said, reloading his Browning 16-gauge.

"Did you see them?"

"Maybe."

"What do you mean, maybe? What are you shootin' at?"

"Just get back inside, will you?"

The door slammed.

Roger was under the Ford pickup, holding his breath, clutching his groin, sweating profusely as he urgently tried to decide whether he should wrap himself around the transmission just inches above him or claw his way down through the pea gravel below him. But he didn't move. The sonic booms were still ringing in his ears. The squealing tires of his cowardly friends made him curse. He was afraid to breathe.

He heard the door open again and the woman say, "Here's a flashlight. Maybe you can see what you're shootin' at."

"Just get back inside and call the sheriff while you're at it."

The door slammed again as the woman was prattling on. A minute or so later she was back. "I called the sheriff's office. They said Dudley's out here somewhere on patrol."

"Fetch my truck keys," the man said. "I'll take a look on the highway."

"You can't drive at night."

"Just get me the damned keys."

The door slammed again. Roger tried wiggling in reverse, but the pea gravel made too much noise. He tried wiggling forward, in the direction of their voices, but again there was too much shuffling and crunching. So he decided to wait. If the pickup started in reverse, he would wait until the last possible second, grab the front bumper as it moved above him, and get himself dragged a few feet until he could bolt and sprint through the darkness. If the old man saw him, it would take several seconds for him to stop, get his gun, get out, and give chase. By then, Roger would be lost in the woods. It was a plan, and it just might work. On the other hand, he could get crushed by the tires, dragged down the highway, or just plain shot.

Buford left the side porch and began searching with his flashlight. From the door, Mrs. Gates yelled, "I hid your keys. You can't drive at night."

Atta girl, thought Roger.

"You'd better get me those damned keys."

"I hid them."

Buford was mumbling in the darkness.

The Dodge raced for several frantic miles before Aggie finally slowed somewhat, then said, "You know we have to go back."

"Why?"

"If he got hit, we have to explain what happened and take care of the details."

"I hope he got hit, and if he did, then he can't talk. If he can't talk, he can't squeal on us. Let's get to Memphis."

"No." Aggie turned around, and they drove in silence until they reached the same country lane where they had stopped before. Close to a fence row, they sat on the hood and contemplated what to do next. Before long, they heard a siren, then saw the blue lights pass by quickly on the highway.

"If the ambulance is next, then we're in big trouble," Aggie said.

"So is Roger."

When Roger heard the siren, he panicked. But as it grew closer, he realized it would conceal some of the noise his escape would need. He found a rock, squirmed to the side of the truck, and flung it in the general direction of the house. It hit something, causing Mr. Gates to say, "What's that?" and to run back to the side porch. Roger slithered like a snake from under the truck, through the fresh urine he'd left earlier, through the wet grass, and all the way to an oak tree just as Dudley the deputy came roaring onto the scene. He hit his brakes and turned violently into the driveway, slinging gravel and sending dust. The commotion saved Roger. Mr. and Mrs. Gates ran out to meet Dudley while Roger eased deeper into the darkness. Within seconds he was behind a line of shrubs, then past an old barn, then lost in a bean field. Half an hour passed.

Aggie said, "I think we just go back to the house, and tell 'em ever'thang. That way we'll know if he's okay."

Calvin said, "But won't they charge us with resistin' arrest, and probably drunk drivin' on top of that?"

"So what do you suggest?"

"The deputy's probably gone now. No ambulance means

Roger's okay, wherever he is. I'll bet he's hidin' somewhere. I say we make one pass by the house, take a good look, then get on to Memphis."

"It's worth a try."

They found Roger beside the road, walking with a limp, headed to Memphis. After a few harsh words by all three, they decided to carry on. Roger took his middle position; Calvin had the door. They drove ten minutes before anyone said another word. All eyes were straight ahead. All three were angry, fuming.

Roger's face was scratched and bloody. He reeked of sweat and urine, and his clothes were covered with dirt and mud. After a few miles, Calvin rolled down his window, and after a few more miles Roger said, "Why don't you roll up that window?"

"We need fresh air," Calvin explained.

They stopped for another six-pack to settle their nerves, and after a few drinks Calvin asked, "Did he shoot at you?"

"I don't know," Roger said. "I never saw him."

"It sounded like a cannon."

"You should've heard it where I was."

At that, Aggie and Calvin became amused and began laughing. Roger, his nerves settled, found their laughter contagious, and soon all three were hooting at the old man with the gun and the wife who hid his truck keys and probably saved Roger's life. And the thought of Dudley the deputy still flying up and down the highway with his blue lights on made them laugh even harder.

Aggie was sticking to the back roads, and when one of them intersected Highway 78 near Memphis, they raced onto the entrance ramp and joined the traffic on the four-lane.

"There's a truck stop just ahead," Roger said. "I need to wash up."

Inside, he bought a NASCAR T-shirt and a cap, then scrubbed his face and hands in the men's room. When he returned to the truck, Aggie and Calvin were impressed with the changes. They raced off again, close to the bright lights now. It was almost 10:00 p.m.

The billboards grew larger, brighter, and closer together, and though the boys had not mentioned the Desperado in an hour, they suddenly remembered the place when they were confronted with a sizzling image of a young woman ready to burst out of what little clothing she was wearing. Her name was Tiffany, and she smirked down at the traffic from a huge billboard that advertised the Desperado, a Gentlemen's Club, with the hottest strippers in the entire South. The Dodge slowed appreciably.

Her legs seemed a mile long, and bare, and her skimpy sheer costume was obviously designed to be shed in a moment's notice. She had teased blond hair, thick red lips, and eyes that absolutely smoldered. The very possibility that she might be working just a few miles up the road, and that they could stop by and see her in the flesh, well, it was all overwhelming.

For a few minutes there was not a word as the Dodge regained its speed. Finally, Aggie said, "I reckon we'd better get to the hospital. Bailey might be dead by now."

It was the first mention of Bailey in hours.

"The hospital's open all night," Roger said. "Never closes. Whatta you thank they do, shut down at night and make ever'body go home?" To show his support, Calvin found this humorous and joined in with a hearty horselaugh.

"So ya'll want to stop by the Desperado?" Aggie asked, playing along.

"Why not?" Roger said.

"Might as well," Calvin said as he sipped a beer and tried to envision Tiffany in the middle of her routine.

"We'll stay for an hour, then hurry on to the hospital," Roger said. After ten beers, he was remarkably coherent.

The bouncer at the door eyed them suspiciously. "Lemme see your ID," he growled at Calvin, who, though twenty-one, looked younger. Aggie looked his age. Roger, twenty-seven, could pass for forty. "Mississippi, huh?" the bouncer said with an obvious bias against people from that state.

"Yep," Roger said.

"Ten-dollar cover charge."

"Just because we're from Mississippi?" Roger asked.

"No, wiseass, everybody pays the cover. If you don't like it, then hop back on your tractor and go home."

"You this nice to all your customers?" Aggie said.

"Yep."

They walked away, huddled up, discussed the cover charge and whether they should stay. Roger explained that there was another club not far away, but warned that it would probably stick them with a similar entry fee. As they whispered and pondered things, Calvin tried to peek in the door for a quick glimpse of Tiffany. He voted to stay, and it was eventually unanimous.

Once inside, they were examined by two more burly and unsmiling bouncers, then led to the main room with a round stage in the center, and on that stage, at that moment, were two young ladies, one white, one black, both naked and gyrating in all directions.

Calvin froze when he saw them. His $10 cover charge was instantly forgotten.

Their table was less than twenty feet from the stage. The club was half-full, and the crowd was young and blue-collar. They were not the only country boys who'd come to town. Their waitress wore nothing but a G-string, and when she popped in with a curt "What'll it be? Three-drink minimum," Calvin almost fainted. He'd never seen so much forbidden flesh.

"Three drinks?" Roger asked, trying to maintain eye contact.

"That's it," she shot back.

"How much is a beer?"

"Five bucks."

"And we have to order three?"

"Three apiece. That's the house rule. If you don't like it, then you can take it up with the bouncers over there." She nodded at the door, but their eyes did not leave her chest.

They ordered three beers each and studied the surroundings. The stage now had four dancers, all gyrating as loud rap rattled the walls. The waitresses moved swiftly between the tables as if they might get fondled if they lingered too long. Many of the customers were drunk and rowdy, and before long a table dance broke out. A waitress climbed onto a table nearby and began her routine while a group of truck drivers stuffed cash into her G-string. Before long, her waistline was bristling with greenbacks.

A platter with nine tall and very skinny glasses of beer arrived, beer that was lighter than light and watered down to the point that it looked more like diluted lemonade. "That'll be $45," the waitress said, and this caused a panicked and prolonged searching of pockets and wallets by all three. They finally rounded up the cash.

"Ya'll still do lap dances?" Roger asked their waitress.

"Depends."

"He's never had one," Roger said, pointing to Calvin, whose heart froze.

"Twenty bucks," she said.

Roger found a $20 bill and forked it over, and within seconds Amber was sitting on top of Calvin, who, at 270 pounds, provided enough lap for a small troupe of dancers. As the music rocked and boomed, Amber bounced and wiggled, and Calvin simply closed his eyes and wondered what true love was really like.

"Rub her legs," Roger instructed, the voice of experience.

"He can't touch," Amber said sternly, while at the same time her rear end was nestled firmly between Calvin's massive thighs. Some brutes at a nearby table watched with amusement and were soon egging Amber on with all sorts of obscene suggestions, and she played to her crowd.

How long will this song last? Calvin asked himself. His broad flat forehead was covered with perspiration.

Suddenly she turned around and faced him without missing a beat, and for at least a minute Calvin held a comely and quivering naked woman in his lap. It was a life-changing experience. Calvin would never be the same.

Sadly, the song ended, and Amber bounced to her feet and hustled off to check on her tables.

"You know you can see her later," Roger said. "One-on-one."

"What's that?" Aggie asked.

"They got little rooms in the back where you can meet the girls after they get off work."

"You're lyin'."

Calvin was still speechless, totally mute as he watched Amber skip around the club taking orders. But he was listening, and during the gap in the music he heard what Roger was saying. Amber could be his, all alone, in some glorious little back room.

They sipped their watery beer and watched other customers arrive. By 11:00 p.m., the place was packed, and more strippers and dancers worked the stage and the crowd. Calvin watched with jealous rage as Amber lap danced on another man, less than ten feet away. He noted with some pride, though, that she did the face-to-face thing for only a few seconds. If he had plenty of cash, he would happily stuff it in her G-string and get lap danced on all night long.

Cash, though, was quickly becoming an issue. During another pause between songs and strippers, Calvin, the unemployed, admitted, "I'm not sure how long I can last here. This is some pretty expensive beer."

Their beer, in eight-ounce glasses, was almost gone, and they had studied the waitresses enough to know that empties didn't sit long on the tables. The customers were expected to drink heavily, tip generously, and throw money at the girls for personal dances. The Memphis skin trade was very profitable.

"I got some cash," Aggie said.

"I got credit cards," Roger said. "Order another round while I take a pee." He stood and for the first time seemed to teeter somewhat, then he disappeared in the smoke and crowd. Calvin flagged down Amber and ordered another round. She smiled and winked her approval. What he wanted much worse than the river water they were drinking was more physical contact with his girl, but it wasn't to be. At that moment, he vowed to redouble his efforts to find a job, save his money, and become a regular at the Desperado. For the first time in his young life, Calvin had a goal.

Aggie was staring at the floor, under Roger's empty seat. "The dumbass dropped his wallet again," he said, and picked up a battered canvas billfold.

"You think he's got any credit cards?" Aggie asked.

"No."

"Let's take a look." He glanced around to make sure there was no sign of Roger, then opened his wallet. There was an expired discount card from a grocery store, then a collection of business cards—two from lawyers, two from bail bondsmen, one from a rehab clinic, and one from a parole officer. Folded neatly and partially hidden was a $20 bill. "What a surprise," Aggie said. "No credit cards, no driver's license."

"And he almost got shot over that," Calvin said.

"He's an idiot, okay?" Aggie closed the wallet and placed it on Roger's chair.

The beer arrived as Roger returned and found his wallet. They scraped together $45 and managed a $3 tip. "Can we put a lap dance on a credit card?" Roger yelled at Amber.

"Nope, just cash," she yelled back as she left them.

"What kinda credit card you got?" Aggie asked.

"Bunch of 'em," he said like a big shot.

Calvin, his lap still on fire, watched his beloved Amber weave through the crowd. Aggie watched the girls too, but he was also watching the time. He had no idea how long it took to give a pint of blood. Midnight was approaching. And though he tried not to, he couldn't help but think about his girlfriend and the tantrum she would throw if she somehow heard about this little detour.

Roger was fading fast. His eyelids were drooping and his head was nodding. "Drink up," he said, thick tongued, as he tried to rally, but his lights were dimming. Between songs, Calvin chatted with two guys at another table and in the course of a quick conversation learned that the legendary stripper, Tiffany, didn't work on Thursday nights.

When the beer was gone, Aggie announced, "I'm leavin'. You boys comin' with me?"

Roger couldn't stand alone, so they half dragged him away from the table. As they headed to the door, Amber glided by and said to Calvin, "Are you leaving me?"

He nodded because he couldn't speak.

"Please come back later," she cooed. "I think you're cute."

One of the bouncers grabbed Roger and helped get him outside. "What time ya'll close?" Calvin asked.

"Three a.m.," the bouncer said and pointed to Roger. "But don't bring him back."

"Say, where's the hospital?" Aggie asked.

"Which one?"

Aggie looked at Calvin and Calvin looked at Aggie, and it was obvious neither had a clue. The bouncer waited impatiently, then said, "You got ten hospitals in this city. Which one?"

"Uh, the nearest one," Aggie said.

"That'll be Lutheran. You know the city?"

"Sure."

"I'll bet you do. Take Lamar to Parkway, Parkway to Poplar. It's just past East High School."

"Thanks."

The bouncer waved them off and disappeared inside. They dragged Roger to the truck, tossed him inside, then spent half an hour roaming midtown Memphis in a hopeless search for Lutheran Hospital. "Are you sure that's the right hospital?" Calvin asked several times.

In various ways, Aggie answered, "Yes," "Sure," "Probably," and "Of course."

When they found themselves downtown, Aggie stopped at a curb and approached a cabdriver who was napping behind the wheel. "Ain't no Lutheran Hospital," the cabdriver said. "We got Baptist, Methodist, Catholic, Central, Mercy, and a few others, but no Lutheran."

"I know, you got ten of 'em."

"Seven, to be exact. Where you from?"

"Mississippi. Look, where's the nearest hospital?"

"Mercy is four blocks away, just down Union Avenue."

"Thanks."

They found Mercy Hospital and left Roger in the truck, comatose. Mercy was the city hospital, the principal destination for late-night victims of crime, domestic abuse, police shootings, gang disputes, drug overdoses, and alcohol-related car wrecks. Almost all of said victims were black. Ambulances and police cars swarmed around the ER entrance. Packs of frantic family members roamed the dungeonlike hallways searching for their victims. Screams and shouts echoed through the place as Aggie and Calvin walked for miles looking for the information desk. They finally found it, tucked away as if it were intentionally hidden. A young Mexican girl was at the desk, smacking gum and reading a magazine.

"Do ya'll admit white people?" Aggie began pleasantly.

To which she replied coolly, "Who are you looking for?"

"We're here to give blood."

"Blood Services is just down the hall," she said, pointing.

"Are they open?"

"I doubt it. Who you giving blood for?"

"Uh, Bailey," Aggie said as he looked blankly at Calvin.

"First name?" She began to peck at a keyboard and look at a monitor.

Aggie and Calvin frowned at each other, clueless. "I thought Bailey was his first name," Calvin said.

"I thought it was his last name. They used to call him Buck, didn't they?"

"Sure, but his momma's last name is Caldwell."

"How many times has she been married?"

The girl watched this back-and-forth with her mouth open. Aggie looked at her and said, "Got anybody with the last name of Bailey?"

She pecked, waited, then said, "A Mr. Jerome Bailey, aged forty-eight, black, gunshot wound."

"Anybody else?"

"No."

"Anybody with the first name of Bailey?"

"We don't enter them by first names."

"Why not?"

⚘

The shooting was a gang skirmish that had begun an hour earlier at a north Memphis housing project. For some reason it resumed in the parking lot of Mercy Hospital. Roger, dead to the world, was jolted from his blackout by a burst of gunfire close by. It took a second or two for his brain to react, but before long he knew damned well that, again, someone was shooting at him. He eased his head up, peeked low through the passenger's window, and was struck by the realization that he had no idea where he was. There were rows of cars parked all around, a tall parking garage nearby, buildings everywhere, and in the distance flashing red and blue lights.

More gunfire, and Roger ducked low, lost his equilibrium, and was on the floorboard, where he frantically searched under the seat for a weapon of some sort. Aggie, like every other boy from Ford County, wouldn't travel anywhere without protection, and Roger knew a gun was close by. He found one under the driver's seat, a 9-millimeter Husk automatic with a twelve-shot clip. Fully loaded. He clutched it, fondled it, kissed the barrel, then quickly rolled down the passenger's window. He heard angry voices, then saw what was most certainly a gangster car easing suspiciously through the parking lot.

Roger fired twice, hit nothing, but succeeded in changing the strategy of the gang shooting. Aggie's Dodge was immediately sprayed with bullets from an assault rifle. The rear window exploded, sending glass throughout the cab and into the long hair of Roger, who hit the floor again and began scrambling to safety. He slid out of the driver's door, ducked low, and began zigzagging through the unlit rows of parked cars. Behind him were more angry voices, then another gunshot. He kept going, his thighs and calves screaming as he kept his head at tire level. He failed to complete a turn between two cars and crashed into the front fender of an old Cadillac. He sat for a moment on the asphalt, listening, breathing, sweating, cursing, but not bleeding. Slowly, he raised his head, saw no one chasing him, but decided to take no chances. He pressed on, cutting between parked cars until he came to a street. A car was approaching, so he stuck the pistol in a front pants pocket.

It was apparent, even to Roger, that this part of town was a war zone. The buildings had thick bars over the windows. The chain-link fences were crowned with razor wire. The alleys were dark and forbidding, and Roger, in a lucid moment, asked himself, What the hell am I doin' here? Only the gun kept him from total panic. He eased along the sidewalk, pondering strategy, and decided it was best to get back to the truck and wait on his friends. The shooting had stopped. Perhaps the police were on the scene and things were secure. There were voices behind him, on the sidewalk, and a quick glance revealed a group of young black men, on his side of the street and gaining. Roger picked up the pace. A rock landed nearby and bounced for twenty feet. They were hollering back there. He eased the gun out of his pocket, put his finger on the trigger, and walked even faster. There were lights ahead, and when he turned a corner, he stepped into a small parking lot outside an all-night convenience store.

There was one car parked directly in front of the store, and beside the car a white man and a white woman were yelling at each other. As Roger stepped onto the scene, the man threw a right hook and clobbered the woman in the face. The sound of her flesh getting smacked was sickening. Roger froze as the scene began to register in his muddled mind.

But the woman took the shot well and counterpunched with an unbelievable combination. She threw a right cross that busted the man's lips, then went low with a left uppercut that crushed his testicles. He squealed like a burned animal and fell in a heap just as Roger took a step closer. The woman looked at Roger, looked at his gun, then saw the gang approaching from the dark street. If there was another conscious white person within four blocks, he or she was not outdoors.

"You in trouble?" she asked.

"I think so. You?"

"I've felt safer. You got a driver's license?"

"Sure," Roger said as he almost reached again for his wallet.

"Let's go." She jumped in the car with Roger behind the wheel and his new friend riding shotgun. Roger squealed tires, and they were soon racing west on Poplar Avenue.

"Who was that guy back there?" Roger asked, his eyes darting back and forth between the street and the rearview mirror.

"My dealer."

"Your dealer!"

"Yep."

"Are we gonna just leave him?"

"Why don't you put that gun down?" she said, and Roger looked at his left hand and realized he was still holding the pistol. He placed it on the seat between them. She immediately grabbed it, pointed it at him, and said, "Just shut up and drive."

The police were gone when Aggie and Calvin returned to the truck. They gawked at the damage, then cursed profusely when they realized Roger had vanished. "He took my Husk," Aggie said, as he searched under the seat.

"Stupid sonofabitch," Calvin kept saying. "I hope he's dead."

They swept glass off the seat and drove away, anxious to get out of downtown Memphis. There was a quick conversation about looking for Roger, but they were fed up with him. The Mexican girl at the information desk had given them directions to Central Hospital, the most likely place to find Bailey.

The lady at the desk at Central explained that the blood unit was closed for the night, would reopen at 8:00 a.m., and had a rigid policy against accepting donations from those who were obviously intoxicated. The hospital did not currently have a patient with either the first or the last name of Bailey. As she was dismissing them, a uniformed security guard appeared from nowhere and asked them to leave. They cooperated, and he walked them out of the front door. As they were saying good night, Calvin asked him, "Say, you know where we might be able to sell a pint of blood?"

"There's a blood bank on Watkins, not too far."

"You think it's open?"

"Yes, it's open all night."

"How do you get there?" Aggie asked.

He pointed this way and that, then said, "Be careful, though. It's where all the addicts go when they need cash. Rough place."

The blood bank was the only destination Aggie found on the first attempt, and by the time they stopped on the street beside it, they were hoping it would be closed. It was not. The reception area was a grungy little room with a row of plastic chairs and magazines scattered everywhere. An addict of some variety was in one corner, on the floor, under a coffee table, curled into the fetal position, and obviously dying. A grim-faced man in surgical scrubs worked the desk, and he greeted them with a nasty "What do you want?"

Aggie cleared his throat, took another glance at the addict in the corner, and managed to spit out, "Ya'll buy blood around here?"

"We will pay for it, and we will accept it for free."

"How much?"

"Fifty bucks a pint."

To Calvin, with $6.25 in his pocket, the price meant a cover charge, three watered-down beers, and another memorable lap dance with Amber. To Aggie, with $18 in his pocket and no credit cards, the deal meant another quick visit to the strip club and enough gas to get home. Both had forgotten about poor Bailey.

Clipboards were handed over. As they filled in the blanks, the attendant asked, "What type of blood?"

The question drew two blank faces.

"What type of blood?" he repeated.

"Red," Aggie said, and Calvin laughed loudly. The attendant did not crack a smile.

"You boys been drinking?" he asked.

"We've had a few," Aggie said.

"But we won't charge you extra for the alcohol," Calvin added quickly, then both roared with laughter.

"What size needle you want?" the man asked, and all humor vanished.

They swore in writing that they had no known allergies or diseases. "Who's first?"

Neither budged. "Mr. Agnor," the man said, "follow me." Aggie followed him through a door and into a large square room with two beds on the right side and three on the left. Lying on the first bed on the right was a thick-chested white woman in gym sweats and hiking boots. A tube ran from her left arm down to a clear plastic bag that was half-filled with a dark red liquid. Aggie glanced at the tube, the bag, the arm, then realized that there was a needle stuck through the skin. He fainted headfirst and landed with a loud thud on the tiled floor.

Calvin, in a plastic chair near the front door nervously flipping through a magazine with one eye on the dying addict, heard a loud noise in the back but thought nothing of it.

Cold water and ammonia brought Aggie around, and he eventually managed to crawl onto one of the beds where a tiny Asian lady with her mouth covered by white gauze began explaining, in a thick accent, that he was going to be fine and there was nothing to worry about. "Keep your eyes closed," she said repeatedly.

"I really don't need fifty bucks," Aggie said, his head spinning. She did not understand. When she placed a tray filled with accessories next to him, he took one look and felt faint again.

"Close eyes, please," she said as she scrubbed his left forearm with alcohol, the odor of which made him nauseous.

"You can have the money," he said. She produced a large black blindfold, stuck it to his face, and suddenly Aggie's world was completely dark.

The attendant returned to the front and Calvin jumped from his chair. "Follow me," the man said, and Calvin did so. When he entered the square room, and when he saw the woman in the hiking boots on one side and Aggie wearing a strange blindfold on the other side, he, too, collapsed and fell hard near the spot where his friend had landed just minutes earlier.

"Who are these bozos?" asked the woman in the hiking boots.

"Mississippi," the attendant said as he patiently hovered over Calvin and waited for him to come around. Cold water and ammonia helped again. Aggie listened to it all from behind his shroud.

Two pints were eventually extracted. A hundred dollars

changed hands. At ten minutes after 2:00 a.m., the battle-scarred Dodge slid into the parking lot of the Desperado, and the two wild bucks arrived for the final hour of the party. Lighter on blood but heavier on testosterone, they paid the cover charge while looking for the lying bouncer who'd sent them off to Lutheran Hospital. He was not there. Inside, the crowd had thinned and the girls were exhausted. An aging stripper went through the motions onstage.

They were led to a table near their first one, and, sure enough, within seconds Amber appeared and said, "What'll it be, boys? Three-drink minimum."

"We're back," Calvin said proudly.

"Wonderful. What'll it be?"

"Beer."

"You got it," she said and vanished.

"I don't think she remembers us," Calvin said, wounded.

"Plop down twenty bucks and she'll remember you," Aggie said. "You ain't wastin' money on a lap dance, are you?"

"Maybe."

"You're as stupid as Roger."

"No one's that stupid. Reckon where he is."

"Floatin' downriver with his throat cut."

"What's his daddy gonna say?"

"He should say, 'That boy was always stupid.' How the hell do I know what he's gonna say? Do you really care?"

Across the room, some corporate types in dark suits were getting plastered. One put his arm around the waist of a waitress, and she quickly jerked away. A bouncer appeared, pointed at the man, and said harshly, "Don't touch the girls!" The suits roared with laughter. Everything was funny.

As soon as Amber delivered their six glasses of beer, Calvin couldn't wait to blurt out, "How 'bout a lap dance?"

She frowned, then said, "Maybe later. I'm pretty tired." Then she was gone.

"She's tryin' to save your money for you," Aggie said. Calvin was crushed. For hours he had relived the brief moment when Amber had straddled his enormous loins and gyrated happily to the music. He could feel her, touch her, even smell her cheap perfume.

A rather large and flabby young lady appeared onstage and began dancing badly. She was soon unclothed but drew little attention. "Must be the graveyard shift," Aggie said. Calvin hardly noticed. He was watching Amber as she sashayed through the club. She was definitely moving slower. It was almost time to go home.

Much to Calvin's dismay, one of the corporate suits enticed Amber into a lap dance. She found the enthusiasm and was soon grinding away as his friends offered all manner of commentary. She was surrounded by gawking drunks. The one upon whom she was dancing evidently lost control of himself. Against club policy and also in violation of a Memphis city ordinance, he reached forward with both hands and grabbed her breasts. It was an enormous mistake.

In a split second, several things happened at once. There was the flash of a camera, and someone yelled, "Vice, you're under arrest!" While this was taking place, Amber jumped from the man's lap and yelled something about his filthy hands. Since the bouncers had been watching the suits closely, they, the bouncers, were at the table instantly. Two cops in plain clothes rushed forward. One was holding a camera, and the other kept saying, "Memphis vice, Memphis vice."

Someone yelled, "Cops!" There was pushing and shoving and lots of profanity. The music stopped cold. The crowd backed away. Things were under control during the first few seconds, until Amber somehow stumbled and fell over a chair. This caused her to wail in an affected, dramatic manner, and it also caused Calvin to rush into the melee and throw the first punch. He swung at the suit who'd groped his girl, and he hit him very hard in the mouth. At that moment, at least eleven grown men, half of them drunk, began throwing punches in every direction and at every target. Calvin was hit hard by a bouncer, and this brought Aggie into the brawl. The suits were swinging wildly at the bouncers, the cops, and the rednecks. Someone threw a glass of beer that landed across the room near a table of middle-aged bikers, who, until that moment, had done nothing more than shout encouragement to everyone throwing punches. However, the breaking glass upset the bikers. They charged. Outside the Desperado, two uniformed cops had been waiting patiently to help carry away victims of the vice squad, and when they were alerted to the excitement inside, they quickly entered the club. When they realized the fight was more like a full-blown riot, they instinctively pulled out their nightsticks and began looking for a skull or two to crack. Aggie's was first, and while he was on the floor, a cop beat him senseless. Glass was shattered. The cheap tables and chairs were splintered. Two of the bikers picked up wooden chair legs and attacked the bouncers. The melee roared on with loyalties shifting rapidly and bodies falling to the floor. Casualties mounted until the cops and the bouncers gained the upper hand and eventually subdued the corporate suits, the bikers, the boys from Ford County, and a few others who'd joined the fun. Blood was everywhere—on the floor, on shirts and jackets, and especially on faces and arms.

More police arrived, then the ambulances. Aggie was unconscious and rapidly losing blood from his already diminished supply. The medics were alarmed at his condition and rushed him into the first ambulance. He was taken to Mercy Hospital. One of the suits had also received a number of blows from a cop's nightstick, and he, too, was unresponsive. He was placed in a second ambulance. Calvin was handcuffed and manhandled into the rear seat of a police car, where he was joined by an angry man in a gray suit and a white shirt soaked with blood.

Calvin's right eye was swollen shut, and through his left he caught a glimpse of Aggie's Dodge pickup sitting forlornly in the parking lot.

Five hours later, from a pay phone in the Shelby County jail, Calvin was finally allowed to make a collect phone call to his mother in Box Hill. Without dwelling on the facts, he explained that he was in jail, that he was charged with felony assault on a police officer, which, according to one of his cell mates, carried up to ten years in prison, and that Aggie was in Mercy Hospital with a busted skull. He had no idea where Roger was. There was no mention of Bailey.

The phone call rippled through the community, and within an hour a carload of friends was headed to Memphis to assess the damage. They learned that Aggie had survived a surgical procedure to remove a blood clot in the brain, and that he, too, was charged with felony assault on a police officer. A doctor told the family that he would be in the hospital for at least a week. The family had no insurance. His truck had been seized by the police, and the procedures required to retrieve it appeared impenetrable.

Calvin's family learned that his bond was $50,000, an unrealistic sum for them to consider. He would be represented by a public defender unless they could raise enough cash to hire a Memphis lawyer. Late Friday afternoon, an uncle was finally allowed to talk to Calvin in the visitors' room of the jail. Calvin wore an orange jumpsuit and orange rubber shower shoes and looked awful. His face was bruised and swollen, his right eye still closed. He was scared and depressed and offered few details.

Still no word from Roger.

After two days in the hospital, Bailey's progress was remarkable. His right leg was broken, not crushed, and his other injuries were minor cuts, bruises, and a very sore chest. His employer arranged for an ambulance, and at noon Saturday Bailey left Methodist Hospital and was driven straight to his mother's house in Box Hill, where he was welcomed home like a prisoner of war. Hours passed before he was told of the efforts by his friends to donate their blood.

Eight days later, Aggie came home to recuperate. His doctor expected a full recovery, but it would take time. His lawyer had managed to reduce the charges to a simple assault. In light of the damage inflicted by the cops, it seemed fair to give Aggie a break. His girlfriend stopped by, but only to end the romance. The legend of the road trip and the brawl in the Memphis strip club would haunt them forever, and she wanted no part of it. Plus, there were significant rumors that perhaps Aggie was a bit brain damaged, and she already had her eye on another boy.

Three months later, Calvin returned to Ford County. His lawyer negotiated a plea to reduce the assault from a felony to a misdemeanor, but the deal required three months in the Shelby County Penal Farm. Calvin didn't like the deal, but the prospect of going to trial in a Memphis courtroom and facing the Memphis police was not appealing. If found guilty on the felony, he would spend years in prison.

In the days following the melee, to the surprise of everyone, the bloody corpse of Roger Tucker was not found in some back alley in downtown Memphis. He wasn't found at all; not that anyone was actively searching for him. A month after the road trip, he called his father from a pay phone near Denver. He claimed to be hitchhiking around the country, alone, and having a grand time. Two months later he was arrested for shoplifting in Spokane, and served sixty days in a city jail.

Almost a year passed before Roger came home.

# Fetching Raymond

·········

$M$r. McBride ran his upholstery shop in the old icehouse on Lee Street, a few blocks off the square in downtown Clanton. To haul the sofas and chairs back and forth, he used a white Ford cargo van with "McBride Upholstery" stenciled in thick black letters above a phone number and the address on Lee. The van, always clean and never in a hurry, was a common sight in Clanton, and Mr. McBride was fairly well-known because he was the only upholsterer in town. He rarely lent his van to anyone, though the requests were more frequent than he would have liked. His usual response was a polite "No, I have some deliveries."

He said yes to Leon Graney, though, and did so for two reasons. First, the circumstances surrounding the request were quite unusual, and, second, Leon's boss at the lamp factory was Mr.

McBride's third cousin. Small-town relationships being what they are, Leon Graney arrived at the upholstery shop as scheduled at four o'clock on a hot Wednesday afternoon in late July.

Most of Ford County was listening to the radio, and it was widely known that things were not going well for the Graney family.

Mr. McBride walked with Leon to the van, handed over the key, and said, "You take care of it, now."

Leon took the key and said, "I'm much obliged."

"I filled up the tank. Should be plenty to get you there and back."

"How much do I owe?"

Mr. McBride shook his head and spat on the gravel beside the van. "Nothing. It's on me. Just bring it back with a full tank."

"I'd feel better if I could pay something," Leon protested.

"No."

"Well, thank you, then."

"I need it back by noon tomorrow."

"It'll be here. Mind if I leave my truck?" Leon nodded to an old Japanese pickup wedged between two cars across the lot.

"That'll be fine."

Leon opened the door and got inside the van. He started the engine, adjusted the seat and the mirrors. Mr. McBride walked to the driver's door, lit an unfiltered cigarette, and watched Leon. "You know, some folks don't like this," he said.

"Thank you, but most folks around here don't care," Leon replied. He was preoccupied and not in the mood for small talk.

"Me, I think it's wrong."

"Thank you. I'll be back before noon," Leon said softly, then backed away and disappeared down the street. He settled into the seat, tested the brakes, slowly gunned the engine to check the power. Twenty minutes later he was far from Clanton, deep in the hills of northern Ford County. Out from the settlement of Pleasant Ridge, the road became gravel, the homes smaller and farther apart. Leon turned in to a short driveway that stopped at a boxlike house with weeds at the doors and an asphalt shingle roof in need of replacement. It was the Graney home, the place he'd been raised along with his brothers, the only constant in their sad and chaotic lives. A jerry-rigged plywood ramp ran to the side door so that his mother, Inez Graney, could come and go in her wheelchair.

By the time Leon turned off the engine, the side door was open and Inez was rolling out and onto the ramp. Behind her was the hulking mass of her middle son, Butch, who still lived with his mother because he'd never lived anywhere else, at least not in the free world. Sixteen of his forty-six years had been behind bars, and he looked the part of the career criminal—long ponytail, studs in his ears, all manner of facial hair, massive biceps, and a collection of cheap tattoos a prison artist had sold him for cigarettes. In spite of his past, Butch handled his mother and her wheelchair with great tenderness and care, speaking softly to her as they negotiated the ramp.

Leon watched and waited, then walked to the rear of the van and opened its double doors. He and Butch gently lifted their mother up and sat her inside the van. Butch pushed her forward to the console that separated the two bucket seats bolted into the floor. Leon latched the wheelchair into place with strips of packing twine someone at McBride's had left in the van, and when Inez was secure, her boys got settled in their seats. The journey began. Within minutes they were back on the asphalt and headed for a long night.

Inez was seventy-two, a mother of three, grandmother of at least four, a lonely old woman in failing health who couldn't remember her last bit of good luck. Though she'd considered herself single for almost thirty years, she was not, at least to her knowledge, officially divorced from the miserable creature who'd practically raped her when she was seventeen, married her when she was eighteen, fathered her three boys, then mercifully disappeared from the face of the earth. When she prayed on occasion, she never failed to toss in an earnest request that Ernie be kept away from her, be kept wherever his miserable life had taken him, if in fact his life had not already ended in some painful manner, which was really what she dreamed of but didn't have the audacity to ask of the Lord. Ernie was still blamed for everything—for her bad health and poverty, her reduced status in life, her seclusion, her lack of friends, even the scorn of her own family. But her harshest condemnation of Ernie was for his despicable treatment of his three sons. Abandoning them was far more merciful than beating them.

By the time they reached the highway, all three needed a cigarette. "Reckon McBride'll mind if we smoke?" Butch said. At three packs a day he was always reaching for a pocket.

"Somebody's been smokin' in here," Inez said. "Smells like a tar pit. Is the air conditioner on, Leon?"

"Yes, but you can't tell it if the windows are down."

With little concern for Mr. McBride's preferences on smoking in his van, they were soon puffing away with the windows down, the warm wind rushing in and swirling about. Once inside the van, the wind had no exit, no other windows, no vents, nothing to let it out, so it roared back toward the front and engulfed the three Graneys, who were staring at the road, smoking intently, seemingly oblivious to everything as the van moved along the county road. Butch and Leon casually flicked their ashes out of the windows. Inez gently tapped hers into her cupped left hand.

"How much did McBride charge you?" Butch asked from the passenger's seat.

Leon shook his head. "Nothing. Even filled up the tank. Said he didn't agree with this. Claimed a lot of folks don't like it."

"I'm not sure I believe that."

"I don't."

When the three cigarettes were finished, Leon and Butch rolled up their windows and fiddled with the air conditioner and the vents. Hot air shot out and minutes passed before the heat was broken. All three were sweating.

"You okay back there?" Leon asked, glancing over his shoulder and smiling at his mother.

"I'm fine. Thank you. Does the air conditioner work?"

"Yes, it's gettin' cooler now."

"I can't feel a thang."

"You wanna stop for a soda or something?"

"No. Let's hurry along."

"I'd like a beer," Butch said, and, as if this was expected, Leon immediately shook his head in the negative and Inez shot forth with an emphatic "No."

"There'll be no drinking," she said, and the issue was laid to rest. When Ernie abandoned the family years earlier, he'd taken nothing but his shotgun, a few clothes, and all the liquor from his private supply. He'd been a violent drunk, and his boys still carried the scars, emotional and physical. Leon, the oldest, had felt more of the brutality than his younger brothers, and as a small boy equated alcohol with the horrors of an abusive father. He had never taken a drink, though with time had found his own vices. Butch, on the other hand, had drunk heavily since his early teens, though he'd never been tempted to sneak alcohol into his mother's home. Raymond, the youngest, had chosen to follow the example of Butch rather than of Leon.

To shift away from such an unpleasant topic, Leon asked his mother about the latest news from a friend down the road, an old spinster who'd been dying of cancer for years. Inez, as always, perked up when discussing the ailments and treatments of her neighbors, and herself as well. The air conditioner finally broke through, and the thick humidity inside the van began to subside. When he stopped sweating, Butch reached for his pocket, fished out a cigarette, lit it, then cracked the window. The temperature rose immediately. Soon all three were smoking, and the windows went lower and lower until the air was again thick with heat and nicotine.

When they finished, Inez said to Leon, "Raymond called two hours ago."

This was no surprise. Raymond had been making calls, col-lect, for days now, and not only to his mother. Leon's phone was ringing so often that his (third) wife refused to answer it. Others around town were also declining to accept charges.

"What'd he say?" Leon asked, but only because he had to reply. He knew exactly what Raymond had said, maybe not ver-batim, but certainly in general.

"Said thangs are lookin' real good, said he'd probably have to fire the team of lawyers he has now so he can hire another team of lawyers. You know Raymond. He's tellin' the lawyers what to do and they're just fallin' all over themselves."

Without turning his head, Butch cut his eyes at Leon, and Leon returned the glance. Nothing was said because words were not necessary.

"Said his new team comes from a firm in Chicago with a thou-sand lawyers. Can you imagine? A thousand lawyers workin' for Raymond. And he's tellin' 'em what to do."

Another glance between driver and right-side passenger. Inez had cataracts, and her peripheral vision had declined. If she had seen the looks being passed between her two oldest, she would not have been pleased.

"Said they've just discovered some new evidence that shoulda been produced at trial but wasn't because the cops and the prosecutors covered it up, and with this new evidence Ray-mond feels real good about gettin' a new trial back here in Clan-ton, though he's not sure he wants it here, so he might move it somewhere else. He's thinkin' about somewhere in the Delta be-cause the Delta juries have more blacks and he says that blacks are more sympathetic in cases like this. What do you thank about that, Leon?"

"There are definitely more blacks in the Delta," Leon said. Butch grunted and mumbled, but his words were not clear.

"Said he don't trust anyone in Ford County, especially the law and the judges. God knows they've never given us a break."

Leon and Butch nodded in silent agreement. Both had been chewed up by the law in Ford County, Butch much more so than Leon. And though they had pled guilty to their crimes in negotiated deals, they had always believed they were persecuted simply because they were Graneys.

"Don't know if I can stand another trial, though," she said, and her words trailed off.

Leon wanted to say that Raymond's chances of getting a new trial were worse than slim, and that he'd been making noise about a new trial for over a decade. Butch wanted to say pretty much the same thing, but he would've added that he was sick of Raymond's jailhouse bullshit about lawyers and trials and new evidence and that it was past time for the boy to stop blaming everybody else and take his medicine like a man.

But neither said a word.

"Said the both of you ain't sent him his stipends for last month," she said. "That true?"

Five miles passed before another word was spoken.

"Ya'll hear me up there?" Inez said. "Raymond says ya'll ain't mailed in his stipends for the month of June, and now it's already July. Ya'll forget about it?"

Leon went first, and unloaded. "Forget about it? How can

we forget about it? That's all he talks about. I get a letter every day, sometimes two, not that I read 'em all, but every letter mentions the stipend. 'Thanks for the money, bro.' 'Don't forget the money, Leon, I'm counting on you, big brother.' 'Gotta have the money to pay the lawyers, you know how much those bloodsuckers can charge.' 'Ain't seen the stipend this month, bro.' "

"What the hell is a stipend?" Butch shot from the right side, his voice suddenly edgy.

"A regular or fixed payment, according to *Webster's*," Leon said.

"It's just money, right?"

"Right."

"So why can't he just say something like, 'Send me the damned money'? Or, 'Where's the damned money?' Why does he have to use the fancy words?"

"We've had this conversation a thousand times," Inez said.

"Well, you sent him a dictionary," Leon said to Butch.

"That was ten years ago, at least. And he begged me for it."

"Well, he's still got it, still wearing it out looking for words we ain't seen before."

"I often wonder if his lawyers can keep up with his vocabulary," Butch mused.

"Ya'll're tryin' to change the subject up there," Inez said. "Why didn't you send him his stipends last month?"

"I thought I did," Butch said without conviction.

"I don't believe that," she said.

"The check's in the mail," Leon said.

"I don't believe that either. We all agreed to send him $100 each, every month, twelve months a year. It's the least we can do. I know it's hard, especially on me, livin' on Social Security and all. But you boys have jobs, and the least you can do is squeeze out $100 each for your little brother so he can buy decent food and pay his lawyers."

"Do we have to go through this again?" Leon asked.

"I hear it every day," Butch said. "If I don't hear from Raymond, on the phone or through the mail, then I hear it from Momma."

"Is that a complaint?" she asked. "Got a problem with your livin' arrangements? Stayin' in my house for free, and yet you want to complain?"

"Come on," Leon said.

"Who'll take care of you?" Butch offered in his defense.

"Knock it off, you two. This gets so old."

All three took a deep breath, then began reaching for the cigarettes. After a long, quiet smoke, they settled in for another round. Inez got things started with a pleasant "Me, I never miss a month. And, if you'll recall, I never missed a month when the both of you was locked up at Parchman."

Leon grunted, slapped the wheel, and said angrily, "Momma, that was twenty-five years ago. Why bring it up now? I ain't had so much as a speedin' ticket since I got paroled." Butch, whose life in crime had been much more colorful than Leon's, and who was still on parole, said nothing.

"I never missed a month," she said.

"Come on."

"And sometimes it was $200 a month 'cause I had two of you

there at one time, as I recall. Guess I was lucky I never had all three behind bars. Couldn't've paid my light bill."

"I thought those lawyers worked for free," Butch said in an effort to deflect attention from himself and hopefully direct it toward a target outside the family.

"They do," Leon said. "It's called pro bono work, and all lawyers are supposed to do some of it. As far as I know, these big firms who come in on cases like this don't expect to get paid."

"Then what's Raymond doin' with $300 a month if he ain't payin' his lawyers?"

"We've had this conversation," Inez said.

"I'm sure he spends a fortune on pens, paper, envelopes, and postage," Leon said. "He claims he writes ten letters a day. Hell, that's over $100 a month right there."

"Plus he's written eight novels," Butch added quickly. "Or is it nine, Momma? I can't remember."

"Nine."

"Nine novels, several volumes of poetry, bunch of short stories, hundreds of songs. Just think of all the paper he goes through," Butch said.

"Are you pokin' fun at Raymond?" she asked.

"Never."

"He sold a short story once," she said.

"Of course he did. What was the magazine? *Hot Rodder*? Paid him forty bucks for a story about a man who stole a thousand hubcaps. They say you write what you know."

"How many stories have you sold?" she asked.

"None, because I haven't written any, and the reason I

haven't written any is because I realize that I don't have the talent to write. If my little brother would also realize that he has no artistic talents whatsoever, then he could save some money and hundreds of people would not be subjected to his nonsense."

"That's very cruel."

"No, Momma, it's very honest. And if you'd been honest with him a long time ago, then maybe he would've stopped writing. But no. You read his books and his poetry and his short stories and told him the stuff was great. So he wrote more, with longer words, longer sentences, longer paragraphs, and got to the point to where now we can hardly understand a damned thang he writes."

"So it's all my fault?"

"Not 100 percent, no."

"He writes for therapy."

"I've been there. I don't see how writin' helps any."

"He says it helps."

"Are these books handwritten or typed up?" Leon asked, interrupting.

"Typed," Butch said.

"Who types 'em?"

"He has to pay some guy over in the law library," Inez said. "A dollar a page, and one of the books was over eight hundred pages. I read it, though, ever' word."

"Did you understand ever' word?" Butch asked.

"Most of 'em. A dictionary helps. Lord, I don't know where that boy finds those words."

"And Raymond sent these books up to New York to get published, right?" Leon asked, pressing on.

"Yes, and they sent 'em right back," she said. "I guess they couldn't understand all his words either."

"You'd think those people in New York would understand what he's sayin'," Leon said.

"No one understands what he's sayin'," Butch said. "That's the problem with Raymond the novelist, and Raymond the poet, and Raymond the political prisoner, and Raymond the songwriter, and Raymond the lawyer. No person in his right mind could possibly have any idea what Raymond says when he starts writin'."

"So, if I understand this correctly," Leon said, "a large portion of Raymond's overhead has been spent to finance his literary career. Paper, postage, typing, copying, shipping to New York and back. That right, Momma?"

"I guess."

"And it's doubtful if his stipends have actually gone to pay his lawyers," Leon said.

"Very doubtful," Butch said. "And don't forget his music career. He spends money on guitar strings and sheet music. Plus, they now allow the prisoners to rent tapes. That's how Raymond became a blues singer. He listened to B. B. King and Muddy Waters, and, according to Raymond, he now entertains his colleagues on death row with late-night sessions of the blues."

"Oh, I know. He's told me about it in his letters."

"He always had a good voice," Inez said.

"I never heard 'im sang," Leon said.

"Me neither," Butch added.

They were on the bypass around Oxford, two hours away from Parchman. The upholstery van seemed to run best at sixty miles an hour; anything faster and the front tires shook a bit. There was no hurry. West of Oxford the hills began to flatten; the Delta was not far away. Inez recognized a little white country church off to the right, next to a cemetery, and it occurred to her that the church had not changed in all the many years she had made this journey to the state penitentiary. She asked herself how many other women in Ford County had made as many of these trips, but she knew the answer. Leon had started the tradition many years earlier with a thirty-month incarceration, and back then the rules allowed her to visit on the first Sunday of each month. Sometimes Butch drove her and sometimes she paid a neighbor's son, but she never missed a visitation and she always took peanut butter fudge and extra toothpaste. Six months after Leon was paroled, he was driving her so she could visit Butch. Then it was Butch and Raymond, but in different units with different rules.

Then Raymond killed the deputy, and they locked him down on death row, which had its own rules.

With practice, most unpleasant tasks become bearable, and Inez Graney had learned to look forward to the visits. Her sons had been condemned by the rest of the county, but their mother would never abandon them. She was there when they were born, and she was there when they were beaten. She had suffered through their court appearances and parole hearings, and she had told anyone who would listen that they were good boys who'd been abused by the man she'd chosen to marry. All of it was her fault. If she'd married a decent man, her children might have had normal lives.

"Reckon that woman'll be there?" Leon asked.

"Lord, Lord," Inez groaned.

"Why would she miss the show?" Butch said. "I'm sure she'll be around somewhere."

"Lord, Lord."

That woman was Tallulah, a fruitcake who'd entered their lives a few years earlier and managed to make a bad situation much worse. Through one of the abolitionist groups, she'd made contact with Raymond, who responded in typical fashion with a lengthy letter filled with claims of innocence and maltreatment and the usual drivel about his budding literary and music careers. He sent her some poems, love sonnets, and she became obsessed with him. They met in the visitation room at death row and, through a thick metal screen window, fell in love. Raymond sang a few blues tunes, and Tallulah was swept away. There was talk of a marriage, but those plans were put on hold until Tallulah's then-current husband was executed by the State of Georgia. After a brief period of mourning, she traveled to Parchman for a bizarre ceremony that was recognized by no identifiable state law or religious doctrine. Anyway, Raymond was in love, and, thus inspired, his prodigious letter writing reached new heights. The family was forewarned that Tallulah was anxious to visit Ford County and see her new in-laws. She indeed arrived, but when they refused to acknowledge her, she instead paid a visit to the *Ford County*

*Times*, where she shared her rambling thoughts, her insights into the plight of poor Raymond Graney, and her promises that new evidence would clear him in the death of the deputy. She also announced that she was pregnant with Raymond's child, a result of several conjugal visits now available to death row inmates.

Tallulah made the front page, photo and all, but the reporter had been wise enough to check with Parchman. Conjugal visits were not allowed for the inmates, especially those on death row. And there was no official record of a marriage. Undaunted, Tallulah continued to wave Raymond's flag, and even went so far as to haul several of his bulky manuscripts to New York, where they were again rejected by publishers with little vision. With time she faded away, though Inez, Leon, and Butch lived with the horror that another Graney might soon be born, somewhere. In spite of the rules regarding conjugal visits, they knew Raymond. He could find a way.

After two years, Raymond informed the family that he and Tallulah would be seeking a divorce and, to properly obtain one, he needed $500. This touched off another nasty episode of bickering and name-calling, and the money was raised only after he threatened suicide, and not for the first time. Not long after the checks had been mailed, Raymond wrote with the great news that he and Tallulah had reconciled. He did not offer to return the money to Inez, Butch, and Leon, though all three suggested that he do so. Raymond declined on the grounds that his new team of lawyers needed the money to hire experts and investigators.

What irked Leon and Butch was their brother's sense of entitlement, as though they, the family, owed him the money because of his persecution. In the early days of his imprisonment, both Leon and Butch had reminded Raymond that he had not sent them the first penny when they were behind bars and he was not. This had led to another nasty episode that Inez had been forced to mediate.

She sat bent and unmoving in her wheelchair, with a large canvas bag in her lap. As the thoughts of Tallulah began to fade, she opened the bag and withdrew a letter from Raymond, his latest. She opened the envelope, plain and white with his swirling cursive writing all over the front, and unfolded two sheets of yellow tablet paper.

Dearest Mother:

It is becoming increasingly obvious and apparent that the cumbersome and unwieldy yes even lethargic machinations of our inequitable and dishonorable yes even corrupt judicial system have inevitably and irrevocably trained their loathsome and despicable eyes upon me.

Inez took a breath, then read the sentence again. Most of the words looked familiar. After years of reading with a letter in one hand and a dictionary in the other, she was amazed at how much her vocabulary had expanded.

Butch glanced back, saw the letter, shook his head, but said nothing.

However, the State of Mississippi will once again be thwarted and stymied and left in thorough and consummate degradation in its resolution to extract blood from Raymond T. Graney. For I have procured and retained the services of a young lawyer with astonishing skills, an extraordinary advocate judiciously chosen by me from the innumerable legions of barristers quite literally throwing themselves at my feet.

Another pause, another quick rereading. Inez was barely hanging on.

Not surprisingly, a lawyer of such exquisite and superlative yes even singular proficiencies and dexterities cannot labor and effectively advocate on my behalf without appropriate recompense.

"What's recompense?" she asked.

"Spell it," Butch said.

She spelled it slowly, and the three pondered the word. This exercise in language skills had become as routine as talking about the weather.

"How's it used?" Butch asked, so she read the sentence.

"Money," Butch said, and Leon quickly agreed. Raymond's mysterious words often had something to do with money.

"Let me guess. He's got a new lawyer and needs some extra money to pay him."

Inez ignored him and kept reading.

It is with great reluctance even trepidation that I desperately beseech you and implore you to procure the quite reasonable sum of $1,500 which will forthrightly find application in my defense and undoubtedly extricate me and emancipate me and otherwise save my ass. Come on, Momma, now is the hour for the family to join hands and metaphorically circle the wagons. Your reluctance yes even your recalcitrance will be deemed pernicious neglect.

"What's recalcitrance?" she asked.

"Spell it," Leon said. She spelled "recalcitrance," then "pernicious," and after a halfhearted debate it was obvious that none of the three had a clue.

One final note before I move on to more pressing correspondence—Butch and Leon have again neglected my stipends. Their latest perfidies concern the month of June, and it's already halfway through July. Please torment, harass, vex, heckle, and badger those two blockheads until they honor their commitments to my defense fund.

Love, as always, from your dearest and favorite son, Raymond

Each letter sent to a death row inmate was read by someone in the mail room at Parchman, and each outgoing letter was likewise scrutinized. Inez had often pitied the poor soul assigned to read Raymond's missives. They never failed to tire Inez, primarily because they required work. She was afraid she would miss something important.

The letters drained her. The lyrics put her to sleep. The novels produced migraines. The poetry could not be penetrated.

She wrote back twice a week, without fail, because if she ne-

glected her youngest by even a day or so, she could expect a tor-
rent of abuse, a four-pager or maybe a five-pager with blistering
language that contained words often not found in a dictionary.
And even the slightest delay in mailing in her stipend would cause
unpleasant collect phone calls.

Of the three, Raymond had been the best student, though
none had finished high school. Leon had been the better athlete,
Butch the better musician, but little Raymond got the brains.
And he made it all the way to the eleventh grade before he got
caught with a stolen motorcycle and spent sixty days in a juve-
nile facility. He was sixteen, five years younger than Butch and
ten younger than Leon, and already the Graney boys were devel-
oping the reputation as skillful car thieves. Raymond joined the
family business and forgot about school.

"So how much does he want this time?" Butch asked.

"Fifteen hundred, for a new lawyer. Said you two ain't sent
his stipends for last month."

"Drop it, Momma," Leon said harshly, and for a long time
nothing else was said.

When the first car theft ring was broken, Leon took the fall
and did his time at Parchman. Upon his release, he married his
second wife and managed to go straight. Butch and Raymond
made no effort at going straight; in fact, they expanded their activities. They fenced stolen guns and appliances, dabbled in the
marijuana trade, ran moonshine, and of course stole cars and sold
them to various chop shops in north Mississippi. Butch got busted
when he stole an 18-wheeler that was supposed to be full of Sony
televisions but in fact was a load of chain-link fencing. Televi-

sions are easy to move on the black market. Chain link proved far more difficult. In the course of events the sheriff raided Butch's hiding place and found the contraband, useless as it was. He pleaded to eighteen months, his first stint at Parchman. Raymond avoided indictment and lived to steal again. He stuck to his first love—cars and pickups—and prospered nicely, though all profits were wasted on booze, gambling, and an astounding string of bad women.

From the beginning of their careers as thieves, the Graney boys were hounded by an obnoxious deputy named Coy Childers. Coy suspected them in every misdemeanor and felony in Ford County. He watched them, followed them, threatened them, harassed them, and at various times arrested them for good cause or for no cause whatsoever. All three had been beaten by Coy in the depths of the Ford County jail. They had complained bitterly to the sheriff, Coy's boss, but no one listens to the whining of known criminals. And the Graneys became quite well-known.

For revenge, Raymond stole Coy's patrol car and sold it to a chop shop in Memphis. He kept the police radio and mailed it back to Coy in an unmarked parcel. Raymond was arrested and would've been beaten but for the intervention of his court-appointed lawyer. There was no proof at all, nothing to link him to the crime except some well-founded suspicion. Two months later, after Raymond had been released, Coy bought his wife a new Chevrolet Impala. Raymond promptly stole it from a church parking lot during Wednesday night prayer meeting and sold it to a chop shop near Tupelo. By then, Coy was openly vowing to kill Raymond Graney.

There were no witnesses to the actual killing, or at least none who would come forward. It happened late on a Friday night, on a gravel road not far from a double-wide trailer Raymond was sharing with his latest girlfriend. The prosecution's theory was that Coy had parked his car and was approaching quietly on foot, alone, with the plan to confront Raymond and perhaps even arrest him. Coy was found after sunrise by some deer hunters. He'd been shot twice in the forehead by a high-powered rifle, and he was positioned in a slight dip in the gravel road, which allowed a large amount of blood to accumulate around his body. The crime scene photos caused two jurors to vomit.

Raymond and his girl claimed to be away at a honky-tonk, but evidently they had been the only customers because no other alibi witnesses could be found. Ballistics traced the bullets to a stolen rifle fenced through one of Raymond's longtime underworld associates, and though there was no proof that Raymond had ever owned, stolen, borrowed, or possessed the rifle, the suspicion was enough. The prosecutor convinced the jury that Raymond had motive—he hated Coy, and he was, after all, a convicted felon; he had opportunity—Coy was found near Raymond's trailer, and there were no neighbors within miles; and he had the means— the alleged murder weapon was waved around the courtroom, complete with an army-issue scope that may have allowed the killer to see through the darkness, though there was no evidence the scope was actually attached to the rifle when it was used to kill Coy.

Raymond's alibi was weak. His girlfriend, too, had a criminal record and made a lousy witness. His court-appointed defense lawyer subpoenaed three people who were supposed to testify that they had heard Coy vow to kill Raymond Graney. All three faltered under the pressure of sitting in the witness chair and being glared at by the sheriff and at least ten of his uniformed deputies. It was a questionable defense strategy to begin with. If Raymond believed Coy was coming to kill him, then did he, Raymond, act in self-defense? Was Raymond admitting to the crime? No, he was not. He insisted he knew nothing about it and was dancing in a bar when someone else took care of Coy.

In spite of the overwhelming public pressure to convict Raymond, the jury stayed out for two days before finally doing so.

A year later, the Feds broke up a methamphetamine ring, and in the aftermath of a dozen hasty plea bargains it was learned that Deputy Coy Childers had been heavily involved in the drug-distribution syndicate. Two other murders, very similar in details, had taken place over in Marshall County, sixty miles away. Coy's stellar reputation among the locals was badly tarnished. The gossip began to fester about who really killed him, though Raymond remained the favorite suspect.

His conviction and death sentence were unanimously affirmed by the state's supreme court. More appeals led to more affirmations, and now, eleven years later, the case was winding down.

West of Batesville, the hills finally yielded to the flatlands, and the highway cut through fields thick with midsummer cotton and soybeans. Farmers on their green John Deeres poked along the highway as if it had been built for tractors and not automobiles. But the Graneys were in no hurry. The van moved on, past an idle cotton gin, abandoned shotgun shacks, new double-wide trailers with satellite dishes and big trucks parked at the doors, and an occasional fine home set back to keep the traffic away from the landowners. At the town of Marks, Leon turned south, and they moved deeper into the Delta.

"I reckon Charlene'll be there," Inez said.

"Most certainly," Leon said.

"She wouldn't miss it for anything," Butch said.

Charlene was Coy's widow, a long-suffering woman who had embraced the martyrdom of her husband with unusual enthusiasm. Over the years she had joined every victims' group she could find, state and national. She threatened lawsuits against the newspaper and anybody else who questioned Coy's integrity. She had written long letters to the editor demanding speedier justice for Raymond Graney. And she had missed not one court hearing along the way, even traveling as far as New Orleans when the federal Fifth Circuit Court of Appeals had the case.

"She's been prayin' for this day," Leon said.

"Well, she better keep prayin' 'cause Raymond said it ain't gonna happen," Inez said. "He promised me his lawyers are much better than the state's lawyers and that they're filin' papers by the truckload."

Leon glanced at Butch, who made eye contact, then gazed at the cotton fields. They passed through the farm settlements of Vance, Tutwiler, and Rome as the sun was finally fading. Dusk brought the swarms of insects that hit the hood and windshield. They smoked with the windows down, and said little. The approach to Parchman always subdued the Graneys—Butch and

Leon for obvious reasons, and Inez because it reminded her of her shortcomings as a mother.

Parchman was an infamous prison, but it was also a farm, a plantation, that sprawled over eighteen thousand acres of rich black soil that had produced cotton and profits for the state for decades until the federal courts got involved and pretty much abolished slave labor. In another lawsuit, another federal court ended the segregated conditions. More litigation had made life slightly better, though violence was worse.

For Leon, thirty months there turned him away from crime, and that was what the law-abiding citizens demanded of a prison. For Butch, his first sentence proved that he could survive another, and no car or truck was safe in Ford County.

Highway 3 ran straight and flat, and there was little traffic. It was almost dark when the van passed the small green highway sign that simply said, Parchman. Ahead there were lights, activity, something unusual happening. To the right were the white stone front gates of the prison, and across the highway in a gravel lot a circus was under way. Death penalty protesters were busy. Some knelt in a circle and prayed. Some walked a tight formation with handmade posters supporting Ray Graney. Another group sang a hymn. Another knelt around a priest and held candles. Farther down the highway, a smaller group chanted pro-death slogans and tossed insults at the supporters of Graney. Uniformed deputies kept the peace. Television news crews were busy recording it all.

Leon stopped at the guardhouse, which was crawling with

prison guards and anxious security personnel. A guard with a clip-board stepped to the driver's door and said, "Your name?"

"Graney, family of Mr. Raymond Graney. Leon, Butch, and our mother, Inez."

The guard wrote nothing, took a step back, managed to say, "Wait a minute," then left them. Three guards stood directly in front of the van, at a barricade across the entry road.

"He's gone to get Fitch," Butch said. "Wanna bet?"

"No," Leon replied.

Fitch was an assistant warden of some variety, a career prison employee whose dead-end job was brightened only by an escape or an execution. In cowboy boots and fake Stetson, and with a large pistol on his hip, he swaggered around Parchman as if he owned it. Fitch had outlasted a dozen wardens and had survived that many lawsuits. As he approached the van, he said loudly, "Well, well, the Graney boys're back where they belong. Here for a little furniture repair, boys? We have an old electric chair ya'll can reupholster." He laughed at his own humor, and there was more laughter behind him.

"Evenin', Mr. Fitch," Leon said. "We have our mother with us."

"Evenin', ma'am," Fitch said as he glanced inside the van. Inez did not respond.

"Where'd you get this van?" Fitch asked.

"We borrowed it," Leon answered. Butch stared straight ahead and refused to look at Fitch.

"Borrowed my ass. When's the last time you boys borrowed

anything? I'm sure Mr. McBride is lookin' for his van right now. Might give him a call."

"You do that, Fitch," Leon said.

"It's Mr. Fitch to you."

"Whatever you say."

Fitch unloaded a mouthful of spit. He nodded ahead as if he and he alone controlled the details. "I reckon you boys know where you're goin'," he said. "God knows you been here enough. Follow that car back to max security. They'll do the search there." He waved at the guards at the barricade. An opening was created, and they left Fitch without another word. For a few minutes, they followed an unmarked car filled with armed men. They passed one unit after another, each entirely separate, each encir-cled by chain link topped with razor wire. Butch gazed at the unit where he'd surrendered several years of his life. In a well-lit open area, the "playground," as they called it, he saw the inevitable basketball game with shirtless men drenched in sweat, always one hard foul away from another mindless brawl. He saw the calmer ones sitting on picnic tables, waiting for the 10:00 p.m. bed check, waiting for the heat to break because the barracks air units sel-dom worked, especially in July.

As usual, Leon glanced at his old unit but did not dwell on his time there. After so many years, he had been able to tuck away the emotional scars of physical abuse. The inmate population was 80 percent black, and Parchman was one of the few places in Mis-sissippi where the whites did not make the rules.

The maximum security unit was a 1950s-style flat-roofed

building, one level, redbrick, much like countless elementary schools built back then. It, too, was wrapped in chain link and razor wire and watched by guards lounging in towers, though on this night everyone in uniform was awake and excited. Leon parked where he was directed, then he and Butch were thoroughly searched by a small battalion of unsmiling guards. Inez was lifted out, rolled to a makeshift checkpoint, and carefully inspected by two female guards. They were escorted inside the building, through a series of heavy doors, past more guards, and finally to a small room they had never seen before. The visitors' room was elsewhere. Two guards stayed with them as they settled in. The room had a sofa, two folding chairs, a row of ancient file cabinets, and the look of an office that belonged to some trifling bureaucrat who'd been chased away for the night.

The two prison guards weighed at least 250 pounds each, had twenty-four-inch necks and the obligatory shaved heads. After five awkward minutes in the room with the family, Butch had had enough. He took a few steps and challenged them with a bold "What, exactly, are you two doing in here?"

"Following orders," one said.

"Whose orders?"

"The warden's."

"Do you realize how stupid you look? Here we are, the family of the condemned man, waiting to spend a few minutes with our brother, in this tiny shit hole of a room, with no windows, cinder-block walls, only one door, and you're standing here guarding us as if we're dangerous. Do you realize how stupid this is?"

Both necks seemed to expand. Both faces turned scarlet. Had

Butch been an inmate, he would have been beaten, but he wasn't. He was a citizen, a former convict who hated every cop, trooper, guard, agent, and security type he'd ever seen. Every man in a uniform was his enemy.

"Sir, please sit down," one said coolly.

"In case you idiots don't realize it, you can guard this room from the other side of that door just as easily as you can from this side. I swear. It's true. I know you probably haven't been trained enough to realize this, but if you just walked through the door and parked your big asses on the other side, then ever'thang would still be secure and we'd have some privacy. We could talk to our little brother without worryin' about you clowns eaves-droppin'."

"You'd better knock it off, pal."

"Go ahead, just step through the door, close it, stare at it, guard it. I know you boys can handle it. I know you can keep us safe in here."

Of course the guards didn't move, and Butch eventually sat in a folding chair close to his mother. After a thirty-minute wait that seemed to last forever, the warden entered with his en-tourage and introduced himself. "The execution is still planned for one minute after midnight," he said officially, as if he were discussing a routine meeting with his staff. "We've been told not to expect a last-minute call from the governor's office." There was no hint of compassion.

Inez placed both hands over her face and began crying softly.

He continued, "The lawyers are busy with all the last-minute stuff they always do, but our lawyers tell us a reprieve is unlikely."

Leon and Butch stared at the floor.

"We relax the rules a little for these events. You're free to stay in here as long as you like, and we'll bring in Raymond shortly. I'm sorry it's come down to this. If I can do anything, just let me know."

"Get those two jackasses outta here," Butch said, pointing to the guards. "We'd like some privacy."

The warden hesitated, looked around the room, then said, "No problem." He left and took the guards with him. Fifteen minutes later, the door opened again, and Raymond bounced in with a big smile and went straight for his mother. After a long hug and a few tears, he bear-hugged his brothers and told them things were moving in their favor. They pulled the chairs close to the sofa and sat in a small huddle, with Raymond clutching his mother's hands.

"We got these sumbitches on the run," he said, still smiling, the picture of confidence. "My lawyers are filin' a truckload of habeas corpus petitions as we speak, and they're quite certain the U.S. Supreme Court will grant certiorari within the hour."

"What does that mean?" Inez asked.

"Means the Supreme Court will agree to hear the case, and it's an automatic delay. Means we'll probably get a new trial in Ford County, though I'm not sure I want it there."

He was wearing prison whites, no socks, and a pair of cheap rubber sandals. And it was clear that Raymond was packing on the pounds. His cheeks were round and puffy. A spare tire hung over his belt. They had not seen him in almost six weeks, and his weight gain was noticeable. As usual, he prattled on about matters they did not understand and did not believe, at least as far as Butch and Leon were concerned. Raymond had been born with a vivid imagination, a quick tongue, and an innate inability to tell the truth.

The boy could lie.

"Got two dozen lawyers scramblin' right now," he said. "State can't keep up with 'em."

"When do you hear somethin' from the court?" Inez asked.

"Any minute now. I got federal judges in Jackson, in New Orleans, and in Washington sittin' by, just ready to kick the state's ass."

After eleven years of having his ass thoroughly kicked by the state, it was difficult to believe that Raymond had now, at this late hour, managed to turn the tide. Leon and Butch nodded gravely, as if they bought this and believed that the inevitable was not about to happen. They had known for many years that their little brother had ambushed Coy and practically blown his head off with a stolen rifle. Raymond had told Butch years earlier, long after he'd landed on death row, that he'd been so stoned he could hardly remember the killing.

"Plus we got some big-shot lawyers in Jackson puttin' pressure on the governor, just in case the Supreme Court chickens out again," he said.

All three nodded, but no one mentioned the comments from the warden.

"You got my last letter, Momma? The one about the new lawyer?"

"Sure did. Read it drivin' over here," she said, nodding.

"I'd like to hire him as soon as we get an order for the new trial. He's from Mobile, and he is one bad boy, lemme tell you. But we can talk about him later."

"Sure, son."

"Thank you. Look, Momma, I know this is hard, but you gotta have faith in me and my lawyers. I been runnin' my own defense for a year now, bossin' the lawyers around 'cause that's what you gotta do these days, and thangs're gonna work out, Momma. Trust me."

"I do, I do."

Raymond jumped to his feet and thrust his arms high above, stretching with his eyes closed. "I'm into yoga now, did I tell ya'll about it?"

All three nodded. His letters had been loaded with the details of his latest fascination. Over the years the family had suffered through Raymond's breathless accounts of his conversion to Buddhism, then Islam, then Hinduism, and his discoveries of meditation, kung fu, aerobics, weight lifting, fasting, and of course his quest to become a poet, novelist, singer, and musician. Little had been spared in his letters home.

Whatever the current passion, it was obvious that the fasting and aerobics had been abandoned. Raymond was so fat his britches strained in the seat.

"Did you bring the brownies?" he asked his mother. He loved her pecan brownies.

"No, honey, I'm sorry. I've been so tore up over this."

"You always bring the brownies."

"I'm sorry."

Just like Raymond. Berating his mother over nothing just hours before his final walk.

"Well, don't forget them again."

"I won't, honey."

"And another thang. Tallulah is supposed to be here any minute. She'd love to meet ya'll because ya'll have always rejected her. She's part of the family regardless of what ya'll thank. As a favor at this unfortunate moment in my life, I ask that ya'll accept her and be nice."

Leon and Butch could not respond, but Inez managed to say, "Yes, dear."

"When I get outta this damned place, we're movin' to Hawaii and havin' ten kids. No way I'm stayin' in Mississippi, not after all this. So she'll be part of the family from now on."

For the first time Leon glanced at his watch with the thought that relief was just over two hours away. Butch was thinking too, but his thoughts were far different. The idea of choking Raymond to death before the state could kill him posed an interesting dilemma.

Raymond suddenly stood and said, "Well, look, I gotta go meet with the lawyers. I'll be back in half an hour." He walked to the door, opened it, then thrust out his arms for the handcuffs. The door closed, and Inez said, "I guess thangs're okay."

"Look, Momma, we'd best listen to the warden," Leon said.

"Raymond's kiddin' himself," Butch added. She started crying again.

The chaplain was a Catholic priest, Father Leland, and he

quietly introduced himself to the family. They asked him to have a seat.

"I'm deeply sorry about this," he said somberly. "It's the worst part of my job."

Catholics were rare in Ford County, and the Graneys certainly didn't know any. They looked suspiciously at the white collar around his neck.

"I've tried to talk to Raymond," Father Leland continued. "But he has little interest in the Christian faith. Said he hadn't been to church since he was a little boy."

"I shoulda took him more," Inez said, lamenting.

"In fact, he claims to be an atheist."

"Lord, Lord."

Of course, the three Graneys had known for some time that Raymond had renounced all religious beliefs and had proclaimed that there was no God. This, too, they had read about in excruciating detail in his lengthy letters.

"We're not church people," Leon admitted.

"I'll be praying for you."

"Raymond stole the deputy's wife's new car outta the church parking lot," Butch said. "Did he tell you that?"

"No. We've talked a lot lately, and he's told me many stories. But not that one."

"Thank you, sir, for bein' so nice to Raymond," Inez said.

"I'll be with him until the end."

"So, they're really gonna do it?" she asked.

"It'll take a miracle to stop things now."

"Lord, help us," she said.

"Let's pray," Father Leland said. He closed his eyes, folded his hands together, and began: "Dear Heavenly Father, please look down upon us at this hour and let your Holy Spirit enter this place and give us peace. Give strength and wisdom to the lawyers and judges who are laboring diligently at this moment. Give courage to Raymond as he makes his preparations." Father Leland paused for a second and barely opened his left eye. All three Graneys were staring at him as if he had two heads. Rattled, he closed his eye and wrapped things up quickly with: "And, Father, grant grace and forgiveness to the officials and the people of Mississippi, for they know not what they're doing. Amen."

He said good-bye, and they waited a few minutes before Raymond returned. He had his guitar, and as soon as he settled into the sofa he strummed a few chords. He closed his eyes and began to hum, then he sang:

*I got time to see you baby*
*I got time to come on by*
*I got time to stay forever*
*'Cause I got no time to die.*

"It's an old tune by Mudcat Malone," he explained. "One of my favorites."

*I got time to see you smilin'*
*I got time to see you cry*
*I got time to hold you baby*
*'Cause I got no time to die.*

The song was unlike any they'd heard before. Butch had once picked the banjo in a bluegrass band, but had given up music many years earlier. He had no voice whatsoever, a family trait shared by his younger brother. Raymond crooned in a painful guttural lurch, an affected attempt to sound like a black blues singer, apparently one in severe distress.

*I got time to be yo' daddy*
*I got time to be yo' guy*
*I got time to be yo' lover*
*'Cause I got no time to die.*

When the words stopped, he kept strumming and did a passable job of playing a tune. Butch, though, couldn't help but think that after eleven years of practice in his cell, his guitar playing was rudimentary.

"That's so nice," Inez said.

"Thanks, Momma. Here's one from Little Bennie Burke, probably the greatest of all. He's from Indianola, you know that?" They did not know. Like most white hill folks, they knew nothing about the blues and cared even less.

Raymond's face contorted again. He hit the strings harder.

*I packed my bags on Monday*
*Tuesday said so long*
*Wednesday saw my baby*
*Thursday she was gone*
*Got paid this Friday mornin'*

*Man said I's all right*
*Told him he could shove it*
*I'm walkin' out tonight.*

Leon glanced at his watch. It was almost 11:00 p.m., just over an hour to go. He wasn't sure he could listen to the blues for another hour, but resigned himself. The singing unnerved Butch as well, but he managed to sit still with his eyes closed, as if soothed by the words and music.

*I'm tired of pickin' cotton*
*I'm tired of shootin' dice*
*I'm tired of gettin' hassled*
*I'm tired of tryin' to be nice*
*I'm tired of workin' for nothing*
*I'm tired of havin' to fight*
*Everything's behind me now*
*I'm walkin' out tonight.*

Raymond then forgot the words, but continued with his humming. When he finally stopped, he sat with his eyes closed for a minute or so, as if the music had transported him to another world, to a much more pleasant place.

"What time is it, bro?" he asked Leon.

"Eleven straight up."

"I gotta go check with the lawyers. They're expectin' a ruling right about now."

He placed his guitar in a corner, then knocked on the door and stepped through it. The guards handcuffed him and led him away. Within minutes a crew from the kitchen arrived with armed escort. Hurriedly, they unfolded a square card table and covered it with a rather large amount of food. The smells were immediately thick in the room, and Leon and Butch were weak with hunger. They had not eaten since noon. Inez was too distraught to think about food, though she did examine the spread. Fried catfish, French-fried potatoes, hush puppies, coleslaw, all in the center of the table. To the right was a mammoth cheeseburger, with another order of fries and one of onion rings. To the left was a medium-size pizza with pepperoni and hot, bubbling cheese. Directly in front of the catfish was a huge slice of what appeared to be lemon pie, and next to it was a dessert plate covered with chocolate cake. A bowl of vanilla ice cream was wedged along the edge of the table.

As the three Graneys gawked at the food, one of the guards said, "For the last meal, he gets anything he wants."

"Lord, Lord," Inez said and began crying again.

When they were alone, Butch and Leon tried to ignore the food, which they could almost touch, but the aromas were overwhelming. Catfish battered and fried in corn oil. Fried onion rings. Pepperoni. The air in the small room was thick with the competing yet delicious smells.

The feast could easily accommodate four people.

At 11:15, Raymond made a noisy entry. He was griping at the guards and complaining incoherently about his lawyers. When he saw the food, he forgot about his problems and his family and took the only seat at the table. Using primarily his fingers, he crammed in a few loads of fries and onion rings and began talking. "Fifth Circuit just turned us down, the idiots. Our habeas petition was beautiful, wrote it myself. We're on the way to Washington, to the Supreme Court. Got a whole law firm up there ready to attack. Thangs look good." He managed to deftly shove food into his mouth, and chew it, while talking. Inez stared at her feet and wiped tears. Butch and Leon appeared to listen patiently while studying the tiled floor.

"Ya'll seen Tallulah?" Raymond asked, still chomping after a gulp of iced tea.

"No," Leon said.

"Bitch. She just wants the book rights to my life story. That's all. But it ain't gonna happen. I'm leavin' all literary rights with the three of ya'll. What about that?"

"Nice," said Leon.

"Great," said Butch.

The final chapter of his life was now close at hand. Raymond had already written his autobiography—two hundred pages—and it had been rejected by every publisher in America.

He chomped away, wreaking havoc with the catfish, burger, and pizza in no particular order. His fork and fingers moved around the table, often headed in different directions, poking, stabbing, grabbing, and shoveling food into his mouth as fast as he could swallow it. A starving hog at a trough would have made less noise. Inez had never spent much time with table manners, and her boys had learned all the bad habits. But eleven years on death row had taken Raymond to new depths of crude behavior.

Leon's third wife, though, had been properly raised. He snapped ten minutes into the last meal. "Do you have to smack like that?" he barked.

"Damn, son, you're makin' more noise than a horse eatin' corn," Butch piled on instantly.

Raymond froze, glared at both of his brothers, and for a few long tense seconds the situation could've gone either way. It could've erupted into a classic Graney brawl with lots of cursing and personal insults. Over the years, there had been several ugly spats in the visitors' room at death row, all painful, all memorable. But Raymond, to his credit, took a softer approach.

"It's my last meal," he said. "And my own family's bitchin' at me."

"I'm not," Inez said.

"Thank you, Momma."

Leon held his hands wide in surrender and said, "I'm sorry. We're all a little tense."

"Tense?" Raymond said. "You think you're tense?"

"I'm sorry, Ray."

"Me too," Butch said, but only because it was expected.

"You want a hush puppy?" Ray said, offering one to Butch.

A few minutes earlier the last meal had been an irresistible feast. Now, though, after Raymond's frenzied assault, the table was in ruins. In spite of this, Butch was craving some fries and a hush puppy, but he declined. There was something eerily wrong with nibbling off the edges of a man's last meal. "No, thanks," he said.

After catching his breath, Raymond plowed ahead, albeit at a slower and quieter pace. He finished off the lemon pie and chocolate cake, with ice cream, belched, and laughed about it, then said, "Ain't my last meal, I can promise you that."

There was a knock on the door, and a guard stepped in and said, "Mr. Tanner would like to see you."

"Send him in," Raymond said. "My chief lawyer," he announced proudly to his family.

Mr. Tanner was a slight, balding young man in a faded navy jacket, old khakis, and even older tennis shoes. He wore no tie. He carried a thick stack of papers. His face was gaunt and pale, and he looked as if he needed a long rest. Raymond quickly introduced him to his family, but Mr. Tanner showed no interest in meeting new people at that moment.

"The Supreme Court just turned us down," he announced gravely to Raymond.

Raymond swallowed hard, and the room was silent.

"What about the governor?" Leon asked. "And all those lawyers down there talkin' to him?"

Tanner shot a blank look at Raymond, who said, "I fired them."

"What about all those lawyers in Washington?" Butch asked.

"I fired them too."

"What about that big firm from Chicago?" Leon asked.

"I fired them too."

Tanner looked back and forth among the Graneys.

"Seems like a bad time to be firin' your lawyers," Leon said.

"What lawyers?" Tanner asked. "I'm the only lawyer working on this case."

"You're fired too," Raymond said, and violently slapped his glass of tea off the card table, sending ice and liquid splashing against a wall. "Go ahead and kill me!" he screamed. "I don't care anymore."

No one breathed for a few seconds, then the door opened suddenly and the warden was back, with his entourage. "It's time, Raymond," he said, somewhat impatiently. "The appeals are over, and the governor's gone to bed."

There was a long heavy pause as the finality sank in. Inez was crying. Leon was staring blankly at the wall where the tea and ice were sliding to the floor. Butch was looking forlornly at the last two hush puppies. Tanner appeared ready to faint.

Raymond cleared his throat and said, "I'd like to see that Catholic guy. We need to pray."

"I'll get him," the warden said. "You can have one last moment with your family, then it's time to go."

The warden left with his assistants. Tanner quickly followed them.

Raymond's shoulders slumped, and his face was pale. All defiance and bravado vanished. He walked slowly to his mother, fell to his knees in front of her, and put his head in her lap. She rubbed it, wiped her eyes, and kept saying, "Lord, Lord."

"I'm so sorry, Momma," Raymond mumbled. "I'm so sorry."

They cried together for a moment while Leon and Butch stood silently by. Father Leland entered the room, and Raymond slowly stood. His eyes were wet and red, and his voice was soft and weak. "I guess it's over," he said to the priest, who nodded sadly and patted his shoulder. "I'll be with you in the isolation room, Raymond," he said. "We'll have a final prayer, if you wish."

"Probably not a bad idea."

The door opened again, and the warden was back. He addressed the Graneys and Father Leland. "Please listen to me," he said. "This is my fourth execution, and I've learned a few things. One is that it is a bad idea for the mother to witness the execution. I strongly suggest, Mrs. Graney, that you remain here, in this room, for the next hour or so, until it's over. We have a nurse who will sit with you, and she has a sedative that I recommend. Please." He looked at Leon and Butch and pleaded with his eyes. Both got the message.

"I'll be there till the end," Inez said, then wailed so loudly that even the warden had a flash of goose bumps.

Butch stepped next to her and stroked her shoulder.

"You need to stay here, Momma," Leon said. Inez wailed again.

"She'll stay," Leon said to the warden. "Just get her that pill."

Raymond hugged both of his brothers, and for the first time ever said that he loved them, an act that was difficult even at that awful moment. He kissed his mother on the cheek and said good-bye.

"Be a man," Butch said with clenched teeth and wet eyes, and they embraced for the final time.

They led him away, and the nurse entered the room. She handed Inez a pill and a cup of water, and within minutes she was slumped in her wheelchair. The nurse sat beside her and said "I'm very sorry" to Butch and Leon.

At 12:15, the door opened and a guard said, "Come with me." The brothers were led from the room, into the hallway that was packed with guards and officials and many other curious onlookers lucky enough to gain access, and then back through the front entrance. Outside, the air was heavy, and the heat had not broken. They quickly lit cigarettes as they walked along a narrow sidewalk next to the west wing of the maximum security unit, past the open windows covered with thick black bars, and as they moved casually to the death room, they could hear the other condemned men banging their cell doors, yelling in protest, all making whatever noise they could in a last-minute farewell to one of their own.

Butch and Leon smoked furiously and wanted to yell something of their own, something in support of the inmates. But neither said a word. They turned a corner and saw a small, flat redbrick building with guards and others milling around its door. There was an ambulance beside it. Their escort led them through a side door to a cramped witness room, and upon entering, they saw faces they expected, but had no interest in seeing. Sheriff Walls was there because the law required it. The prosecutor was there, by choice. Charlene, Coy's long-suffering widow, sat next to the sheriff. She was joined by two hefty young gals who were no doubt her daughters. The victims' side of the witness room was separated by a wall of Plexiglas that allowed them to glare at the condemned man's family but prevented them from speaking, or cursing. Butch and Leon sat in plastic chairs. Strangers shuffled in behind them, and when everyone was in place, the door was closed. The witness room was packed and hot.

They stared at nothing. The windows before them were shielded by black curtains so that they could not see the sinister preparations under way on the other side. There were sounds, indistinguishable movements. Suddenly the curtains were yanked open, and they were looking at the death room, twelve feet by fifteen, with a freshly painted concrete floor. In the center of it was the gas chamber, an octagon-shaped silver cylinder with windows of its own to allow proper witnessing and verification of death.

And, there was Raymond, strapped to a chair inside the gas chamber, his head secured with some hideous brace that forced him to look ahead and prevented him from seeing the witnesses. At that moment he seemed to be looking up as the warden spoke to him. The prison attorney was present, as were some guards and of course the executioner and his assistant. All went about their tasks, whatever they were supposed to be doing, with grim determined looks, as if they were bothered by this ritual. In fact, all were volunteers, except for the warden and the attorney.

A small speaker hung from a nail in the witness room and conveyed the final sounds.

The attorney stepped close to the chamber door and said: "Raymond, by law I'm required to read your death warrant." He lifted a sheet of paper and continued: "Pursuant to a verdict of guilty and a sentence of death returned against you in the Circuit Court of Ford County, you are hereby sentenced to death by lethal gas in the gas chamber of the Mississippi State Penitentiary at Parchman. May God have mercy on your soul." He then stepped away and lifted a telephone from its receiver on the wall. He listened, then said, "No stays."

The warden said, "Any reason why this execution should not go forward?"

"No," said the attorney.

"Any last words, Raymond?"

Raymond's voice was barely audible, but in the perfect stillness of the witness room he was heard: "I am sorry for what I did. I ask the forgiveness of the family of Coy Childers. I have been forgiven by my Lord. Let's get this over with."

The guards left the death room, leaving the warden and the attorney, who shuffled backward as far from Raymond as possible. The executioner stepped forward and closed the narrow chamber door. His assistant checked the seals around it. When the chamber was ready, they glanced around the death room—a quick inspection. No problems. The executioner disappeared into a small closet, the chemical room, where he controlled his valves.

Long seconds passed. The witnesses gawked in horror and fascination and held their breaths. Raymond held his too, but not for long.

The executioner placed a plastic container of sulfuric acid into a tube that ran from the chemical room to a bowl in the bottom of the chamber, just under the chair that Raymond now occupied. He pulled a lever to release the canister. A clicking sound occurred, and most of those watching flinched. Raymond flinched too. His fingers clutched the arms of the chair. His spine stiffened. Seconds passed, then the sulfuric acid mixed with a collection of cyanide pellets already in the bowl, and the lethal steam began rising. When Raymond finally exhaled, when he could no longer hold his breath, he sucked in as much poison as possible to speed things along. His entire body reacted instantly with jolts and gyrations. His shoulders jumped back. His chin and forehead fought mightily against the leather head brace. His hands, arms, and legs shook violently as the steam rose and grew thicker.

His body reacted and fought for a minute or so, then the cyanide took control. The convulsions slowed. His head became still. His fingers loosened their death grip on the arms of the chair. The air continued to thicken as Raymond's breathing slowed, then stopped. Some final twitching, a jolt in his chest muscles, a vibration in his hands, and finally it was over.

He was pronounced dead at 12:31 a.m. The black curtains were closed, and the witnesses hustled from the room. Outside, Butch and Leon leaned on a corner of the redbrick building and smoked a cigarette.

Inside the death room, a vent above the chamber was opened, and the gas escaped into the sticky air over Parchman. Fifteen minutes later, guards with gloves unshackled Raymond and wrestled his body out of the chamber. His clothing was cut off, to be burned. His corpse was hosed off with cold water, then dried with kitchen towels, reclothed in prison whites, and laid inside a cheap pine coffin.

Leon and Butch sat with their mother and waited for the warden. Inez was still sedated, but she clearly understood what had taken place in the last few minutes. Her head was buried in her hands, and she cried softly, mumbling occasionally. A guard entered and asked for the keys to Mr. McBride's van. An hour dragged by.

The warden, fresh from his press announcement, finally entered the room. He offered some sappy condolences, managed to look sad and sympathetic, then asked Leon to sign some forms. He explained that Raymond left almost $1,000 in his prison account, and a check would be sent within a week. He said the van was loaded with the coffin and four boxes of Raymond's belongings— his guitar, clothing, books, correspondence, legal materials, and manuscripts. They were free to go.

The coffin was moved to one side so Inez could be rolled through the back of the van, and when she touched it, she broke down again. Leon and Butch rearranged boxes, secured the wheel-chair, then moved the coffin again. When everything was in its place, they followed a car full of guards back to the front of the prison, through the entrance, and when they turned onto High-way 3, they drove past the last of the protesters. The television crews were gone. Leon and Butch lit cigarettes, but Inez was too emotional to smoke. No one spoke for miles as they hurried through the cotton and soybean fields. Near the town of Marks, Leon spotted an all-night convenience store. He bought a soda for Butch and tall coffees for his mother and himself.

When the Delta yielded to the hill country, they felt better.

"What did he say last?" Inez asked, her tongue thick.

"He apologized," Butch said. "Asked Charlene for forgive-ness."

"So she watched it?"

"Oh yes. You didn't think she'd miss it."

"I should've seen it."

"No, Momma," Leon said. "You can be thankful for the rest of your days that you didn't witness the execution. Your last mem-ory of Raymond was a long hug and a nice farewell. Please don't think you missed anything."

"It was horrible," Butch said.

"I should've seen it."

In the town of Batesville they passed a fast-food place that advertised chicken biscuits and twenty-four-hour service. Leon turned around. "I could use the ladies' room," Inez said. There were no other customers inside at 3:15 in the morning. Butch rolled his mother to a table near the front, and they ate in silence. The van with Raymond's coffin was less than thirty feet away.

Inez managed a few bites, then lost her appetite. Butch and Leon ate like refugees.

They entered Ford County just after 5:00 a.m., and it was still very dark, the roads empty. They drove to Pleasant Ridge in the north end of the county, to a small Pentecostal church where they parked in the gravel lot, and waited. At the first hint of sunlight, they heard an engine start somewhere in the distance.

"Wait here," Leon said to Butch, then left the van and disappeared. Behind the church there was a cemetery, and at the far end of it a backhoe had just begun digging the grave. The backhoe was owned by a cousin's boss. At 6:30, several men from the church arrived and went to the grave site. Leon drove the van down a dirt trail and stopped near the backhoe, which had finished its digging and was now just waiting. The men pulled the coffin from the van. Butch and Leon gently placed their mother's wheelchair on the ground and pushed her as they followed the coffin.

They lowered it with ropes, and when it settled onto the four-by-four studs at the bottom, they withdrew the ropes. The preacher read a short verse of Scripture, then said a prayer. Leon and Butch shoveled some dirt onto the coffin, then thanked the men for their assistance.

As they drove away, the backhoe was refilling the grave.

The house was empty—no concerned neighbors waiting, no relatives there to mourn. They unloaded Inez and rolled her into the house and into her bedroom. She was soon fast asleep. The four boxes were placed in a storage shed, where their contents would weather and fade along with the memories of Raymond.

It was decided that Butch would stay home that day to care for Inez, and to ward off the reporters. There had been many calls in the past week, and someone was bound to show up with a camera. He worked at a sawmill, and his boss would understand.

Leon drove to Clanton and stopped on the edge of town to fill up with gas. At 8:00 a.m. sharp he pulled in to the lot at McBride Upholstery and returned the van. An employee explained that Mr. McBride wasn't in yet, was probably still at the coffee shop, and usually got to work around 9:00. Leon handed over the keys, thanked the employee, and left.

He drove to the lamp factory east of town, and punched the clock at 8:30, as always.

# Fish Files

**✦** · · · · · · · · · · · · · · · · · · · **✦**

*A*fter seventeen years of grinding out a living in a law
practice that, for some forgotten reason, had gradually
been reduced to little more than bankruptcy and divorce work, it
was astonishing, even years later, that one phone call could change
so much. As a busy lawyer who handled the desperate problems
of others, Mack Stafford had made and received all sorts of life-
altering phone calls: calls to initiate or settle divorces; calls to pass
along grim court rulings on child custody; calls to inform honest
men that they would not be repaid. Unpleasant calls, for the most
part. He had never thought about the possibility that one call
could so quickly and dramatically lead to his own divorce and
bankruptcy.

It came during lunch on a bleak and dreary and otherwise
slow Tuesday in early February, and because it was just after

noon, Mack took it himself. Freda, the secretary, had stepped out for an errand and a sandwich, and since his little firm employed no one else, Mack was left to guard the phone. As things evolved, the fact that he was alone was crucial. If Freda had answered it, there would have been questions, and lots of them. In fact, most of what followed would not have happened had she been at her post in the reception area near the front door of a little shop known as: Law Offices of Jacob McKinley Stafford, LLC.

After the third ring, Mack grabbed the phone on his desk in the back and offered the usual, brusque "Law office." He received on average fifty calls a day, most from warring spouses and disgruntled creditors, and he had long since developed the habit of disguising his voice and withholding his name when forced to take calls unfiltered by Freda. He hated answering the phone cold, but he also needed the business. Like every other lawyer in Clanton, and there were plenty, he never knew when the next call might be the big one, the big catch, the big case that could lead to a handsome fee and maybe even a way out. Mack had been dreaming of such a phone call for more years than he cared to admit.

And on this cold winter day, with a slight chance of snow in the air, the call finally arrived.

A male voice with a different accent, from somewhere up north, replied, "Yes, Mr. Mack Stafford, please."

The voice was too polished and too far away to worry him, so he replied, "This is Mack."

"Mr. Mack Stafford, the attorney?"

"Correct. Who's calling?"

"My name is Marty Rosenberg, and I'm with the Durban &
Lang firm in New York."

"New York City?" Mack asked, and much too quickly. Of
course it was New York City. Though his practice had never
taken him anywhere near the big city, he certainly knew of Durban & Lang. Every lawyer in America had at least heard of the
firm.

"That's correct. May I call you Mack?" The voice was quick
but polite, and Mack suddenly had a visual of Mr. Rosenberg sitting in a splendid office with art on the walls and associates and
secretaries scurrying about tending to his needs. Yet in the midst
of such power he wanted to be friendly. A wave of insecurity
swept over Mack as he looked around his dingy little room and
wondered if Mr. Rosenberg had already decided he was just another small-town loser because he answered his own phone.

"Sure. And I'll just call you Marty."

"Great."

"Sorry, Marty, to grab the phone, but my secretary stepped
out for lunch." It was important for Mack to clear the air and let
this guy know that he was a real lawyer with a real secretary.

"Yes, well, I forgot that you're an hour behind us," Marty
said with a trace of contempt, the first hint that perhaps they
were separated by far more than just a simple hour.

"What can I do for you?" Mack said, seizing control of the
conversation. Enough of the small talk. Both were busy, important attorneys. His mind was in overdrive as he tried to think of
any case, any file, any legal matter that could conceivably merit interest from such a large and prestigious law firm.

"Well, we represent a Swiss company that recently purchased most of the Tinzo group out of South Korea. You're familiar with Tinzo?"

"Of course," Mack replied quickly, while his mind racked its memory for some recollection of Tinzo. It did indeed ring a bell, though a very distant one.

"And according to some old Tinzo records, you at one time represented some loggers who claimed to have been injured by defective chain saws manufactured by a Tinzo division in the Philippines."

Oh, that Tinzo! Now Mack was in the game. Now he remembered, though the details were still not at his fingertips. The cases were old, stale, and almost forgotten because Mack had tried his best to forget them.

"Terrible injuries," he said anyway. Terrible as they might have been, they had never been so grievous as to prompt Mack to actually file suit. He'd signed them up years earlier but lost interest when he couldn't bluff a quick settlement. His theory of liability was shaky at best. The Tinzo chain saws in question actually had an impressive safety record. And, most important, product liability litigation was complicated, expensive, way over his head, and usually involved jury trials, which Mack had always tried to avoid. There was comfort in filing divorces and personal bankruptcies and doing an occasional will or deed. Little in the way of fees, but he and most of the other lawyers in Clanton could eke out a living while avoiding almost all risk.

"We have no record of any lawsuits being filed down there," Marty was saying.

"Not yet," Mack said with as much bluster as he could manage.

"How many of these cases do you have, Mack?"

"Four," he said, though he wasn't certain of the exact number.

"Yes, that's what our records show. We have the four letters you sent to the company sometime back. However, there doesn't seem to have been much activity since the original correspondence."

"The cases are active," Mack said, and for the most part it was a lie. The office files were still open, technically, but he hadn't touched them in years. Fish files, he called them. The longer they sit there untouched, the more they stink. "We have a six-year statute of limitations," he said, somewhat smugly, as if he just might crank up things tomorrow and commence all manner of hardball litigation.

"Kind of unusual, if I must say so," Marty mused. "Not a thing in the files in over four years."

In an effort to steer the conversation away from his own procrastination, Mack decided to get to the point. "Where is this going, Marty?"

"Well, our Swiss client wants to clean up the books and get rid of as much potential liability as possible. They're European, of course, and they don't understand our tort system. Frankly, they're terrified of it."

"With good reason," Mack jumped in, as if he routinely extracted huge sums of money from corporate wrongdoers.

"They want these things off the books, and they've instructed me to explore the possibility of settlement."

Mack was on his feet, phone wedged between his jaw and shoulder, his pulse racing, his hands scrambling for a fish file in a pile of debris on the sagging credenza behind his desk, a frantic search for the names of his clients who'd been maimed years ago by the sloppy design and production of Tinzo chain saws. Say what? Settlement? As in money changing hands from the rich to the poor? Mack couldn't believe what he was hearing.

"Are you there, Mack?" Marty asked.

"Oh yes, just flipping through a file here. Let's see, the chain saws were all the same, a model 58X, twenty-four-inch with the nickname of LazerCut, a heavy-duty pro model that for some reason had a chain guard that was defective and dangerous."

"You got it, Mack. I'm not calling to argue about what might have been defective, that's what trials are for. I'm talking about settlement, Mack. Are you with me?"

Damned right I am, Mack almost blurted. "Certainly. I'm happy to talk settlement. You obviously have something in mind. Let's hear it." He was seated again, tearing through the file, looking for dates, praying that the six-year statute of limitations had not expired on any of these now critically important cases.

"Yes, Mack, I have some money to offer, but I must caution you up front that my client has instructed me not to negotiate. If we can settle these matters quickly, and very quietly, then we'll write the checks. But when the dickering starts, the money disappears. Are we clear on this, Mack?"

Oh yes. Crystal clear. Mr. Marty Rosenberg in his fancy office high above Manhattan had no idea how quickly and quietly and cheaply he could make the fish files disappear. Mack would take anything. His badly injured clients had long since stopped calling. "Agreed," Mack said.

Marty shifted gears, and his words became even crisper. "We figure it would cost a hundred thousand to defend these cases in federal court down there, assuming we could lump them together and have just one trial. This is obviously a stretch since the cases have not been filed, and, frankly, litigation seems unlikely, given the thinness of the file. Add another hundred thousand for the injuries, none of which have been documented, mind you, but we understand some fingers and hands have been lost. Anyway, we'll pay a hundred thousand per claim, throw in the cost of defense, and the total on the table comes to half a million bucks."

Mack's jaw dropped, and he almost swallowed the phone. He was prepared to demand at least three times any amount Marty first mentioned, the usual lawyer's routine, but for a few seconds he could neither speak nor breathe.

Marty went on: "All up-front money, confidential, no admission of liability, with the offer good for thirty days, until March 10."

An offer of $10,000 per claim would have been a shock, and a windfall. Mack gasped for air and tried to think of a response.

Marty went on: "Again, Mack, we're just trying to clean up the balance sheet. Whatta you think?"

What do I think? Mack repeated to himself. I think my cut is 40 percent and the math is easy. I think that last year I grossed $95,000 and burned half of it in overhead—Freda's salary and the office bills—which left me with a net of about $46,000 before taxes, which I think was slightly less than my wife earned as an assistant principal at Clanton High School. I'm thinking a lot of things right now, some really random stuff like (1) Is this a joke? (2) Who from my law school class could be behind this? (3) Assuming it's real, how can I keep the wolves away from this wonderful fee? (4) My wife and two daughters would burn through this money in less than a month; (5) Freda would demand a healthy bonus; (6) How can I approach my chain-saw clients after so many years of neglect? And so on. I'm thinking about a lot of stuff, Mr. Rosenberg.

"That's very generous, Marty," Mack managed to say, finally. "I'm sure my clients will be pleased." After the shock, his brain was beginning to focus again.

"Good. Do we have a deal?"

"Well, let me see. I, of course, will need to run this by my clients, and that might take a few days. Can I call you in a week?"

"Of course. But we're anxious to wrap this up, so let's hurry. And, Mack, I cannot stress enough our desire for confidentiality. Can we agree to bury these settlements, Mack?"

For that kind of money, Mack would agree to anything. "I understand," he said. "Not a word to anyone." And Mack meant it. He was already thinking of all the people who would never know about this lottery ticket.

"Great. You'll call me in a week?"

"You got it, Marty. And, listen, my secretary has a big mouth. It's best if you don't call here again. I'll call you next Tuesday. What time?"

"How about eleven, eastern?"

"You got it, Marty."

They swapped phone numbers and addresses, and said good-bye. According to the digital timer on Mack's phone, the call lasted eight minutes and forty seconds.

The phone rang again just after Marty hung up, but Mack could only stare at it. He wouldn't dare push his luck. Instead, he walked to the front of his office, to the large front window with his name painted on it, and he looked across the street to the Ford County Courthouse, where, at that moment, some garden-variety ham-and-egg lawyers were upstairs munching on cold sandwiches in the judge's chambers and haggling over another $50 a month in child support, and whether the wife should get the Honda and hubby should get the Toyota. He knew they were there because they were always there, and he was often with them. And down the hall in the clerk's office more lawyers were poring over land records and lien books and dusty old plats while they bantered back and forth in their tired humor, jokes and stories and quips he'd heard a thousand times. A year or two earlier, someone had counted fifty-one lawyers in the town of Clanton, and virtually all were packed together around the square, their offices facing the courthouse. They ate in the same cafés, met in the same coffee shops, drank in the same bars, hustled the same clients, and almost all of them harbored the same gripes and complaints about their chosen profession. Somehow, a town of ten thousand people provided enough conflict to support fifty-one lawyers, when in reality less than half that number were needed.

Mack had rarely felt needed. To be sure, he was needed by his wife and daughters, though he often wondered if they wouldn't be happier without him, but the town and its legal needs would certainly survive nicely without him. In fact, he had realized long ago that if he suddenly closed shop, few would notice. No client would go without representation. The other lawyers would secretly grin because they had one less competitor. No one in the courthouse would miss him after a month or so. This had saddened him for many years. But what really depressed him was not the present or the past but the future. The prospect of waking up one day at the age of sixty and still trudging to the office—no doubt the same office—and filing no-fault divorces and nickel-and-dime bankruptcies on behalf of people who could barely pay his modest fees, well, it was enough to sour his mood every day of his life. It was enough to make Mack a very unhappy man.

He wanted out. And he wanted out while he was still young.

A lawyer named Wilkins passed by on the sidewalk without glancing at Mack's window. Wilkins was a jackass who worked four doors down. Years ago, over a late-afternoon drink with three other lawyers, one of whom was Wilkins, Mack had talked too much and divulged the details of his grand scheme to make a killing with chain-saw litigation. Of course the scheme went nowhere, and when Mack could not convince any of the more competent trial lawyers in the state to sign on, his chain-saw files began to stink. Wilkins, ever the prick, would catch Mack in the presence of other lawyers and say something like, "Hey, Mack, how's that chain-saw class action coming along?" Or, "Hey, Mack, you settled those chain-saw cases yet?" With time, though, even Wilkins forgot about the cases.

Hey, Wilkins, take a look at this settlement, old boy! Half a million bucks on the table, $200,000 of it goes into my pocket. At least that much, maybe more. Hey, Wilkins, you haven't cleared $200,000 in the last five years combined.

But Mack knew that Wilkins would never know. No one would know, and that was fine with Mack.

Freda would soon make her usual noisy entrance. Mack hurried to his desk, called the number in New York, asked for Marty Rosenberg, and when his secretary answered, Mack hung up and smiled. He checked his afternoon schedule, and it was as dreary as the weather. One new divorce at 2:30, and an ongoing one at 4:30. There was a list of fifteen phone calls to make, not a single one of which he looked forward to. The fish files on the credenza were festering in neglect. He grabbed his overcoat, left his briefcase, and sneaked out the back door.

His car was a small BMW with 100,000 miles on the odometer. The lease expired in five months, and he was already fretting about what to drive next. Since lawyers, regardless of how broke they may be, are supposed to drive something impressive, he had been quietly shopping around, careful to keep things to himself. His wife would not approve of whatever he chose, and he simply wasn't ready for that fight.

His favorite beer trail began at Parker's Country Store, eight miles south of town in a small community where no one ever recognized him. He bought a six-pack of bright green bottles, imported, good stuff for this special day, and continued south on narrow back roads until there was no other traffic. He listened to Jimmy Buffett sing about sailing and drinking rum and living a life that Mack had been dreaming about for some time. In the summer before he started law school, he spent two weeks scuba diving in the Bahamas. It had been his first trip out of the country, and he longed to do it again. Over the years, as the tedium of practicing law overwhelmed him, and as his marriage became less and less fulfilling, he listened to Buffett more and more. He could handle life on a sailboat. He was ready.

He parked in a secluded picnic area at Lake Chatulla, the largest body of water within fifty miles, and left the engine running, the heat on, a window cracked. He sipped beer and gazed across the lake, a busy place in the summer with ski boats and small catamarans, but deserted in February.

Marty's voice was still fresh and clear. Their conversation was still easy to replay, almost word for word. Mack talked to himself, then sang along with Buffett.

This was his moment, an opportunity that in all likelihood would never pass his way again. Mack finally convinced himself that he wasn't dreaming, that the money was on the table. The math was calculated, then recalculated over and over.

A light snow began, flurries that melted as soon as they touched the ground. Even the chance of an inch or two thrilled the town, and now that a few flakes were falling, he knew that the kids at school were standing at the windows, giddy at the thought of being dismissed and sent home to play. His wife was probably calling the office with instructions to go fetch the girls. Freda was looking for him. After the third beer, he fell asleep.

He missed his 2:30 appointment, and didn't care. He missed his 4:30 as well. He saved one beer for the return trip, and at a quarter past five he walked through the rear door of his office and was soon face-to-face with an extremely agitated secretary.

"Where have you been?" Freda demanded.

"I went for a drive," he said as he removed his overcoat and hung it in the hallway. She followed him into his office, hands on hips, just like his wife. "You missed two appointments—the Maddens and the Garners—and they are not happy at all. You smell like a brewery."

"They make beer at breweries, don't they?"

"I suppose. That's $1,000 in fees you just pissed away."

"So what?" He fell into his chair, knocked some files off his desk.

"So what? So we need all the fees we can get around here. You're in no position to run off clients. We didn't cover the overhead last month, and this month is even slower." Her voice was pitched, shrill, rapid, and the venom had been building for hours. "There's a stack of bills on my desk and no money in the bank. The other bank would like some progress on that line of credit you decided to create, for some reason."

"How long have you worked here, Freda?"

"Five years."

"That's long enough. Pack your things and get out. Now."

She gasped. Both hands flew up to her mouth. She managed to say, "You're firing me?"

"No. I'm cutting back on the overhead. I'm downsizing."

She fought back quickly, laughing in a loud nervous cackle. "And who'll answer the phone, do all the typing, pay the bills, organize the files, babysit the clients, and keep you out of trouble?"

"No one."

"You're drunk, Mack."

"Not drunk enough."

"You can't survive without me."

"Please, just leave. I'm not going to argue."

"You'll lose your ass," she growled.

"I've already lost it."

"Well, now you're losing your mind."

"That too. Please."

She huffed off, and Mack put his feet on his desk. She slammed drawers and stomped around the front for ten minutes, then yelled, "You're a lousy son of a bitch, you know that?"

"Got that right. Good-bye."

The front door slammed, and all was quiet. The first step had been taken.

An hour later, he left again. It was dark and cold, and the snow had given up. He was still thirsty and didn't want to go home, nor did he want to be seen in one of the three bars in down-town Clanton.

The Riviera Motel was east of town, on the highway to Memphis. It was a 1950s-style dump with tiny rooms, some known to be available by the hour, and a small café and a small lounge. Mack parked himself at the bar and ordered a draft beer. There was country music from a jukebox, college basketball on the screen above, and the usual collection of low-budget travelers and bored locals, all well over the age of fifty. Mack recognized no one but the bartender, an old-timer whose name escaped him. Mack was not exactly a regular at the Riviera.

He asked for a cigar, lit it, sipped his beer, and after a few minutes pulled out a small notepad and began scribbling. To hide much of his financial mess from his wife, he had organized his law firm as a limited liability company, or an LLC, the current rage among lawyers. He was the sole owner, and most of his debts were gathered there: a $25,000 line of credit that was now six years old and showing no signs of being reduced; two law firm credit cards that were used for small expenses, both personal and business, and were also maxed out at the $10,000 limit and kept afloat with minimum payments; and the usual office debts for equipment. The LLC's largest liability was a $120,000 mortgage on the office building Mack had purchased eight years earlier, against the rather vocal objections of his wife. The monthly strain was $1,400, and not eased one bit by the empty space on the second floor Mack was certain he would rent to others when he bought the place.

On this wonderful, dreary day in February, Mack was two months in arrears on his office mortgage.

He ordered another beer as he added up the misery. He could bankrupt it all, give his files to a lawyer friend, and walk away a free man with no trace of embarrassment or humiliation because he, Mack Stafford, wouldn't be around for folks to point at and whisper about.

The office was easy. The marriage would be another matter.

He drank until ten, then drove home. He pulled in to the driveway of his modest little home in an old section of

Clanton, turned off the engine and the lights, sat behind the wheel, and stared at the house. The lights in the den were on. She was waiting.

They had purchased the house from her grandmother not long after they were married fifteen years earlier, and for about fifteen years now Lisa had wanted something larger. Her sister was married to a doctor, and they lived in a fine home out by the country club, where all the other doctors, and bankers, and some of the lawyers lived. Life was much better out there because the homes were newer, with pools and tennis courts and a golf course just around the corner. For much of his married life, Mack had been reminded that they were making little progress in their climb up the social ladder. Progress? Mack knew they were actually sliding. The longer they stayed in Granny's house, the smaller it became.

Lisa's family had owned Clanton's only concrete plant for generations, and though this kept them at the top of the town's social class, it did little for their bank accounts. They were afflicted with "family money," a status that had much to do with snobbery and precious little to do with hard assets. Marrying a lawyer seemed like a good move at the time, but fifteen years later she was having doubts and Mack knew it.

The porch light came on.

If the fight was to be like most others, the girls—Helen and Margo—would have front-row seats. Their mother had probably been making calls and throwing things for several hours, and in the midst of her rampage she made sure the girls knew who was right and who was wrong. Both were now young teenagers and showing every sign of growing up to be just like Lisa. Mack certainly loved them, but he had already made the decision, on beer number three at the lake, that he could live without them.

The front door opened, then there she was. She took one step onto the narrow porch, crossed her bare arms, and glared across the frigid lawn, directly into the shivering eyes of Mack. He stared back, then opened the driver's door and got out of the car. He slammed the door, and she let loose with a nasty "Where have you been?"

"At the office," he shot back as he took a step and told himself to walk carefully and not stagger like a drunk. His mouth was full of peppermint gum, not that he planned to fool anyone. The driveway declined slightly from the house to the street.

"Where have you been?" she inquired again, even louder.

"Please, the neighbors." He didn't see the patch of ice between his car and hers, and by the time he discovered it, things were out of control. He flipped forward, yelping, and crashed into the rear bumper of her car with the front of his head. His world went black for a few moments, and when he came to, he heard the frantic female voices, one of which announced, "He's drunk."

Thanks, Lisa.

His head was split, and his eyes wouldn't focus. She hovered over him, saying things like, "There's blood, oh my God!" And, "Your father's drunk!" And, "Go call 911!"

Mercifully, he blacked out again, and when he could hear again, there was a male voice in control. Mr. Browning from next door. "Watch the ice, Lisa, and hand me that blanket. There's a lot of blood."

"He's been drinking," Lisa said, always looking for allies.

"He probably doesn't feel a thing," Mr. Browning added helpfully. He and Mack had feuded for years.

Though he was groggy and could've said something, Mack decided, lying there in the cold, to just close his eyes and let someone else worry about him. Before long, he heard an ambulance.

☿

He actually enjoyed the hospital. The drugs were delightful, the nurses thought he was cute, and it provided a perfect excuse to stay away from the office. He had six stitches and a nasty bruise on his forehead, but, as Lisa had informed someone on the phone when she thought he was asleep, there was "no additional brain damage." Once it was determined that his wounds were slight, she avoided the hospital and kept the girls away. He was in no hurry to leave, and she was in no hurry for him to come home. But after two days, the doctor ordered his release. As he was gathering his things and saying good-bye to the nurses, Lisa entered his room and shut the door. She sat in the only chair, crossed her arms and legs as if she planned to stay for hours, and Mack relaxed on the bed. The last dose of Percocet was still lingering, and he felt wonderfully light-headed.

"You fired Freda," she said, jaws clenched, eyebrows arched.

"Yes."

"Why?"

"Because I got tired of her mouth. What do you care? You hate Freda."

"What will happen to the office?"

"It'll be a helluva lot quieter for one thing. I've fired secretaries before. It's no big deal."

A pause as she uncrossed her arms and began twirling a strand of hair. This meant that she was pondering serious stuff and was about to unload it.

"We have an appointment with Dr. Juanita tomorrow at five," she announced. Done deal. Nothing to negotiate.

Dr. Juanita was one of three licensed marriage counselors in Clanton. Mack knew them professionally through his work as a divorce lawyer. He knew them personally because Lisa had dragged him to all three for counseling. He needed counseling. She, of course, did not. Dr. Juanita always sided with the women, and so her selection was no surprise.

"How are the girls?" Mack asked. He knew the answer would be ugly, but if he didn't ask, then she would later complain to Dr. Juanita, "He didn't even ask about the girls."

"Humiliated. Their father comes home drunk late at night and falls in the driveway, cracks his skull, gets hauled to the hospital, where his blood alcohol is twice the legal limit. Everybody in town knows it."

"If everybody knows it, then it's because you've spread the word. Why can't you just keep your mouth shut?"

Her face flashed red, and her eyes glowed with hatred. "You, you, you're pathetic. You're a miserable pathetic drunk, you know that?"

"I disagree."

"How much are you drinking?"

"Not enough."

"You need help, Mack, serious help."

"And I'm supposed to get this help from Dr. Juanita?"

She suddenly bolted to her feet and stormed for the door. "I'm not going to fight in a hospital."

"Of course not. You prefer to fight at home in front of the girls."

She yanked open the door and said, "Five o'clock tomorrow, and you'd better be there."

"I'll think about it."

"And don't come home tonight."

She slammed the door, and Mack heard her heels click angrily away.

⚘

The first client in Mack's chain-saw class-action scheme was a career pulpwood cutter by the name of Odell Grove. Almost five years earlier, Mr. Grove's nineteen-year-old son needed a quick divorce and found his way to Mack's office. In the course of representing the kid, himself a pulpwood cutter, Mack learned of Odell's encounter with a chain saw that proved more dangerous than most. During routine operations, the chain snapped, the guard failed, and Odell lost his left eye. He wore a patch now, and it was the patch that helped identify this long-forgotten client when Mack entered the truck-stop café outside the small town of Karraway. It was a few minutes past eight, the morning after Mack's discharge from the hospital, the morning after he'd slept at the office. He had sneaked by the house after the girls left for school and picked up some clothes. To mix with the locals, he was wearing boots and a camouflage suit he put on occasionally when hunting deer. The fresh wound on his forehead was covered with a green wool ski cap pulled low, but he couldn't hide all the bruising. He was taking painkillers and had a buzz. The pills were giving him the courage to somehow wade through this unpleasant encounter. He had no choice.

Odell with his black eye patch was eating pancakes and talking loudly three tables away, and never glanced at Mack. According to the file, they had met at the same truck stop four years and ten months earlier, when Mack first informed Odell that he had a good, solid case against the maker of the chain saw. Their last contact had been almost two years ago, when Odell called the office with some rather pointed inquiries about the progress of his good, solid case. After that, the file became odorous.

Mack drank coffee at the counter, glanced at a newspaper, and waited for the early-morning crowd to leave for work. Eventually, Odell and his two co-workers finished breakfast and stopped at the cash register. Mack left a dollar for his coffee and followed them outside. As they headed for their pulpwood truck, Mack swallowed hard and said, "Odell." All three stopped as Mack hustled over for a friendly hello.

"Odell, it's me, Mack Stafford. I handled the divorce for your son Luke."

"The lawyer?" Odell asked, confused. He took in the boots, the hunting garb, the ski cap not far above the eyes.

"Sure, from Clanton. You gotta minute?"

"What—"

"Just take a minute. A small business matter."

Odell looked at the other two, and all three shrugged. "We'll wait in the truck," one of them said.

Like most men who spend their time deep in the woods knocking down trees, Odell was thick through the shoulders and chest, with massive forearms and weathered hands. And with his one good eye he was able to convey more contempt than most men could dish out with two.

"What is it?" he snarled, then spat. A toothpick was stuck in the corner of his mouth. There was a scar on his left cheek, courtesy of Tinzo. The accident had cost him one eyeball and a month's worth of pulpwood, little more.

"I'm winding down my practice," Mack said.

"What the hell does that mean?"

"Means I'm closing up the office. I think I might be able to squeeze some money out of your case."

"I think I've heard this before."

"Here's the deal. I can get you twenty-five thousand cash, hard cash, in two weeks, but only if you keep it extremely confidential. I mean graveyard quiet. You can't tell a soul."

For a man who'd never seen $5,000 in cash, the prospect was instantly appealing. Odell glanced around to make sure they were alone. He worked the toothpick as if it helped him think.

"Somethin' don't smell right," he said, his eye patch twitching.

"It's not complicated, Odell. It's a quick settlement because the company that made the chain saw is getting bought out by another company. Happens all the time. They'd like to forget about these old claims."

"All nice and legal?" Odell asked, with suspicion, as if this lawyer couldn't be trusted.

"Of course. They'll pay the money, but only if it's kept confidential. Plus, think of all the problems you'd face if folks knew you had that kind of cash."

Odell looked straight at the pulpwood truck and his two buddies sitting inside. Then he thought of his wife, and her mother, and his son in jail for drugs, and his son who was unemployed, and before long he'd thought of lots of people who'd happily help him go through the money. Mack knew what he was thinking, and added, "Cold cash, Odell. From my pocket to yours, and nobody will know anything. Not even the IRS."

"No chance of gettin' more?" Odell asked.

Mack frowned and kicked a rock. "Not a dime, Odell. Not a dime. It's twenty-five thousand or nothing. And we have to move quick. I can hand you the cash in less than a month."

"What do I have to do?"

"Meet me here Friday of next week, 8:00 a.m. I'll need one signature, then I can get the money."

"How much you makin' off this?"

"It's not important. You want the cash or not?"

"That's not much money for an eyeball."

"You're right about that, but it's all you're gonna get. Yes or no?"

Odell spat again and moved the toothpick from one side to the other. Finally, he said, "I reckon."

"Good. Next Friday, 8:00 a.m., here, and come alone."

During their first meeting years earlier, Odell had mentioned that he knew of another pulpwood cutter who'd lost a hand while using the same model Tinzo chain saw. This second injury had inspired Mack to begin dreaming of a broader attack, a class action on behalf of dozens, maybe hundreds of maimed plaintiffs. He could almost feel the money, years earlier.

Plaintiff number two had been tracked down next door in Polk County, in a desolate hollow deep in a pine forest. His name was Jerrol Baker, aged thirty-one, a former logger who'd been unable to pursue that career with only one hand. Instead, he and a cousin had built a methamphetamine lab in their double-wide trailer, and Jerrol the chemist made much more money than Jerrol the logger. His new career, however, proved just as dangerous, and Jerrol narrowly escaped a fiery death when their lab exploded, incinerating the equipment, the inventory, the trailer, and the cousin. Jerrol was indicted, sent to prison, and from there wrote several unanswered letters to his class-action lawyer seeking updates on the good, solid case they had against Tinzo. He was paroled after a few months, and rumored to be back in the area. Mack had not spoken to him in at least two years.

And speaking to him now would be a challenge, if not an impossibility. Jerrol's mother's house was abandoned. A neighbor down the road was most uncooperative until Mack explained that he owed Jerrol $300 and needed to deliver a check. Since it was likely that Jerrol owed money to most of his mother's neighbors, a few details emerged. Mack certainly didn't appear to be a drug agent, a process server, or a parole officer. The neighbor pointed up the road and over the hill, and Mack followed his directions. He dropped more hints about delivering money as he worked his way deeper into the pine forests of Polk County. It was almost noon when the gravel road came to a dead end. An ancient mobile home sat forlornly on cinder blocks wrapped in wild vines. Mack, a .38-caliber handgun in one pocket, slowly approached the trailer. The door opened slowly, sagging on its hinges.

Jerrol stepped onto the rickety plank porch and glared at Mack, who froze twenty feet away. Jerrol was shirtless but wearing ink, his arms and chest adorned with a colorful collection of prison tattoos. His hair was long and dirty, his thin body no doubt ravaged by meth. He'd lost his left hand thanks to Tinzo, but in his right he held a sawed-off shotgun. He nodded, but didn't speak. His eyes were deep-set, ghostlike.

"I'm Mack Stafford, a lawyer from Clanton. I believe you're Jerrol Baker, aren't you?"

Mack half expected the shotgun to come up firing, but it didn't move. Oddly enough, the client smiled, a toothless offering that was more frightening than the weapon. "'At's me," he grunted.

They talked for ten minutes, a surprisingly civil exchange given the setting and given their history. As soon as Jerrol realized he was about to receive $25,000 in cash, and that no one would know about it, he turned into a little boy and even invited Mack inside. Mack declined.

⚑

By the time they settled into their leather seats and faced the counselor across the desk, Dr. Juanita had been fully briefed on all issues and only pretended to be open-minded. Mack almost asked how many times the girls had chatted, but his strategy was all about avoiding conflict.

After a few comments designed to relax the husband and wife, and to instill confidence and warmth, Dr. Juanita invited them to say something. Not surprisingly, Lisa went first. She prattled nonstop for fifteen minutes about her unhappiness, her emptiness, her frustrations, and she minced no words in describing her husband's lack of affection and ambition, and his increasing reliance upon alcohol.

Mack's forehead was black-and-blue, and a fairly large white bandage covered a third of it, so not only was he described as a drunk, he in fact looked like one. He bit his tongue, listened, tried to appear dismal and depressed. When it was his turn to speak, he expressed some of the same concerns but didn't drop any bombs. Most of their problems were caused by him, and he was ready to take the blame.

When he finished, Dr. Juanita split them up. Lisa left first and went back to the lobby to flip through magazines while she reloaded. Mack was left to face the counselor alone. The first time he'd endured this torture, he'd been nervous. Now, though, he'd been through so many sessions that he really didn't care. Nothing he said would help save their marriage, so why say much at all?

"I have a sense that you want out of this marriage," Dr. Juanita began softly, wisely, eyeing him carefully.

"I want out because she wants out. She wants a bigger life, a bigger house, a bigger husband. I'm just too small."

"Do you and Lisa ever share a laugh?"

"Maybe if we're watching something funny on television. I laugh, she laughs, the girls laugh."

"How about sex?"

"Well, we're both forty-two years old, and we average about once a month, which is sad because an encounter takes five minutes, max. There's no passion, no romance, just something to knock off the edge. Pretty methodical, like connect the dots. I get the impression that she could forget the entire business."

Dr. Juanita took some notes, in much the same manner that Mack took notes with a client who said nothing but something needed to be written nonetheless.

"How much are you drinking?" she asked.

"Not nearly as much as she says. She's from a family of non-drinkers, so a three-beer night is a regular bender."

"But you are drinking too much."

"I came home the other night, the day it snowed, slipped on some ice, hit my head, and now most of Clanton has heard that I staggered home drunk and fell out in the driveway, cracked my skull, and now I'm acting weird. She's lining up allies, Juanita, you understand? She's telling everyone how lousy I am because she wants folks on her side when she files for divorce. The battle lines are already drawn. It's inevitable."

"You're giving up?"

"I'm surrendering. Total. Unconditional."

⚥

Sunday just happened to be the second Sunday of the month, a day Mack hated above all others. Lisa's family, the Bunning clan, was required by law to meet at her parents' home for an after-church brunch the second Sunday of every month. No excuses were tolerated, unless a family member happened to be out of town, and even then such an absence was frowned upon and the missing one usually subjected to withering gossip, outside the presence of the children of course.

Mack, his forehead an even deeper shade of blue and the swelling still evident, couldn't resist the temptation of a final, glorious farewell. He skipped church, decided to neither shower nor shave, dressed himself in old jeans and a soiled sweatshirt, and for dramatic effect removed the white gauze that covered his wound so that the entire brunch would be ruined when all the Bunnings saw his gruesome stitches. He arrived just a few minutes late, but early enough to prevent the adults from enjoying a few preliminary rounds of excoriating chitchat. Lisa completely ignored him, as did almost everyone else. His daughters hid in the sunroom with their cousins, who, of course, had heard all about the scandal and wanted details about his crack-up.

At one point, just before they were seated at the table, Lisa brushed by him and through gritted teeth managed to utter, "Why don't you just leave?" To which Mack cheerfully responded, "Because I'm starving and I haven't had a burned casserole since the second Sunday of last month."

All were present, sixteen total, and after Lisa's father, still wearing his white shirt and tie from church, blessed the day with his standard petition to the Almighty, they passed the food and the meal began. As always, about thirty seconds passed before her father began discussing the price of cement. The women drifted off into little side pockets of gossip. Two of Mack's nephews across the table just stared at his stitches, unable to eat. Finally, Lisa's mother, the grandam, reached the inevitable point at which she could no longer hold her tongue. During a lull, she announced at full volume, "Mack, your poor head looks dreadful. That must be painful."

Mack, anticipating just such a salvo, shot back, "Can't feel a thing. I'm on some wonderful drugs."

"What happened?" The question came from the brother-in-law, the doctor, the only other person at the table with access to Mack's hospital records. There was little doubt the doctor had practically memorized Mack's charts, grilled the attending physicians, nurses, and orderlies, and knew more about Mack's condition than he did himself. As Mack made his plans to exit the legal profession, perhaps his only regret was that he'd never sued his brother-in-law for medical malpractice. Others certainly had, and collected.

"I'd been drinking," Mack said proudly. "Came home late, slipped on some ice, hit my head."

Spines stiffened in unison around the table from the fiercely teetotaling family.

Mack pressed on: "Don't tell me you guys haven't heard all the details. Lisa was an eyewitness. She's told everyone."

"Mack, please," Lisa said as she dropped her fork. All forks were suddenly still, except for Mack's. He plunged his into a pile of rubber chicken and stuffed it into his mouth.

"Please what?" he said, mouth full, chicken visible. "You've made sure that every person at this table knows your version of what happened." He was chewing, talking, and pointing his fork at his wife, who was at the other end of the table close to her father. "And you've probably told them all about our visit to the marriage counselor, right?"

"Oh my God," Lisa gasped.

"And I'm sleeping at the office, don't we all know that?" he said. "Can't go home anymore, because, well, hell, I might slip and fall again. Or whatever. I might get drunk and beat my kids. Who knows? Right, Lisa?"

"That's enough, Mack," her father said, the voice of authority.

"Yes, sir. Sorry. This chicken is practically raw. Who cooked it?"

His mother-in-law bristled. Her spine stiffened even more. Her eyebrows arched. "Well, I did, Mack. Any more complaints about the food?"

"Oh, tons of complaints, but what the hell."

"Watch your language, Mack," her father-in-law said.

"See what I mean." Lisa leaned in low. "He's cracking up." Most of them nodded gravely. Helen, their younger daughter, began crying softly.

"You love to say that, don't you?" Mack yelled from his end. "You said the same thing to the marriage counselor. You've said it to everyone. Mack bumped his head, and now he's losing his shit."

"Mack, I don't tolerate such language," her father said sternly. "Please leave the table."

"Sorry. I'll be happy to leave." He rose and kicked back his chair. "And you'll be delighted to know that I'll never be back. That'll give you all a thrill, won't it?"

The silence was thick as he left the table. The last thing he heard was Lisa saying, "I'm so sorry."

Monday, he walked around the square to the large and busy office of Harry Rex Vonner, a friend who was undoubtedly the nastiest divorce lawyer in Ford County. Harry Rex was a loud, burly brawler who chewed black cigars, growled at his secretaries, growled at the court clerks, controlled the dockets, intimidated the judges, and terrified every divorcing party on the other side. His office was a landfill, with boxes of files in the foyer, over-flowing wastebaskets, stacks of old magazines in the racks, a thick layer of blue cigarette smoke just below the ceiling, another thick layer of dust on the furniture and bookshelves, and, always, a motley collection of clients waiting forlornly near the front door. The place was a zoo. Nothing ran on time. Someone was always yelling in the back. The phones rang constantly. The copier was always jammed. And so on. Mack had been there many times before on business and loved the chaos of the place.

"Heard you're crackin' up, boy," Harry Rex began as they met at his office door. The room was large, windowless, and situated at the back of the building, far away from the waiting clients. It was filled with bookshelves, storage boxes, trial exhibits, enlarged photos, and stacks of thick depositions, and the walls were covered with cheap matted photos, primarily of Harry Rex holding rifles and grinning over slain animals. Mack could not remember his last visit, but he was certain nothing had changed.

They sat down, Harry Rex behind a massive desk with sheets of paper falling off the sides, and Mack in a worn canvas chair that tottered back and forth.

"I just busted my head, that's all," Mack said.

"You look like hell."

"Thanks."

"Has she filed yet?"

"No. I just checked. She said she'll use some gal from Tupelo, can't trust anyone around here. I'm not fighting, Harry Rex. She can have everything—the girls, the house, and everything in it. I'm filing for bankruptcy, closing up shop, and moving away."

Harry Rex slowly cut the end off another black cigar, then shoved it into the corner of his mouth. "You are crackin' up, boy." Harry Rex was about fifty but seemed much older and wiser. To anyone younger, he habitually added the word "boy" as a term of affection.

"Let's call it a midlife crisis. I'm forty-two years old, and I'm fed up with being a lawyer. The marriage ain't working. Neither is the career. It's time for a change, some new scenery."

"Look, boy, I've had three marriages. Gettin' rid of a woman ain't no reason to tuck tail and run."

"I'm not here for career advice, Harry Rex. I'm hiring you to handle my divorce and my bankruptcy. I've already prepared the paperwork. Just get one of your flunkies to file everything and make sure I'm protected."

"Where you going?"

"Somewhere far away. I'm not sure right now, but I'll let you know when I get there. I'll come back when I'm needed. I'm still a father, you know?"

Harry Rex slumped in his chair. He exhaled and looked around at the piles of files stacked haphazardly on the floor around his desk. He looked at his phone with five red lights blinking. "Can I go with you?" he asked.

"Sorry. You gotta stay here and be my lawyer. I have eleven active divorce files, almost all uncontested, plus eight bankruptcies, one adoption, two estates, one car wreck, one workers' comp case, and two small business disputes. Total fees of about $25,000 over the next six months. I'd like you to take 'em off my hands."

"It's a pile of crap."

"Yes, the same stuff I've been shoveling for seventeen years. Dump it on one of your little associates back there and give him a bonus. Believe me, there's nothing complicated about it."

"How much child support can you stand?"

"Max is three thousand a month, which is a helluva lot more than I contribute now. Start at two thousand and see how it goes. Irreconcilable differences, she can file, I'll join in. She gets full custody, but I get to see the girls whenever I'm in town. She gets the house, her car, bank accounts, everything. She's not involved in the bankruptcy. The joint assets are not included."

"What are you bankrupting?"

"The Law Offices of Jacob McKinley Stafford, LLC. May it rest in peace."

Harry Rex chewed the cigar and looked at the petition for bankruptcy. There was nothing remarkable about it, the usual run-up on credit cards, the ever-present unsecured line of credit, the burdensome mortgage. "You don't have to do this," he said. "This stuff is manageable."

"The petition has already been prepared, Harry Rex. The decision has been made, along with several others. I'm bolting, okay? Outta here. Gone."

"Pretty gutsy."

"No. Most folks would say that running away is the act of a coward."

"How do you see it?"

"I could not care less. If I don't leave now, then I'll be here forever. This is my only chance."

"Attaboy."

At precisely 10:00 a.m., Tuesday, one glorious week after the first phone call, Mack made the second. As he punched the numbers, he smiled and congratulated himself on the amazing accomplishments of the past seven days. The plan was working perfectly, not a single hitch so far, except perhaps the head wound, but even that had been skillfully woven into the escape. Mack was hurt, hospitalized with a blow to the head. No wonder he's acting weird.

"Mr. Marty Rosenberg," he said pleasantly, then waited until the great man was notified. He answered quickly, and they exchanged preliminaries. Marty seemed unhurried, willing to go with the flow of meaningless chatter, and Mack was suddenly worried that this lack of efficiency would lead to a change in plans, some bad news. He decided to get to the point.

"Say, Marty, I've met with all four of my clients, and as you might guess, they're all anxious to accept your offer. We'll put this baby to sleep for half a million bucks."

"Yes, well, was it half a million, Mack?" He seemed uncertain.

Mack's heart froze and he gasped. "Of course, Marty," he said, then added a fake chuckle as if ol' Marty here was up to another prank. "You offered a hundred grand for each of the four, plus a hundred for the cost of defense."

Mack could hear papers being yanked around up in New York. "Hmmm, let's see, Mack. We're talking about the Tinzo cases, right?"

"That's right, Marty," Mack said with no small amount of fear and frustration. And desperation. The man with the checkbook wasn't even sure what they were talking about. One week earlier he'd been perfectly efficient. Now he was floundering. Then the most horrifying statement of all: "I'm afraid I've got these cases confused with some others."

"You gotta be kidding!" Mack barked, much too sharply. Be cool, he told himself.

"We really offered that much for these cases?" Marty said, obviously scanning notes while he talked.

"Damned right you did, and I, in good faith, conveyed the offers to my clients. We gotta deal, Marty. You made reasonable offers, we accepted. You can't back out now."

"Just seems a little high, that's all. I'm working on so many of these product liability cases these days."

Well, congratulations, Mack almost said. You have tons of work to do for clients who can pay you tons of money. Mack wiped sweat from his forehead and saw it all slipping away. Don't panic, he said to himself. "It's not high at all, Marty. You should see Odell Grove with only one eye, and Jerrol Baker minus his left hand, and Doug Jumper with his mangled and useless right hand, and Travis Johnson with little nubs where his fingers used to be. You should talk to these men, Marty, and see how miserable their lives are, how much they've been damaged by Tinzo chain saws, and I think you'd agree that your offer of half a million is not only reasonable but perhaps a bit on the low side." Mack exhaled and almost smiled to himself when he finished. Not a bad closing argument. Maybe he should have spent more time in the courtroom.

"I don't have time to hash out these details or argue liability, Mark, I—"

"It's Mack. Mack Stafford, attorney-at-law, Clanton, Mississippi."

"Right, sorry." More papers shuffled in New York. Muted voices in the background as Mr. Rosenberg directed other people. Then he was back, his voice refocused. "You realize, Mack, that Tinzo has gone to trial four times with this chain saw and won every trial. Slam dunk, no liability."

Of course Mack did not know this, because he'd forgotten about his little class action. But in desperation he said, "Yes, and I've studied those trials. But I thought you were not going to argue liability, Marty."

"Okay, you're right. I'll fax down the settlement documents."
Mack breathed deeply.

"How long before you can get them back to me?" Marty
asked.

"Couple of days."

They haggled over the wording of the documents. They went
back and forth about how to distribute the money. They stayed
on the phone for another twenty minutes doing what lawyers are
expected to do.

When Mack finally hung up, he closed his eyes, propped his
feet on his desk, and kicked back in his swivel rocker. He was
drained, exhausted, still frightened, but quickly getting over it.
He smiled, and was soon humming a Jimmy Buffett tune.

His phone kept ringing.

¥

The truth was, he had not been able to locate either Travis
Johnson or Doug Jumper. Travis was rumored to be out west
driving a truck, something he evidently could do with only seven
full-length fingers. Travis had an ex-wife with a house full of kids
and a ledger full of unpaid child support. She worked a night shift
in a convenience store in Clanton, and had few words for Mack.
She remembered his promises to collect some money when Travis
lost part of three fingers. According to some sketchy friends,
Travis had fled a year earlier and had no plans to return to Ford
County.

Doug Jumper was rumored to be dead. He had gone to prison
in Tennessee on assault charges and had not been seen in three

years. He'd never had a father. His mother had moved away. There were some relatives scattered around the county, but as a whole they showed little interest in talking about Doug and even less interest in talking to a lawyer, even one wearing hunter's camouflage, or faded jeans and hiking boots, or any of the other ensembles Mack used to blend in with the natives. His well-practiced routine of dangling the carrot of some vague check payable to Doug Jumper did not work. Nothing worked, and after two weeks of searching, Mack finally gave up when he heard for the third or fourth time the rumor "That boy's probably dead."

He obtained the legitimate signatures of Odell Grove and Jerrol Baker—Jerrol's being little more than a pathetic wiggle across the page with his right hand—and then committed his first crime. Notarizations on the settlement-and-release forms were required by Mr. Marty Rosenberg up in New York, but this was standard practice in every case. Mack had fired his notary, though, and procuring the services of another was far too complicated.

At his desk, with the doors locked, Mack carefully forged Freda's name as a notary public, then applied the notary seal with an expired stamp he'd kept in a locked file cabinet. He notarized Odell's signature, then Jerrol's, then stopped to admire his handiwork. He had been planning this deed for days now, and he was convinced he would never be caught. The forgeries were beautiful, the altered notary stamp was scarcely noticeable, and no one up in New York would take the time to analyze them. Mr. Rosenberg and his crack staff were so anxious to close their files that they would glance at Mack's paperwork, confirm a few details, then send the check.

His crimes grew more complicated when he forged the signatures of Travis Johnson and Doug Jumper. This, of course, was justified since he had made good-faith efforts to find them, and if they ever surfaced, he would be willing to offer them the same $25,000 he was paying to Odell and Jerrol. Assuming, of course, that he was around when they surfaced.

But Mack had no plans to be around.

The next morning, he used the U.S. Postal Service—another possible violation of the law, federal, but, again, nothing that troubled him—and sent the package by express to New York.

Then Mack filed for bankruptcy, and in the process broke another law by failing to disclose the fees that were on the way from his chain-saw masterpiece. It could be argued, and perhaps it would be argued if he got caught, that the fees had not yet been collected, and so forth, but Mack could not even win this debate with himself. Not that he really tried. The fees would never be seen by anyone in Clanton, or Mississippi, for that matter.

He hadn't shaved in two weeks, and in his opinion the salt-and-pepper beard was rather becoming. He stopped eating and stopped wearing coats and ties. The bruises and stitches were gone from his head. When he was seen around town, which was not that often, folks hesitated and whispered because word was hot on the streets that poor Mack was losing it all. News of his bankruptcy raced through the courthouse, and when coupled with the news that Lisa had filed for divorce, the lawyers and clerks and secretaries talked of little else. His office was locked during business hours, and after. His phones went unanswered.

The chain-saw money was wired to a new bank account in Memphis, and from there it was quietly dispersed. Mack took $50,000 in cash, paid off Odell Grove and Jerrol Baker, and felt good about it. Sure they were entitled to more, at least under the terms of the long-forgotten contracts Mack had shoved under their noses when they'd hired him. But, at least for Mack, the occasion called for a more flexible interpretation of said contracts, and there were several reasons. First, his clients were very happy. Second, his clients would certainly squander anything above $25,000, so in the interest of preserving the money, Mack argued that he should simply keep the bulk of it. Third, $25,000 was a fair settlement in light of their injuries, and especially in light of the fact that the two would have received nothing if Mack had not been shrewd enough to dream up the chain-saw litigation scheme in the first place.

Reasons four, five, and six followed the same line of thinking. Mack was already tired of rationalizing his actions. He was screwing his clients and he knew it.

He was now a crook. Forging documents, hiding assets, swindling clients. And if he had allowed himself to brood on these actions, he would have been miserable. The reality was that Mack was so thrilled with his escape that he caught himself laughing at odd times. When the crimes were done, there was no turning back, and this pleased him too.

He handed Harry Rex a check for $50,000 to cover the initial fallout from the divorce, and he executed the necessary papers to allow his lawyer to act on his behalf in tidying up his affairs. The rest of the money was wired to a bank in Central America.

☥

The last act in his well-planned and brilliantly executed farewell was a meeting with his daughters. After several testy phone conversations, Lisa had finally relented and agreed to allow Mack to enter the house for one hour, on a Thursday night. She would leave, but return in exactly sixty minutes.

Somewhere in the unwritten rules of human behavior a wise person once decided that such meetings are mandatory. Mack certainly could have skipped it, but then he was not only a crook but also a coward. No rule was safe. He supposed it was important for the girls to have the chance to vent, to cry, to ask why. He need not have worried. Lisa had so thoroughly prepped them that they could barely manage a hug. He promised to see them as often as possible, even though he was leaving town. They accepted this with more skepticism than he thought possible. After thirty long and awkward minutes, Mack squeezed their stiff bodies one more time and hurried to his car. As he drove away, he was convinced the three women were planning a happy new life without him.

And if he had allowed himself to dwell on his failures and shortcomings, he could have become melancholy. He fought the urge to remember the girls when they were smaller and life was happier. Or had he ever been truly happy? He really couldn't say.

He returned to his office, entered, as always now, through the rear door, and gave the place one final walk-through. All active files had been delivered to Harry Rex. The old ones had been burned. The law books, office equipment, furniture, and cheap art on the wall had been either sold or given away. He loaded up one medium-size suitcase, the contents of which had been carefully selected. No suits, ties, dress shirts, jackets, dress shoes—all that garb had been given to charity. Mack was leaving with the lighter stuff.

He took a bus to Memphis, flew from there to Miami, then on to Nassau, where he stayed one night before catching a flight to Belize City, Belize. He waited an hour in the sweltering airport there, sipping a beer from the tiny bar, listening to some rowdy Canadians talk excitedly about bonefishing, and dreaming of what was ahead. He wasn't really sure what was ahead, but it was certainly far more attractive than the wreckage behind.

The money was in Belize, a country with a U.S. extradition treaty that was more formal than practical. If his trail got hot, and he was supremely confident it would not, then Mack would quietly ease on down to Panama. His odds of getting caught were less than slim, in his opinion, and if someone began poking around Clanton, Harry Rex would know it soon enough.

The plane to Ambergris Cay was an aging Cessna Caravan, a twenty-seater that was stuffed with well-fed North Americans too wide for the narrow seats. But Mack didn't mind. He gazed out the window, down to the brilliant aquamarine water three thousand feet below, warm salty water in which he would soon be swimming. On the island, and north of the main town of San Pedro, he found a room at a quaint little waterfront place called

Rico's Reef Resort. All rooms were thatched-roof cabins, each with a small front porch. Each porch had a long hammock, leaving little doubt as to the priorities at Rico's. He paid cash for a week, no credit cards ever again, and quickly changed into his new work clothes—T-shirt, old denim shorts, baseball cap, no shoes. He soon found the watering hole, ordered a rum drink, and met a man named Coz. Coz anchored one end of the teakwood bar and gave the impression that he had been attached to it for quite some time. His long gray hair was pulled back into a ponytail. His skin was burned bronze and leathery. His accent was faded New England, and before long Coz, chain-smoking and drinking dark rum, let it slip that at one time he'd been involved with a vaguely undefined firm in Boston. He poked and prodded into Mack's background, but Mack was too nervous to divulge anything.

"How long you staying?" Coz asked.

"Long enough to get a tan," Mack answered.

"Might take a while. Watch the sun. It's brutal."

Coz had advice for lots of things in Belize. When he realized he was getting little from his drinking buddy, he said, "You're smart. Don't talk too much around here. You got a lot of Yanks running from something."

Later, in the hammock, Mack rocked with the breeze, gazed at the ocean, listened to the surf, sipped a rum and soda, and asked himself if he was really running. There were no warrants, court orders, or creditors chasing him. At least none that he knew of. Nor did he expect any. He could go home tomorrow if he chose, but that thought was distasteful. Home was gone. Home was something he had just escaped. The shock of leaving weighed heavy, but the rum certainly helped.

Mack spent the first week either in the hammock or by the pool, carefully soaking up the sun before hustling back to the porch for a reprieve. When he wasn't napping, tanning, or loitering at the bar, he took long walks by the water. A companion would be nice, he said to himself. He chatted with the tourists at the small hotels and fishing lodges, and he finally got lucky with a pleasant young lady from Detroit. At times he was bored, but being bored in Belize was far better than being bored in Clanton.

On March 25, Mack awoke from a bad dream. For some awful reason he remembered the date because a new term of chancery court began on that day in Clanton, and under usual circumstances Mack would be at the docket call in the main courtroom. There, along with twenty other lawyers, he would answer when his name was called and inform the judge that Mr. and Mrs. So-and-So were present and ready to get their divorce. He had at least three on the docket for that day. Sadly, he could still remember their names. It was nothing but an assembly line, and Mack was a low-paid and very replaceable worker.

Lying naked under thin sheets, he closed his eyes. He inhaled and sniffed the musty oak and leather smell of the old courtroom. He heard the voices of the other lawyers as they bickered importantly over the last-minute details. He saw the judge in his faded black robe sitting low in a massive chair waiting impatiently for papers to sign to dissolve yet another marriage made in heaven.

Then he opened his eyes, and as he watched the slow silent

spin of the ceiling fan, and listened to the early-morning sounds of the ocean, Mack Stafford was suddenly and thoroughly consumed with the joys of freedom. He quickly pulled on some gym shorts and ran down the beach to a pier that jutted two hundred feet into the water. Sprinting, he raced along the pier and never slowed as it came to an end. Mack was laughing as he launched himself through the air and landed in a mighty splash. The sauna-like water pushed him to the top, and he started swimming.

# Casino

❧ · · · · · · · · · · · · · · · · · · · · ❧

Clanton's most ambitious hustler was a tractor dealer named
Bobby Carl Leach. From a large gravel sales lot on the highway north of town, Bobby Carl built an empire that, at one time
or another, included a backhoe and dozer service, a fleet of pulpwood trucks, two all-you-can-eat catfish cabins, a motel, some raw
timberland upon which the sheriff found marijuana in cultivation,
and a collection of real estate that primarily comprised empty
buildings scattered around Clanton. Most of them eventually
burned. Arson followed Bobby Carl, as did litigation. He was no
stranger to lawsuits; indeed, he loved to brag about all the lawyers
he kept busy. With a colorful history of shady deals, divorces,
IRS audits, fraudulent insurance claims, and near indictments,
Bobby Carl was a small industry unto himself, at least to the local
bar association. And though he was always in the vicinity of trou-

ble, he had never been seriously prosecuted. Over time, his ability to elude the law added to his reputation, and most of Clanton enjoyed repeating and embellishing stories about Bobby Carl's dealings.

His car of choice was a Cadillac DeVille, always maroon and new and spotless. He traded every twelve months for the latest model. No one else dared drive the same car. He once bought a Rolls-Royce, the only one within two hundred miles, but kept it less than a year. When he realized such an exotic vehicle had little impact on the locals, he got rid of it. They had no idea where it was made and how much it cost. None of the mechanics in town would touch it; not that it mattered because they couldn't find parts for it anyway.

He wore cowboy boots with dangerously pointed toes, starched white shirts, and dark three-piece suits, the pockets of which were always stuffed with cash. And every outfit was adorned with an astonishing collection of gold—thick watches, bulky neck chains, bracelets, belt buckles, collar pins, tie bars. Bobby Carl gathered gold the way some women hoard shoes. There was gold trim in his cars, office, briefcases, knives, portrait frames, even his plumbing fixtures. He liked diamonds too. The IRS could not keep track of such portable wealth, and the black market was a natural shopping place for Bobby Carl.

Gaudy as he was in public, he was fanatical about his private life. He lived quietly in a weird contemporary home deep in the hills east of Clanton, and the fact that so few people had ever seen his place fueled rumors that it was used for all sorts of illegal and immoral activities. There was some truth to these rumors. A man of his status quite naturally attracted women of the looser variety, and Bobby Carl loved the ladies. He married several of them, always to his regret. He enjoyed booze, but never to excess. There were wild friends and rowdy parties, but Bobby Carl Leach never missed an hour of work because of a hangover. Money was much too important.

At 5:00 every morning, including Sundays, his maroon DeVille made a quick loop around the Ford County Courthouse in downtown Clanton. The stores and offices were always empty and dark, and this pleased him greatly. Let 'em sleep. The bankers and lawyers and real estate agents and merchants who told stories about him while they envied his money were never at work at 5:00 in the morning. He relished the darkness and tranquillity, the absence of competition at that hour. After his daily victory lap, he sped away to his office, which was on the site of his tractor sales lot and was, without question, the largest in the county. It covered the second floor of an old redbrick building built before Pearl Harbor, and from behind its darkly tinted windows Bobby Carl could keep an eye on his tractors while also watching the highway traffic.

Alone and content at that early hour, he began each day with a pot of strong coffee, which he drained as he read his newspapers. He subscribed to every daily he could get—Memphis, Jackson, Tupelo—and the weeklies from the surrounding counties. Reading and gulping coffee with a vengeance, he combed the papers not for the news but for the opportunities. Buildings for sale, farmland, foreclosures, factories coming and going, auctions, bankruptcies, liquidations, requests for bids, bank mergers, upcoming public works. The walls of his office were covered with plats of land and aerial photos of towns and counties. The local land rolls were in his computer. He knew who was behind on their property taxes, and for how long and how much, and he gathered and stored this information in the predawn hours while everyone else was asleep.

His greatest weakness, far ahead of women and whiskey, was gambling. He had a long and ugly history with Las Vegas and poker clubs and sports bookies. He routinely dropped serious cash at the dog track in West Memphis and once nearly bankrupted himself on a cruise ship to Bermuda. And when casino gambling arrived, quite unexpectedly, in Mississippi, his empire began taking on worrisome levels of debt. Only one local bank would deal with him anyway, and when he tapped out there to cover his losses at the craps tables, he was forced to hock some gold in Memphis to meet his payroll. Then a building burned. He bullied the insurance company into a settlement, and his cash crisis abated, for the moment.

※

The Choctaw Indians built the only landlocked casino in the state. It was in Neshoba County, two hours south of Clanton, and there one night Bobby Carl rolled the dice for the last time. He lost a small fortune, and driving home under the influence, he swore he would never gamble again. Enough was enough. It was a sucker's game. There was an excellent reason the smart boys keep building new casinos.

Bobby Carl Leach considered himself a smart boy.

His research soon revealed that the Department of the Interior recognized 562 tribes of Native Americans across the country, but only the Choctaw in Mississippi. The state had once been covered with Indians—at least nineteen major tribes—but most had been forcibly relocated in the 1830s and sent to Oklahoma. Only three thousand Choctaw remained, and they were prospering nicely from their casino.

Competition was needed. Further research revealed that at one time the second-largest population had belonged to the Yazoo, and long before the white man arrived, their territory had covered virtually all of what is now the north half of Mississippi, including Ford County. Bobby Carl paid a few bucks to a genealogical research firm which produced a suspicious family tree that purported to prove that his father's great-grandfather had been one-sixteenth Yazoo.

A business plan began to take shape.

Thirty miles west of Clanton, on the Polk County line, there was a country grocery store owned by a slightly dark-skinned old man with long braided hair and turquoise on every finger. He was known simply as Chief Larry, primarily because he claimed to be a full-blooded Indian and said he had papers to prove it. He was a Yazoo, and proud of it, and to convince folks of his authenticity, he stocked all manner of cheap Indian artifacts and souvenirs along with the eggs and cold beer. A tepee made in China sat next to the highway, and there was a lifeless, geriatric black bear asleep in a cage by the door. Since Chief's was the only store within ten miles, he managed a decent traffic from the locals and some gas and a snapshot from the occasional lost tourist.

Chief Larry was an activist of sorts. He seldom smiled, and he gave the impression that he carried the weight of his long-suffering and forgotten people. He wrote angry letters to congressmen and governors and bureaucrats, and their responses were tacked to the wall behind the cash register. At the slightest provocation, he would launch into a bitter diatribe against the latest round of injustices imposed upon "his people." History was a favorite topic, and he would and could go on for hours about the colorful and heartbreaking theft of "his land." Most of the locals knew to keep their comments brief as they paid for their goods. A few, though, enjoyed pulling up a chair and letting Chief rant.

For almost two decades Chief Larry had been tracking down other Yazoo descendants in the area. Most of those he wrote to had no inkling of their Indian heritage and certainly wanted no part of it. They were thoroughly assimilated, mixed, intermarried, and ignorant of his version of their gene pool. They were white! This was, after all, Mississippi, and any hint of tainted blood meant something far more ominous than a little ancestral frolicking with the natives. Of those who bothered to write back, almost all claimed to be of Anglo stock. Two threatened to sue him, and one threatened to kill him. But he labored on, and when he had organized a motley crew of two dozen desperate souls, he founded the Yazoo Nation and made application to the Department of the Interior.

Years passed. Gambling arrived on reservations throughout the country, and suddenly Indian land became more valuable.

When Bobby Carl decided he was part Yazoo, he quietly got involved. With the help of a prominent law firm in Tupelo, pressure was applied to the proper places in Washington, and official tribal status was granted to the Yazoo. They had no land, but then none was needed under federal guidelines.

Bobby Carl had the land. Forty acres of scrub brush and loblolly pine just down the highway from Chief Larry's tepee.

When the charter arrived from Washington, the proud new tribe met in the rear of Chief's store for a ceremony. They invited their congressman, but he was occupied at the Capitol. They invited the governor, but there was no response. They invited other state officials, but more important duties called them. They invited the local politicians, but they, too, were working too hard elsewhere. Only a lowly and pale-faced undersecretary of some strain showed up from the DOI and handed over the paperwork. The Yazoo, most as pale faced as the bureaucrat, were nonetheless impressed by the moment. Not surprisingly, Larry was unanimously elected as chief for a lifetime. There was no mention of a salary. But there was a lot of talk about a home, a piece of land on which they could build an office or a headquarters, a place of identity and purpose.

The following day, Bobby Carl's maroon DeVille slid into the gravel parking lot at Chief's. He had never met Chief Larry and had never stepped inside the store. He took in the fake tepee, noticed the peeling paint on the exterior walls, sneered at the ancient gas pumps, stopped at the bear's cage long enough to determine that the creature was in fact alive, then walked inside to meet his blood brother.

Fortunately, Chief had never heard of Bobby Carl Leach. Otherwise, he may have sold him a diet soda and wished him farewell. After a few sips, and after it became obvious that the customer was in no hurry to leave, Chief said, "You live around here?"

"Other side of the county," Bobby Carl said as he touched a fake spear that was part of an Apache warrior set on a rack near the counter. "Congratulations on the federal charter," he said.

Chief's chest swelled immediately, and he offered his first smile. "Thank you. How did you know? Was it in the paper?"

"No. I just heard. I'm part Yazoo."

With that, the smile instantly vanished, and Chief's black eyes focused harshly on Bobby Carl's expensive wool suit, vest, starched white shirt, loud paisley tie, gold bracelets, gold watch, gold cuff links, gold belt buckle, all the way down to the javelin-tipped cowboy boots. Then he studied the hair—tinted and permed with little strands wiggling and bouncing around the ears. The eyes were bluish green, Irish and shifty. Chief, of course, preferred someone who resembled himself, someone with at least a few Native American characteristics. But these days he had to take what he could get. The gene pool had become so shallow that calling oneself a Yazoo was all that mattered.

"It's true," Bobby Carl pressed on, then he touched his inside coat pocket. "I have documentation."

Chief waved him off. "No, it's not necessary. A pleasure, Mr.—"

"Leach, Bobby Carl Leach."

Over a sandwich, Bobby Carl explained that he was well acquainted with the chief of the Choctaw Nation, and suggested that the two great men meet. Chief Larry had long envied the

Choctaw for their standing and their efforts to preserve themselves. He had also read about their wildly profitable casino business, the proceeds of which supported the tribe, built schools and
clinics, and sent the young people away to college on scholarship.
Bobby Carl, the humanitarian, seized upon the social advances of
the Choctaw due to their wisdom in tapping into the white man's
lust for gambling and drinking.

The following day, they left for a tour of the Choctaw reservation. Bobby Carl drove and talked nonstop, and by the time
they arrived at the casino, he had convinced Chief Larry that
they, the proud Yazoo, could duplicate the venture and prosper
as a young nation. The Choctaw chief was curiously tied up with
other business, but an underling provided a halfhearted tour of
the sprawling casino and hotel, as well as the two eighteen-hole
golf courses, convention center, and private airstrip, all in a very
rural and forlorn part of Neshoba County.

"He's afraid of competition," Bobby Carl whispered to Chief
Larry as their tour guide showed them around with no enthusiasm whatsoever.

Driving home, Bobby Carl laid out the deal. He would donate the forty-acre tract of land to the Yazoo. The tribe would finally have a home! And on the land they would build themselves
a casino. Bobby Carl knew an architect and a contractor and a
banker, and he knew the local politicians, and it was clear that he
had been planning this for some time. Chief Larry was too dazed
and too unsophisticated to ask many questions. The future suddenly held great promise, and money had little to do with it.
Respect was the issue. Chief Larry had dreamed of a home for his

people, a definable place where his brothers and sisters could live and prosper and try to recapture their heritage.

Bobby Carl was dreaming too, but his dreams had little to do with the glory of a long-lost tribe.

His deal would give him a half interest in the casino, and for this he would donate the forty acres, secure financing for the casino, and hire the lawyers to satisfy the hands-off and distracted regulators. Since the casino would be on Indian land, there was actually very little to be regulated. The county and state certainly couldn't stop them; this had already been firmly settled by prior litigation around the country.

At the end of the long day, and over a soft drink in the back of Chief's store, the two blood brothers shook hands and toasted the future.

The forty-acre tract changed owners, the bulldozers shaved every inch of it, the lawyers charged ahead, the banker finally saw the light, and within a month Clanton was consumed with the horrific news that a casino was coming to Ford County. For days, the rumors raged in the coffee shops around the square, and in the courthouse and downtown offices there was talk of little else. Bobby Carl's name was linked to the scandal from the very beginning, and this gave it an air of ominous credibility. It was a perfect fit for him, just the type of immoral and profitable venture that he would pursue with a vengeance. He denied it in public and confirmed it in private, and leaked it to anyone he deemed worthy of spreading it.

When the first concrete was poured two months later, there was no ceremonial shoveling of dirt by local leaders, no speeches with promises of jobs, none of the usual posturing for cameras. It was a non-event, by design, and had it not been for a cub reporter acting on a tip, the commencement of construction would have gone unnoticed. However, the following edition of the *Ford County Times* ran a large front-page photo of a cement truck with workers around it. The headline screamed: "Here Comes the Casino." A brief report added few details, primarily because no one wanted to talk. Chief Larry was too busy behind the meat counter. Bobby Carl Leach was out of town on urgent business. The Bureau of Indian Affairs within the DOI was thoroughly uncooperative. An anonymous source did contribute by confirming, off the record, that the casino would be open "in about ten months."

The front-page story and photo confirmed the rumors, and the town erupted. The Baptist preachers got themselves organized, and the following Sunday unloaded vile condemnations of gambling and its related evils upon their congregations. They called their people to action. Write letters! Call your elected officials! Keep an eye on your neighbors to make sure they don't succumb to the sin of gambling! They had to stop this cancer from afflicting their community. The Indians were attacking again.

The next edition of the *Times* was laden with screeching letters to the editor, and not a single one supported the idea of a casino. Satan was advancing on them, and all decent folk should "circle the wagons" to fend off his evil intentions. When the County Board of Supervisors met as usual on a Monday morning, the meeting was moved into the main courtroom to accommodate the angry crowd. The five supervisors hid behind their lawyer, who tried to explain to the mob that there was nothing the county could do to stop the casino. It was a federal issue, plain and simple. The Yazoo had become officially recognized. They owned the land. Indians had built casinos in at least twenty-six other states, usually with local opposition. Lawsuits had been filed by groups of concerned citizens, and they had lost every one of them.

Was it true that Bobby Carl Leach was the real force behind the casino? someone demanded.

The lawyer had been drinking with Bobby Carl two nights earlier. He couldn't deny what the entire town suspected. "I believe so," he said cautiously. "But we are not entitled to know everything about the casino. And besides, Mr. Leach is of Yazoo descent."

A wave of raucous laughter swept through the room, followed by boos and hissing.

"He'd claim to be a midget if he could make a buck!" someone yelled, and this caused even more laughter, more jeers.

They yelled and booed and hissed for an hour, but the meeting eventually ran out of gas. It became obvious that the county could do nothing to stop the casino.

And so it went. More letters to the editor, more sermons, more phone calls to elected officials, a few updates in the newspaper. As the weeks and months dragged on, the opposition lost interest. Bobby Carl lay low and was seldom seen around town. He was, however, at the construction site every morning by 7:00, yelling at the superintendent and threatening to fire someone.

✿

The Lucky Jack Casino was finished just over a year after the Yazoo charter arrived from Washington. Everything about it was cheap. The gaming hall itself was a hastily designed combination of three prefab metal buildings wedged together and fronted with fake facades of white brick and lots of neon. A fifty-room hotel was attached to it and designed to be as towering as possible. With six floors of small, cramped rooms available for $49.95 a night, it was the tallest building in the county. Inside the casino, the motif was the Wild West, cowboys and Indians, wagon trains, gunslingers, saloons, and tepees. The walls were plastered with garish paintings of western battle scenes, with the Indians having the slight advantage in the body count, if anyone cared to notice. The floors were covered with a thin tacky carpet inlaid with colorful images of horses and livestock. The atmosphere was that of a rowdy convention hall thrown together as quickly as possible to attract gamblers. Bobby Carl had handled most of the design. The staff was rushed through training. "One hundred new jobs," Bobby Carl retorted to anyone who criticized his casino. Chief Larry was outfitted in full Yazoo ceremonial garb, or at least his version of it, and his routine was to roam the gambling floor and chat with the clients and make them feel as though they were on real Indian territory. Of the two dozen official Yazoo, fifteen signed up for work. They were given headbands and feathers and taught how to deal blackjack, one of the more lucrative jobs.

The future was full of plans—a golf course, a convention center, an indoor pool, and so on—but first they had to make some money. They needed gamblers.

The opening was without fanfare. Bobby Carl knew that cameras and reporters and too much attention would scare away many of the curious, so the Lucky Jack opened quietly. He ran ads in the newspapers of the surrounding counties, with promises of better odds and luckier slots and "the largest poker room in Mississippi." It was a blatant falsehood, but no one would dare contest it in public. Business was slow at first; the locals were indeed staying away. Most of the traffic was from the surrounding counties, and few of the first gamblers cared to spend the night. The high-rise hotel was empty. Chief Larry had almost no one to talk to as he roamed the floor.

After the first week, word spread around Clanton that the casino was in trouble. Experts on the subject held forth in the coffee shops around the square. Several of the braver ones admitted to visiting the Lucky Jack and happily reported that the place was virtually deserted. The preachers crowed from their pulpits—Satan had been defeated. The Indians had been crushed once again.

After two weeks of lackluster activity, Bobby Carl decided it was time to cheat. He found an old girlfriend, one willing to have her face splashed across the newspapers, and rigged the slots so she would win an astounding $14,000 with a $1 chip. Another mole, one from Polk County, won $8,000 at the "luckiest slots this side of Vegas." The two winners posed for photos with Chief Larry as he ceremoniously handed over greatly enlarged checks, and Bobby Carl paid for full-page ads in eight weekly newspapers, including the *Ford County Times*.

The lure of instant riches was overwhelming. Business doubled, then tripled. After six weeks, the Lucky Jack was breaking even. The hotel offered free rooms with weekend packages, and often had no vacancies. RVs began arriving from other states. Billboards all over north Mississippi advertised the good life at the Lucky Jack.

⚥

The good life was passing Stella by. She was forty-eight, the mother of one fully grown daughter, and the wife of a man she no longer loved. When she had married Sidney decades earlier, she had known he was dull, quiet, and not particularly handsome and lacked ambition, and now as she approached the age of fifty she could not remember why or how he had attracted her. The romance and lust didn't last long, and by the time their daughter was born, they were simply going through the motions. On Stella's thirtieth birthday she confided to a sister that she really wasn't happy. Her sister, once divorced with another one in the works, advised her to unload Sidney and find a man with a personality, someone who enjoyed life, someone with assets preferably. Instead, Stella doted on her daughter and secretly began taking birth control pills. The thought of another child with even a few of Sidney's genes was not appealing.

Eighteen years had passed now, and the daughter was gone. Sidney had put on a few pounds and was graying and sedentary and duller than ever. He worked as a data collector for a midsize life insurance company, and was content to put in his years and dream of some glorious retirement that he, for some reason, believed would be far more exciting than the first sixty-five years of his life. Stella knew better. She knew that Sidney, whether working or retired, would be the same insufferable mouse of a man whose silly little daily rituals would never change and would eventually drive her crazy.

She wanted out.

She knew he still loved her, adored her even, but she could not return the affection. She tried for years to convince herself that their marriage was still anchored in love, that of the long-lasting, non-romantic, deeply embedded type that survives decade after decade. But she finally gave up this fatal notion.

She hated to break his heart, but he would eventually get over it.

She dropped twenty pounds, darkened her hair, went a bit heavier with the makeup, and flirted with the idea of some new breasts. Sidney watched this with amusement. His cute wife now looked ten years younger. What a lucky man he was!

His luck ran out, though, when he came home one night to an empty house. Most of the furniture was still there, but his wife was not. Her closets were empty. She had taken some linens and kitchen accessories but had not been greedy about it. Truth was, Stella wanted nothing from Sidney but a divorce.

The paperwork was on the kitchen table—a joint petition for a divorce on the grounds of irreconcilable differences. Prepared by a lawyer already! It was an ambush. He wept as he read it, then cried even harder as he read her rather terse two-page farewell. For a week or so they bickered on the phone, back and forth, back and forth. He begged her to come home. She declined, said it was over, so please just sign the paperwork and stop crying.

They had lived for years on the outskirts of the small town of Karraway, a desolate little place, well suited for a man like Sidney. Stella, however, had had enough. She was now in Clanton, the county seat, a larger town with a country club and a few lounges. She was living with an old girlfriend, sleeping in the basement, looking for a job. Sidney tried to find her, but she avoided him. Their daughter called from Texas and quickly sided with her mother.

The house, always on the quiet side, was now like a tomb, and Sidney couldn't stand it. He developed the ritual of waiting until dark, then driving to Clanton, around the square, up and down the streets of the town, eyes moving from side to side, hoping fervently that he would see his wife, and that she would see him, and that her cruel heart would melt and life would be good again. He never saw her, and he kept driving, out of the town and into the countryside.

One night he passed Chief Larry's store and down the road turned in to the crowded parking lot of the Lucky Jack Casino. Maybe she'd be there. Maybe she was so desperate for the bright lights and the fast life that she would stoop to hang out in such a trashy place. It was just a thought, just an excuse to see the action that everyone had been talking about. Who would have ever dreamed that a casino would exist in the hidebound rural outback of Ford County? Sidney roamed the tacky carpet, spoke to Chief Larry, watched a group of drunk rednecks lose their paychecks shooting craps, sneered at the pathetic geezers stuffing their savings into rigged slot machines, and listened briefly to a dreadful country crooner trying to imitate Hank Williams on a small stage in the rear. A few middle-aged and very overweight swingers wobbled and shifted listlessly on the dance floor in front of the band. Some real hell-raisers. Stella wasn't there. She wasn't in the bar, nor the buffet cafeteria, nor the poker room. Sidney was somewhat relieved, but his heart was still broken.

He hadn't played cards in years, but he remembered the basic rules of twenty-one, a game his father had taught him. After circling the blackjack tables for half an hour, he finally mustered the courage to slide into a seat at the $5 table and get change for a $20 bill. He played for an hour and won $85. He spent the next day studying the rules of blackjack—the basic odds, doubling down, splitting pairs, the ins and outs of buying insurance—and returned to the same table the following night and won over $400. He studied some more, and the third night he played for three hours, drank nothing but black coffee, and walked away with $1,750. He found the game to be simple and straightforward. There was a perfect way to play each hand, based on what the dealer was showing, and following the standard odds, a player can win six hands out of ten. Add the two-for-one payout for hitting a blackjack, and the game provided the best odds against the house.

Why, then, did so many people lose? Sidney was appalled at the other players' lack of knowledge and their foolish bets. The nonstop alcohol didn't help, and in a land where drinking was repressed and still considered a major sin, the free flow of booze at the Lucky Jack was irresistible for many.

Sidney studied, played, drank free black coffee brought in by the cocktail waitresses, and played some more. He bought books and self-help videos and taught himself to count cards, a difficult strategy that often worked beautifully but would also get a gambler thrown out of most casinos. And, most important, he taught himself the discipline necessary to play the odds, to quit when he was losing, and to radically change his bets as the deck grew smaller.

He stopped driving to Clanton to look for his wife and instead drove straight to the Lucky Jack, where, on most nights, he would play for an hour or two and take home at least $1,000. The more he won, the more he noticed the hard frowns from the pit bosses. The beefy young men in cheap suits—security, he guessed—seemed to watch him a bit closer. He continually refused to be rated—the process of signing up for the "club membership" that gave all sorts of freebies to those regulars who gambled hard. He refused to register in any way. His favorite book was *How to Break the Casino*, and the author, an ex-gambler turned writer, preached the message of disguise and deceit. Never wear the same clothes, jewelry, hats, caps, glasses. Never play at the same table for more than an hour. Never give them your name. Take a friend and tell him to call you Frank or Charlie or something. Make a stupid bet occasionally. Change your drink routine, but stay away from alcohol. The reason was simple. The law allowed any casino in the country to simply ask a gambler to leave. If they suspect you're counting cards, or cheating, or if you're winning too much and they're just tired of it, they can give you the boot. No reason is necessary. An assortment of identities keeps them guessing.

The success of the gambling gave Sidney a new purpose in life, but in the darkness of the night he still awoke and reached for Stella. The divorce decree had been signed by a judge. She was not coming back, but he reached anyway, still dreaming of the woman he would always love.

Stella was not suffering from loneliness. The news of an attractive new divorced woman in town spread quickly, and before long she found herself at a party where she met the infamous Bobby Carl Leach. Though she was somewhat older than most of the women he chased, he nonetheless found her attractive and sexy. He charmed her with his usual stream of compliments and seemed to hang on every word she uttered. They had dinner the following night and went to bed right after dessert. Though he was rough and vulgar, she found the experience exhilarating. It was so wonderfully different from the stoic and chilly copulating she had endured with Sidney.

Before long, Stella had a well-paying job as an assistant/ secretary for Mr. Leach, the latest in a long line of women who were added to the payroll for reasons other than their organizational skills. But if Mr. Leach expected her to do little more than answer the phone and strip on demand, he miscalculated badly. She quickly surveyed his empire and found little of interest. Timber, raw land, rental property, farm equipment, and low-budget motels were all as dull as Sidney, especially when weighed against the glitz of a casino. She belonged at the Lucky Jack, and soon commandeered an office upstairs above the gaming floor, where Bobby Carl roamed in the late evenings, gin and tonic in hand, staring at the innumerable video cameras and counting his money. Her title shifted to that of director of operations, and she began planning an expansion of the dining area and maybe an indoor pool. She had lots of ideas, and Bobby Carl was pleased to have an easy bedmate who felt just as much passion for the business.

Back in Karraway, Sidney soon heard the rumors that his beloved Stella had taken up with that rogue Leach, and this further depressed him. It made him ill. He thought of murder, then suicide. He dreamed of ways to impress her, and to win her back. When he heard that she was running the casino, he stopped going. But he did not stop gambling. Instead, he broadened his game with long weekends at the casinos in Tunica County, on the Mississippi River. He won $14,000 in a marathon session at the Choctaw casino in Neshoba County, and was asked to leave the Grand Casino in Biloxi after wiping out two tables to the tune of $38,000. He took a week of vacation and went to Vegas, where he played at a different casino every four hours and left town with over $60,000 in winnings. He quit his job and spent two weeks in the Bahamas, raking in piles of $100 chips at every casino in Freeport and Nassau. He bought an RV and toured the country, prowling for any reservation with a casino. Of the dozen or so he found, all were glad to see him leave. Then he spent a month back in Vegas, studying at the private table of the world's greatest teacher, the man who'd written *How to Break the Casino*. The one-on-one tutorial cost Sidney $50,000, but it was worth every penny. His teacher convinced him he had the talent, the disci-

some of her new friends and a few of Bobby Carl's, then announced the winners in yet another large ad in the local newspapers. And away they went. Bobby Carl and Stella, a handful of casino executives (Chief Larry declined, much to their relief), and the ten lucky couples left Clanton in limos for the trip to the airport in Memphis. From there, they flew to Miami and boarded a ship with four thousand others for an intimate jaunt through the islands.

When they were out of the country, the Valentine's Day massacre began. Sidney entered the Lucky Jack on a busy night—Stella had advertised all sorts of cheap romantic freebies, and the place was packed. He was Sidney, but he looked nothing like the Sidney last seen at the casino. His hair was long and stringy, darkly tinted, and hanging over his ears. He hadn't shaved in a month, and his beard was colored with the same cheap dye he'd used on his hair. He wore large, round tortoiseshell glasses, also tinted, and his eyes were hard to see. He wore a leather biker's jacket and jeans, and six of his fingers bore rings of various stones and metals. A baffling black beret covered most of his head and drooped to the left. For the benefit of the security boys upstairs at their monitors, the back of each hand was adorned with an obscene fake tattoo.

No one had ever seen this Sidney.

Of the twenty blackjack tables, only three catered to the high rollers. Their minimum bets were $100 a hand, and these tables generally saw little traffic. Sidney assumed a chair at one, tossed out a bundle of cash, and said, "Five thousand, in $100 chips." The dealer smiled as he took the cash and spread it across the table. A pit boss watched carefully over his shoulder. Stares and nods were exchanged around the pit, and the eyes upstairs came to life. There were two other gamblers at the table, and they hardly noticed. Both were drinking and were down to their last few chips.

Sidney played like an amateur and lost $2,000 in twenty minutes. The pit boss relaxed; nothing to worry about. "Do you have a club card?" he asked Sidney.

"No," came the curt reply. And don't offer me one.

The other two men left the table, and Sidney spread out his operations. Playing three seats and betting $500 at each one, he quickly recaptured his $2,000 and added another $4,500 to his stack of chips. The pit boss paced a little and tried not to stare. The dealer shuffled the cards as a cocktail waitress brought a vodka and orange juice, a drink Sidney sipped but barely consumed. Playing four seats at $1,000 each, he broke even for the next fifteen minutes, then won six hands in a row, for a total of $24,000. The $100 chips were too numerous to move around quickly, so he said, "Let's switch to those purple ones." The table had only twenty of the $1,000 chips. The dealer was forced to call time-out as the pit boss sent for more money. "Would you like dinner?" he asked, somewhat nervously.

"Not hungry," Sidney said. "But I'll run to the men's room."

When play resumed, Sidney, still alone at the table and attracting a few onlookers, played four seats at $2,000 each. He broke even for fifteen minutes, then glanced at the pit boss and abruptly asked, "Can I have another dealer?"

"Certainly."

"I prefer a female."

"No problem."

A young Hispanic lady stepped to the table and offered a feeble "Good luck." Sidney did not respond. He played $1,000 at each of the four seats, lost three in a row, then increased his bets to $3,000 a hand and won four straight.

The casino was down over $60,000. The blackjack record so far at the Lucky Jack was $110,000 for one night. A doctor from Memphis had made the haul, only to lose it and much more the following night. "Let 'em win," Bobby Carl loved to say. "We'll get it right back."

"I'd like some ice cream," Sidney said in the general direction of the pit boss, who immediately snapped his fingers. "What flavor?"

"Pistachio."

A plastic bowl and spoon soon arrived, and Sidney tipped the waitress with his last $100 chip. He took a small bite, then placed $5,000 at four seats. Playing $20,000 a hand was indeed rare, and the gossip spread through the casino. A crowd hovered behind him, but he was oblivious. He won seven of the next ten hands and was up $102,000. As the dealer shuffled the decks, Sidney slowly ate the ice cream and did nothing else but stare at the cards.

With a fresh shoe, he varied his bets from $10,000 to $20,000 per hand. When he won $80,000 more, the pit boss stepped in and said, "That's enough. You're counting cards."

"You're wrong," Sidney said.

"Let him go," someone said behind him, but the pit boss ignored it.

The dealer backed away from the confrontation. "You're counting," the pit boss said again.

"It's not illegal," Sidney shot back.

"No, but we make our own rules."

"You're full of crap," Sidney growled, then took another bite.

"That's it. I'll ask you to leave."

"Fine. I want cash."

"We'll cut a check."

"Hell no. I walked in here with cash, and I'm leaving with cash."

"Sir, would you please come with me?"

"Where?"

"Let's handle this over at the cashier's."

"Great. But I demand cash."

The crowd watched them disappear. In the cashier's office, Sidney produced a fake driver's license that declared him to be a Mr. Jack Ross from Dothan, Alabama. The cashier and the pit boss filled out the required IRS form, and after a heated argument Sidney walked out of the casino with a canvas bank bag filled with $184,000 in $100 bills.

He was back the following night in a dark suit, white shirt, and tie, and looking considerably different. The beard, long hair, rings, tattoos, beret, and goofy glasses were gone. His head was shaved slick, and he sported a narrow gray mustache and wire-rimmed reading glasses perched on his nose. He chose a different table with a different dealer. Last night's pit boss was not on duty. He put cash on the table and asked for twenty-four $1,000 chips. He played for thirty minutes, won twelve hands out of fifteen, then asked for a private table. The pit boss led him to a small room near the poker pit. The security boys upstairs were standing at their posts, watching every move.

"I'd like $10,000 chips," Sidney announced. "And a male dealer."

No problem. "Something to drink?"

"A Sprite, with some pretzels."

He pulled some more cash from his pocket and counted the chips after the exchange. There were twenty of them. He played three seats at a time, and fifteen minutes later he owned thirty-two chips. Another pit boss and the manager on duty had joined the occasion and stood behind the dealer, watching grimly.

Sidney munched on pretzels as if he were playing $2 slots. Instead, he was now betting $10,000 at each of four seats. Then $20,000, then back to $10,000. When the shoe was low, he suddenly bet $50,000 at all six seats. The dealer was showing a five, his worst card. Sidney calmly split two sevens and doubled down on a hard ten. The dealer flipped a queen, then very slowly pulled his next card. It was a nine, for a bust of twenty-four. The hand netted Sidney $400,000, and the first pit boss was ready to faint.

"Perhaps we should take a break," the manager said.

"Oh, I say we finish the shoe, then take a break," Sidney said.

"No," the manager said.

"You want the money back, don't you?"

The dealer hesitated and cast a desperate look at the manager. Where was Bobby Carl when they needed him?

"Deal," Sidney said with a grin. "It's just money. Hell, I've never walked out of a casino with cash in my pocket."

"Could we have your name?"

"Sure. It's Sidney Lewis." He removed his wallet, tossed over his real driver's license, and didn't care if they had his real name. He had no plans to return. The manager and pit bosses studied it, anything to buy some time.

"Have you been here before?" the manager asked.

"I was here a few months ago. Are we gonna play? What kind of casino is this? Now deal the cards."

The manager reluctantly returned the license, and Sidney left it on the table, next to his towering collection of chips. The manager then nodded slowly at the dealer. Sidney had a single $10,000 chip at each of the six seats, then quickly added four more to each. Three hundred thousand dollars was suddenly in play. If he won half of the seats, he planned to keep playing. If he lost, he'd quit and walk out with a two-night net of about $600,000, a pleasant sum of money that would do much to satisfy his hatred of Bobby Carl Leach.

Cards slowly hit the table, and the dealer gave himself a six as his up card. Sidney split two jacks, a gutsy move that most experts warned against, then he waved off further draws. When the dealer flipped his down card and revealed a nine, Sidney showed no expression, but the manager and both pit bosses turned pale. The dealer was required to draw on a fifteen, and he did so with great reluctance. He pulled a seven, for a bust of twenty-two.

The manager jumped forward and said, "That's it. You're counting cards." He wiped beads of sweat from his forehead.

Sidney said, "You must be kidding. What kind of dump is this?"

"It's over, buddy," the manager said, then glanced at two thick security guards who had suddenly materialized behind Sidney, who calmly stuck a pretzel in his mouth and crunched it loudly. He grinned at the manager and the pit bosses and decided to call it a night.

"I want cash," he said.

"That might be a problem," the manager said.

They escorted Sidney to the manager's office upstairs, where the entire entourage gathered behind a closed door. No one sat down.

"I demand cash," Sidney said.

"We'll give you a check," the manager said again.

"You don't have the cash, do you?" Sidney said, taunting. "This two-bit casino doesn't have the cash and cannot cover its exposure."

"We have the money," the manager said without conviction. "And we're happy to write a check."

Sidney glared at him, and the two pit bosses, and the two security guards, then said, "The check will bounce, won't it?"

"Of course not, but I'll ask you to hold it for seventy-two hours."

"Which bank?"

"Merchants, in Clanton."

At nine o'clock the next morning, Sidney and his lawyer walked into the Merchants Bank on the square in Clanton and demanded to see the president. When they were in his office, Sidney pulled out a check from the Lucky Jack Casino in the amount of $945,000, postdated three days. The president examined it, wiped his face, then said in a cracking voice, "I'm sorry, but we can't honor this check."

"And in three days?" the lawyer asked.

"I seriously doubt it."

"Have you talked to the casino?"

"Yes, several times."

An hour later, Sidney and his lawyer walked into the Ford County Courthouse, to the office of the chancery clerk, and filed a petition for a temporary restraining order seeking an immediate closing of the Lucky Jack and the payment of the debt. The judge, the Honorable Willis Bradshaw, set an emergency hearing for 9:00 the following morning.

⚜

Bobby Carl jumped ship in Puerto Rico and scrambled to find flights back to Memphis. He arrived in Ford County late that evening and drove, in a rented Hertz subcompact, straight to the casino, where he found few gamblers, and even fewer employees who knew anything about what had happened the previous night. The manager had quit and could not be found. One of the pit bosses who'd dealt with Sidney was likewise rumored to have fled the county. Bobby Carl threatened to fire everyone else, except for Chief Larry, who was overwhelmed by the chaos. At midnight, Bobby Carl was meeting with the bank president and a team of lawyers, and the anxiety level was through the roof.

Stella was still on the cruise ship, but unable to enjoy herself. In the midst of the chaos, when Bobby Carl was screaming into the phones and throwing things, she had heard him yell, "Sidney Lewis! Who the hell is Sidney Lewis?"

She said nothing, at least nothing about the Sidney Lewis she knew, and found it impossible to believe that her ex-husband had been capable of breaking a casino. Still, she was very uncomfortable, and when the ship docked at George Town on Grand Cayman, she took a cab to the airport and headed home.

Judge Bradshaw welcomed the throng of spectators to his courtroom. He thanked them for coming and invited them back in the future. Then he asked if the lawyers were ready to proceed.

Bobby Carl, red eyed and haggard and unshaven, was seated at one table with three of his lawyers and Chief Larry, who'd never been near a courtroom and was so nervous that he simply closed his eyes and appeared to be meditating. Bobby Carl, who'd seen many courtrooms, was nonetheless just as stressed. Everything he owned had been mortgaged for the bank loan, and now the future of his casino, as well as all his other assets, was in great jeopardy.

One of his lawyers stood quickly and said, "Yes, Judge, we are ready, but we have filed a motion to dismiss this proceeding because of a lack of jurisdiction. This matter belongs in federal court, not state."

"I've read your motion," Judge Bradshaw said, and it was obvious he did not like what he had read. "I'm keeping jurisdiction."

"Then we'll file in federal court later this morning," the lawyer shot back.

"I can't stop you from filing anything."

Judge Bradshaw had spent most of his career trying to sort out ugly disputes between feuding couples, and over the years he had developed an intense dislike for the causes of divorce. Alcohol, drugs, adultery, gambling—his involvement with the major vices was never ending. He taught Sunday school in the Methodist church and had strict beliefs about right and wrong. Gambling was an abomination, in his opinion, and he was delighted to have a crack at it.

Sidney's lawyer argued loud and hard that the casino was undercapitalized and maintained insufficient cash reserves; thus, it was an ongoing threat to other gamblers. He announced he was filing a full-blown lawsuit at 5:00 that afternoon if the casino did not honor its debt to his client. In the meantime, though, the casino should be closed.

Judge Bradshaw seemed to favor this idea.

And so did the crowd. The spectators included quite a few preachers and their followers, all good registered voters who had always supported Judge Bradshaw, and all bright-eyed and happy at the possibility of shutting down the casino. This was the miracle they had been praying for. And though they silently condemned Sidney Lewis for his sinful ways, they couldn't help but admire the guy—a local boy—for breaking the casino. Go, Sidney.

As the hearing dragged on, it came to light that the Lucky Jack had cash on hand of about $400,000, and in addition to this there was a $500,000 reserve fund secured with a bond. Also, Bobby Carl admitted on the witness stand that the casino had averaged about $80,000 a month in profits for the first seven months, and that this number was rising steadily.

After a grueling five-hour hearing, Judge Bradshaw ordered the casino to pay the entire $945,000, immediately, and closed its doors until the debt was satisfied. He also instructed the sheriff to block the entrance off the state highway and to arrest any gambler who tried to enter. Lawyers for the Lucky Jack ran to federal court in Oxford and filed papers to reopen. A hearing would take several days to organize. As promised, Sidney filed suit in both state and federal courts.

Over the next few days, more lawsuits flew back and forth. Sidney sued the insurance company that issued the bond, then sued the bank as well. The bank, suddenly nervous about the $2 million it had loaned the Lucky Jack, soured on the once-exciting gaming business. It called the loan and sued the Yazoo Nation, Chief Larry, and Bobby Carl Leach. They countersued, alleging all sorts of unfair practices. The burst of litigation electrified the local lawyers, most of whom jockeyed for a piece of the action.

When Bobby Carl learned that Stella's recently divorced husband was in fact Sidney, he accused her of conspiring with him and fired her. She sued. Days passed and the Lucky Jack remained closed. Two dozen unpaid employees filed suit. Federal regulators issued subpoenas. The federal judge wanted no part of the mess, and dismissed the casino's efforts to reopen.

After a month of frantic legal maneuvering, reality settled in. The casino's future looked dire. Bobby Carl convinced Chief Larry that they had no choice but to file for bankruptcy protection. Two days later, Bobby Carl reluctantly did the same. After two decades of wheeling and dealing and operating on the edge, he was finally bankrupt.

Sidney was in Las Vegas when he received a call from his lawyer with the great news that the insurance company would settle for the full amount of its bond—$500,000. In addition, the frozen accounts of the Lucky Jack would be thawed just enough so that another check for $400,000 would be issued in his favor. He immediately hopped in his RV and made a leisurely and triumphant journey back to Ford County, but not before hitting three Indian casinos along the way.

☙

Bobby Carl's favorite arsonists were a husband-and-wife duo from Arkansas. Contact was made, cash changed hands. A set of building plans and keys were passed along. The nighttime security guards at the casino were fired. Its water supply was cut off. The building had no sprinkler system because no building code required one.

By the time the Springdale Volunteer Fire Brigade arrived on the scene at 3:00 a.m., the Lucky Jack was fully ablaze. Its metal-framed structures were melting. Inspectors later suspected arson but found no trace of gasoline or other incendiaries. A natural gas leak and explosion had started the fire, they decided. During the ensuing litigation, investigators for the insurance company would produce records which revealed that the casino's natural gas tanks had been mysteriously filled only a week before the fire.

Chief Larry returned to his store and fell into a state of severe depression. Once again, his tribe had been demolished by the white man's greed. His Yazoo Nation scattered, never to be seen again.

Sidney hung around Karraway for a while, but grew weary of the attention and gossip. Since he'd quit his job and busted the casino, folks quite naturally referred to him as a professional gambler, a rarity indeed for rural Mississippi. And though Sidney didn't fit the mold of a high-rolling rogue, the topic of his new lifestyle was irresistible. It was well-known that he was the only man in town with $1 million, and this caused problems. Old friends materialized. Single women of all ages schemed of ways to meet him. All the charities wrote letters and pleaded for money. His daughter in Texas became more involved in his life and was quick to apologize for taking sides during the divorce. When he put a For Sale sign in his front yard, Karraway talked of little else. The heartiest rumor was that he was moving to Las Vegas.

He waited.

He played poker online for hours, and when he got bored, he drove his RV to the casinos in Tunica, or to the Gulf Coast. He won more than he lost, but was careful not to attract too much attention. Two casinos in Biloxi had banned him months earlier. He always returned to Karraway, though he really wanted to leave it forever.

He waited.

The first move was made by his daughter. She called and talked for an hour one night, and toward the end of a rambling conversation let it slip that Stella was lonely and sad and really missed her life with Sidney. According to the daughter, Stella was consumed with remorse and desperate to reconcile with the only man she would ever love. As Sidney listened to his daughter prattle on, he realized that he needed Stella far more than he disliked her. Still, he made no promises.

The next phone call was more to the point. The daughter began an effort to broker a meeting between her parents, sort of a first step to normalize relations. She was willing to return to Karraway and mediate matters if necessary. All she wanted was for her parents to be together. How odd, thought Sidney, since she expressed no such thoughts before he broke the casino.

After a week or so of shadowboxing, Stella showed up one night for a glass of tea. In a lengthy, emotional meeting, she confessed her sins and begged for forgiveness. She left and returned the next night for another discussion. On the third night, they went to bed and Sidney was in love again.

Without discussing marriage, they loaded up the RV and took off to Florida. Near Ocala, the Seminole tribe was operating a fabulous new casino and Sidney was eager to attack it. He was feeling lucky.

# Michael's Room

➤┼ · · · · · · · · · · · · · · · · · · · ┼◄

The encounter was probably inevitable in a town of ten thousand people. Sooner or later, you're bound to bump into almost everyone, including those whose names are long forgotten and whose faces are barely familiar. Some names and faces are registered and remembered and withstand the erosion of time. Others are almost instantly discarded, and most for good reason.

For Stanley Wade, the encounter was caused in part by his wife's lingering flu and in part by their need for sustenance, along with other reasons. After a long day at the office, he called home to check on her and to inquire about dinner. She rather abruptly informed him that she had no desire to cook and little desire to eat, and that if he was hungry, he'd better stop by the store. When was he not hungry at dinnertime? After a few more sentences, they agreed on frozen pizza, about the only dish Stanley could prepare and, oddly, the only thing she might possibly want to nibble on. Preferably sausage and cheese. Please enter through the kitchen and keep the dogs quiet, she instructed. She might be asleep on the sofa.

The nearest food store was the Rite Price, an old discount house a few blocks off the square, with dirty aisles and low prices and cheap giveaways that attracted the lower classes. Most uppity whites used the new Kroger south of town, far out of Stanley's way. But it was only a frozen pizza. What difference did it make? He wasn't shopping for the freshest organic produce on this occasion. He was hungry and looking for junk and just wanted to get home.

He ignored the shopping carts and baskets and went straight to the frozen section, where he selected a fourteen-inch creation with an Italian name and freshness guaranteed. He was closing the icy glass door when he became aware of someone standing very near him, someone who'd seen him, followed him, and was now practically breathing on him. Someone much larger than Stanley. Someone who had no interest in frozen foods, at least not at that moment. Stanley turned to his right and locked eyes with a smirking and unhappy face he'd seen somewhere before. The man was about forty, roughly ten years younger than Stanley, at least four inches taller, and much thicker through the chest. Stanley was slight, almost fragile, not the least bit athletic.

"You're Lawyer Wade, ain't you?" the man said, but it was far more an accusation than a question. Even the voice was vaguely familiar—unusually high-pitched for such a hulking figure, rural but not ignorant. A voice from the past, no doubt about that.

Stanley correctly assumed that their previous meeting, whenever and wherever, concerned a lawsuit of some variety, and it didn't take a genius to surmise that they had not been on the same side. Coming face-to-face with old courtroom adversaries long after trial is a hazard for many small-town lawyers. As much as he was tempted, Stanley could not bring himself to deny who he was. "That's right," he said, clutching his pizza. "And you are?"

With that, the man suddenly moved past Stanley and, in doing so, lowered his shoulder slightly and landed a solid hit against Lawyer Wade, who was knocked against the icy door he'd just closed. The pizza fell to the floor, and as Stanley balanced himself and reached for his dinner, he turned and saw the man head down the aisle and disappear around a corner in the direction of the breakfast foods and coffee. Stanley caught his breath, glanced around, started to yell something provocative, but quickly thought better of it, then stood for a moment and tried to analyze the only harsh physical contact he could remember during his adult life. He'd never been a fighter, athlete, drinker, hell-raiser. Not Stanley. He'd been the thinker, the scholar, top third of his law class.

It was an assault, pure and simple. The least touching of another in anger. But there were no witnesses, and Stanley wisely decided to forget about it, or at least try. Given the disparity in their sizes and dispositions, it certainly could have been much worse.

And it would be, very shortly.

For the next ten minutes he tried to collect himself as he moved cautiously around the grocery store, peeking around corners, reading labels, inspecting meats, watching the other shoppers for signs of his assailant or perhaps another one. When he was somewhat convinced the man was gone, he hurried to the lone open cashier, quickly paid for his pizza, and left the store. He strolled to his car, eyes darting in all directions, and was safely locked inside with the engine on when he realized there would be more trouble.

A pickup had wheeled to a stop behind Stanley's Volvo, blocking it. A parked van faced it and prevented a forward escape. This angered Stanley. He turned off the ignition, yanked open his driver's door, and was climbing out when he saw the man approaching quickly from the pickup. Then he saw the gun, a large black pistol.

Stanley managed to offer a weak "What the hell" before the hand without the gun slapped him across the face and knocked him against the driver's door. For a moment he saw nothing, but was aware of being grabbed, then dragged and thrown into the pickup, and slid across the vinyl front seat. The hand around the back of his neck was thick, strong, violent. Stanley's neck was skinny and weak, and for some reason, in the horror of the moment, he admitted to himself that this man could easily snap his neck, and with only one hand.

Another man was driving, a very young man, probably just a kid. A door slammed. Stanley's head was stuffed down near the floorboard, cold steel jammed into the base of his skull. "Go," the man said, and the pickup jerked forward.

"Don't move and don't say a word or I'll blow your brains out," the man said, his high voice quite agitated.

"Okay, okay," Stanley managed to say. His left arm was pinned behind his back, and for good measure the man jerked it up until Stanley flinched in pain. The pain continued for a minute or so, then suddenly the man let go. The pistol was taken away from Stanley's head. "Sit up," the man said, and Stanley raised himself, shook his head, adjusted his glasses, and tried to focus. They were on the outskirts of town, headed west. A few seconds passed and nothing was said. To his left was the kid driving, a teenager of no more than sixteen, a slight boy with bangs and pimples and eyes that revealed an equal amount of surprise and bewilderment. His youth and innocence were oddly comforting—surely this thug wouldn't shoot him in front of a boy! To his right, with their legs touching, was the man with the gun, which was temporarily resting on his beefy right knee and aimed at no one in particular.

More silence as they left Clanton behind. Lawyer Wade took deep, quiet breaths and managed to calm himself somewhat as he tried to arrange his thoughts and address the scenario of being abducted. Okay, Lawyer Wade, what have you done in twenty-three years of practicing law to deserve this? Whom did you sue? Who got left out of a will? Maybe a bad divorce? Who was on the losing side of a lawsuit?

When the boy turned off the highway and onto a paved

county road, Stanley finally said, "Mind if I ask where we're going?"

Ignoring the question, the man said, "Name's Cranwell. Jim Cranwell. That's my son Doyle."

That lawsuit. Stanley swallowed hard and noticed, for the first time, the dampness around his neck and collar. He was still wearing his dark gray suit, white cotton shirt, drab maroon tie, and the entire outfit suddenly made him hot. He was sweating, and his heart thumped like a jackhammer. *Cranwell v. Trane*, eight or nine years ago. Stanley defended Dr. Trane in a nasty, contentious, emotional, and ultimately successful trial. A bitter loss for the Cranwell family. A great win for Dr. Trane and his lawyer, but Stanley didn't feel so victorious now.

The fact that Mr. Cranwell so freely divulged his name, and that of his son, meant only one thing, at least to Stanley. Mr. Cranwell had no fear of being identified because his victim would not be able to talk. That black pistol over there would find some action after all. A wave of nausea vibrated through Stanley's midsection, and for a second he considered where to unload his vomit. Not to the right and not to the left. Straight down, between his feet. He clenched his teeth and swallowed rapidly, and the moment passed.

"I asked where we're going," he said, a rather feeble effort to show some resistance. But his words were hollow and scratchy. His mouth was very dry.

"It's best if you just shut up," Jim Cranwell said. Being in no position to argue, or press his inquiries, Stanley decided to shut up. Minutes passed as they drove deeper into the county along Route 32, a busy road during the day but deserted at night. Stanley knew the area well. He'd lived in Ford County for twenty-five years and it was a small place. His breathing slowed again, as did his heart rate, and he concentrated on absorbing the details around him. The truck, a late-1980s Ford, half ton, metallic gray on the outside, he thought, and some shade of dark blue on the inside. The dash was standard, nothing remarkable. On the sun visor above the driver there was a thick rubber band holding papers and receipts. A hundred and ninety-four thousand miles on the odometer, not unusual for this part of the world. The kid was driving a steady fifty miles an hour. He turned off Route 32 and onto Wiser Lane, a smaller paved road that snaked through the western part of the county and eventually crossed the Talla-hatchie River at the Polk County line. The roads were getting narrower, the woods thicker, Stanley's options fewer, his chances slimmer.

He glanced at the pistol and thought of his brief career as an assistant prosecutor many years earlier, and the occasions when he took the tagged murder weapon, showed it to the jurors, and waved it around the courtroom, trying his best to create drama, fear, and a sense of revenge.

Would there be a trial for his murder? Would that rather large pistol—he guessed it was a .44 Magnum, capable of splattering his brains across a half acre of rural farmland—one day be waved around a courtroom as the system dealt with his gruesome homicide?

"Why don't you say something?" Stanley asked without look-ing at Jim Cranwell. Anything was better than silence. If Stanley had a chance, it would be because of his words, his ability to reason, or beg.

"Your client Dr. Trane, he left town, didn't he?" Cranwell said.

Well, at least Stanley had the right lawsuit, which gave him no comfort whatsoever. "Yes, several years ago."

"Where'd he go?"

"I'm not sure."

"He got in some trouble, didn't he?"

"Yes, you could say that."

"I just did. What kind of trouble?"

"I don't remember."

"Lyin' ain't gonna help you, Lawyer Wade. You know damned well what happened to Dr. Trane. He was a drunk and a drug head, and he couldn't stay out of his own little pharmacy. Got hooked on painkillers, lost his license, left town, tried to hide back home in Illinois."

These details were offered as if they were common knowledge, available every morning at the local coffee shops and dissected over lunch at the garden clubs, when in fact the meltdown of Dr. Trane had been handled discreetly by Stanley's firm, and buried. Or so he thought. The fact that Jim Cranwell had so closely monitored things after the trial made Stanley wipe his brow and shift his weight and once again fight thoughts of throwing up.

"That sounds about right," Stanley said.

"You ever talk to Dr. Trane?"

"No. It's been years."

"Word is he disappeared again. You heard this?"

"No." It was a lie. Stanley and his partners had heard several rumors about the puzzling disappearance of Dr. Trane. He'd fled to Peoria, his home, where he regained his license and resumed his medical practice but couldn't stay out of trouble. Roughly two years earlier, his then-current wife had called around Clanton asking old friends and acquaintances if they'd seen him.

The boy turned again, onto a road with no sign, a road Stanley thought perhaps he'd driven past but never noticed. It was also paved, but barely wide enough for two vehicles to pass. So far the kid had not made a sound.

"They'll never find him," Jim Cranwell said, almost to himself, but with a brutal finality.

Stanley's head was spinning. His vision was blurred. He blinked, rubbed his eyes, breathed heavily with his mouth open, and felt his shoulders sag as he absorbed and digested these last words from the man with the gun. Was he, Stanley, supposed to believe that these backwoods people from deep in the county somehow tracked down Dr. Trane and rubbed him out without getting caught?

Yes.

"Stop up there by Baker's gate," Cranwell said to his son. A hundred yards later, the truck stopped. Cranwell opened his door, waved the pistol, and said, "Get out." He grabbed Stanley by the wrist and led him to the front of the truck, shoved him against the hood spread eagle, and said, "Don't move an inch." Then he whispered some instructions to his son, who got back in the truck.

Cranwell grabbed Stanley again, yanked him to the side of the road and down into a shallow ditch, where they stood as the truck drove away. They watched the taillights disappear around a curve.

Cranwell pointed the gun at the road and said, "Start walkin'."

"You won't get away with this, you know," Stanley said.

"Just shut up and walk." They began walking down the dark, potholed road. Stanley went first, with Cranwell five feet behind him. The night was clear, and a half-moon gave enough light to keep them in the center of the road. Stanley looked to his right and left, and back again, in a hopeless search for the distant lights of a small farm. Nothing.

"You run and you're a dead man," Cranwell said. "Keep your hands out of your pockets."

"Why? You think I have a gun?"

"Shut up and keep walkin'."

"Where would I run to?" Stanley asked without missing a step. Without a sound, Cranwell suddenly lunged forward and threw a mighty punch that landed on the back of Stanley's slender neck and dropped him quickly to the asphalt. The gun was back, at his head, and Cranwell was on top of him, growling.

"You're a little smart-ass, you know that, Wade? You were a smart-ass at trial. You're a smart-ass now. You were born a smart-ass. I'm sure your Momma was a smart-ass, and I'm sure your kids, both of 'em, are too. Can't help it, can you? But, listen to me, you little smart-ass, for the next hour you will not be a smart-ass. You got that, Wade?"

Stanley was stunned, groggy, aching, and not sure if he could hold back the vomit. When he didn't respond, Cranwell jerked his collar, yanked him back so that Stanley was on his knees. "Got any last words, Lawyer Wade?" The barrel of the gun was stuck in his ear.

"Don't do this, man," Stanley pleaded, suddenly ready to cry.

"Oh, why not?" Cranwell hissed from above.

"I have a family. Please don't do this."

"I got kids too, Wade. You've met both of them. Doyle is drivin' the truck. Michael's the one you met at trial, the little brain-damaged boy who'll never drive, walk, talk, eat, or take a piss by himself. Why, Lawyer Wade? Because of your dear client Dr. Trane, may he burn in hell."

"I'm sorry. Really, I mean it. I was just doing my job. Please."

The gun was shoved harder so that Stanley's head tilted to the left. He was sweating, gasping, desperate to say something that might save him.

Cranwell grabbed a handful of Stanley's thinning hair, yanked it. "Well, your job stinks, Wade, because it includes lyin', bullyin', badgerin', coverin' up, and showin' no compassion whatsoever for folks who get hurt. I hate your job, Wade, almost as much as I hate you."

"I'm sorry. Please."

Cranwell pulled the barrel out of Stanley's ear, aimed down the dark road, and, with the gun about eight inches from Stanley's head, pulled the trigger. A cannon would have made less noise in the stillness.

Stanley, who'd never been shot, shrieked in horror and pain and death and fell to the pavement, his ears screaming and his body convulsing. A few seconds passed as the gunshot's echo was absorbed into the thick woods. A few more seconds, and Cranwell said, "Get up, you little creep."

Stanley, still un-shot but uncertain about it, slowly began to realize what had happened. He got up, unsteady, still gasping and unable to speak or hear. Then he realized his pants were wet. In his moment of death, he'd lost control of his bladder. He touched his groin, then his legs.

"You pissed on yourself," Cranwell said. Stanley heard him, but barely. His ears were splitting, especially the right one. "You poor boy, all wet with piss. Michael wets himself five times a day. Sometimes we can afford diapers; sometimes we can't. Now walk."

Cranwell shoved him again, roughly, while pointing down the road with the pistol. Stanley stumbled, almost fell, but caught himself and staggered for a few steps until he could focus and balance and convince himself that he had not, in fact, been shot.

"You ain't ready to die," Cranwell said from behind.

Thank God for that, Stanley almost said but caught himself because it would most certainly be taken as another smart-ass comment. Lurching down the road, he vowed to avoid all other smart-ass comments, or anything even remotely similar. He put a finger in his right ear in an effort to stop the ringing. His crotch and legs felt cold from the moisture.

They walked for another ten minutes, though it seemed like an eternal death march to Stanley. Rounding a curve in the road, he saw lights ahead, a small house in the distance. He picked up his pace slightly as he decided that Cranwell was not about to fire again with someone within earshot.

The house was a small brick split-level a hundred yards off the road, with a gravel drive and neat hedges just below the front windows. Four vehicles were parked haphazardly along the drive and in the yard, as if the neighbors had hurried over for a quick supper. One was the Ford pickup, once driven by Doyle, now parked in front of the garage. Two men were smoking under a tree.

"This way," Cranwell said, pointing with the gun and shoving Stanley toward the house. They walked by the two smokers. "Look what I got," Cranwell said. The men blew clouds of smoke but said nothing.

"He pissed on himself," he added, and they thought that was amusing.

They walked across the front yard, past the door, past the garage, around the far side of the house, and in the back they approached a cheap, unpainted plywood addition someone had stuck on like a cancerous growth. It was attached to the house but could not be seen from the road. It had unbalanced windows, exposed pipes, a flimsy door, the dismal look of a room added as cheaply and quickly as possible.

Cranwell stuck a hand on Stanley's bruised neck and shoved him toward the door. "In here," he said, the gun, as always, giving direction. The only way in was up a short wheelchair ramp, one as rickety as the room itself. The door opened from the inside. People were waiting.

✿

Eight years earlier, during the trial, Michael had been three years old. He had been displayed for the jury only once. During his lawyer's emotional final summation, the judge allowed Michael to be rolled into the courtroom in his special chair for a quick viewing. He wore pajamas, a large bib, no socks or shoes. His oblong head fell to one side. His mouth was open, his eyes were closed, and his tiny misshapen body wanted to curl into itself. He was severely brain damaged, blind, with a life expectancy of only a few years. He was a pitiful sight then, though the jury eventually showed no mercy.

Stanley had endured the moment, along with everyone else in the courtroom, but when Michael was rolled away, he got back to business. He was convinced he would never see the child again.

He was wrong. He was now looking at a slightly larger version of Michael, though a more pathetic one. He was wearing pajamas and a bib, no socks or shoes. His mouth was open, his eyes still closed. His face had grown upward into a long sloping forehead, covered in part by thick black matted hair. A tube ran from his left nostril back to some unseen place. His arms were bent at the wrists and curled under. His knees were drawn to his chest. His belly was large, and for an instant he reminded Stanley of those sad photos of starving children in Africa.

Michael was arranged on his bed, an old leftover from some hospital, propped up with pillows and lashed down with a Velcro strap that fit loosely across his chest. At the foot of his bed was his mother, a gaunt, long-suffering soul whose name Stanley could not immediately recall.

He'd made her cry on the witness stand.

At the other end of the bed was a small bathroom with the door open, and next to the door was a black metal file cabinet with two drawers, legal size, and enough scratches and dents to prove it had passed through a dozen flea markets. The wall next to Michael's bed had no windows, but the two walls along the sides had three narrow windows each. The room was fifteen feet long at most and about twelve feet wide. The floor was covered with cheap yellow linoleum.

"Sit here, Lawyer Wade," Jim said, shoving his prisoner into a folding chair in the center of the small room. The pistol was no longer in sight. The two smokers from outside entered and closed the door. They took a few steps and joined two other men who were standing near Mrs. Cranwell, only a few feet from Wade. Five men, all large and frowning and seemingly ready for violence. And there was Doyle somewhere behind Stanley. And Mrs. Cranwell, Michael, and Lawyer Wade.

The stage was set.

Jim walked over to the bed, kissed Michael on the forehead, then turned and said, "Recognize him, Lawyer Wade?"

Stanley could only nod.

"He's eleven years old now," Jim said, gently touching his son's arm. "Still blind, still brain damaged. We don't know how much he hears and understands, but it ain't much. He'll smile once a week when he hears his momma's voice, and sometimes he'll smile when Doyle tickles him. But we don't get much of a response. Are you surprised to see him alive, Lawyer Wade?"

Stanley was staring at some cardboard boxes stuffed under Michael's bed, and he did so to avoid looking at the child. He was listening with his head turned to his right because his right ear wasn't working, as far as he could tell. His ears were still traumatized from the gunshot, and if faced with lesser problems, he might have spent some time worrying about a loss of hearing. "Yes," he answered truthfully.

"I thought so," Jim said. His high-pitched voice had settled down an octave or two. He was not agitated now. He was at home, in front of a friendly crowd. "Because at trial you told the jury that Michael wouldn't reach the age of eight. Ten was impossible, accordin' to one of the many bogus experts you trotted into the courtroom. And your goal was obviously to shorten his life and lessen the damages, right? Do you recall all this, Lawyer Wade?"

"Yes."

Jim was pacing now, back and forth alongside Michael's bed, talking to Stanley, glancing at the four men bunched together along the wall. "Michael's now eleven, so you were wrong, weren't you, Lawyer Wade?"

Arguing would make matters worse, and why argue the truth? "Yes."

"Lie number one," Jim announced, and held up an index finger. Then he stepped to the bed and touched his son again. "Now, most of his food goes through a tube. A special formula, costs $800 a month. Becky can get some solid foods down him every now and then. Stuff like instant puddin', ice cream, but not much. He takes all sorts of medications to prevent seizures and infections and the like. His drugs cost us about a thousand a month. Four times a year we haul him to Memphis to see the specialists, not sure why, because they can't do a damned thang, but anyway off we go because they tell us to come. Fifteen hundred bucks a trip. He goes through a box of diapers every two days, $6 a box, a hundred bucks a month, not much, but when you can't always afford them, then they're pretty damned expensive. A few other odds and ends and we figure we spend thirty thousand a year taking care of Michael."

Jim was pacing again, laying out his case and doing a fine job. His handpicked jury was with him. His numbers sounded more ominous this far from the courtroom. "As I recall, your expert scoffed at the numbers, said it would take less than ten grand a year to care for Michael. You recall this, Lawyer Wade?"

"I think so, yes."

"Can we agree that you were wrong? I have the receipts."

"They're right over there," Becky said, pointing to the black metal cabinet. Her first words.

"No. I'll take your word."

Jim thrust forward two fingers. "Lie number two. Now, the same expert testified that a full-time nurse would not be necessary. Made it sound like little Michael would just lie around on the sofa like some zombie for a couple of years, then die and ever'thang would be fine. He disagreed with the notion that Michael would require constant care. Becky, you want to talk about constant care?"

Her long hair was all gray and pulled into a ponytail. Her eyes were sad and fatigued. She made no effort to hide the dark circles under them. She stood and took a step to a door next to the bed. She opened it and pulled down a small foldaway cot. "This is where I sleep, almost every night. I can't leave him because of the seizures. Sometimes Doyle will sleep here, sometimes Jim, but somebody has to be here during the night. The seizures always come at night. I don't know why." She shoved the cot back and closed the door. "I feed him four times a day, an ounce at a time. He urinates at least five times and has at least two bowel movements. You can't predict when. They happen at different times. Eleven years now, and there's no schedule for them. I bathe him twice a day. And I read to him, tell him stories. I seldom leave this room, Mr. Wade. And when I'm not here, I feel guilty because I should be. The word 'constant' doesn't begin to describe it." She sat back down in her old recliner at the foot of Michael's bed and stared at the floor.

Jim resumed the narrative. "Now, as you will recall, at trial our expert said that a full-time nurse would be required. You told the jury this was a bunch of baloney. 'Hogwash,' I believe is what you said. Just another effort by us to grab some money. Made us sound like a bunch of greedy bastards. Remember this, Lawyer Wade?"

Stanley nodded. He could not remember the exact words, but it certainly sounded like something he would say in the heat of a trial.

Three fingers. "Lie number three," Cranwell announced to his jury, four men with the same general body type, hair color, hard faces, and well-worn dungarees as Jim. Clearly, they were all related.

Jim continued. "I made forty thousand bucks last year, Lawyer Wade, and I paid taxes on all of it. I don't get the write-offs that you smart folks are entitled to. Before Michael was born, Becky here worked as a teacher's assistant at a school in Karraway, but she can't work now, for obvious reasons. Don't ask me how we get by, because I can't tell you." He waved at the four men and said, "We get a lot of help from friends and local churches. We get nothin' from the State of Mississippi. It doesn't make much sense, does it? Dr. Trane walked away without payin' a dime. His insurance company, a bunch of crooks from up north, walked away without payin' a dime. The rich folks do the damage, then get off scot-free. You care to explain this, Lawyer Wade?"

Stanley just shook his head. There was nothing to be gained by trying to argue. He was listening, but he was also jumping ahead to the point in the near future when he would be forced to again beg for his life.

"Let's talk about another lie," Cranwell was saying. "Our expert said we could probably hire a part-time nurse for thirty thousand a year, and that's the low end. Thirty for the nurse, thirty for the other expenses, a total of sixty a year, for twenty years. The math was easy, one point two million. But that scared our lawyer because no jury in this county has ever given a million dollars. Highest verdict, at that time, eight years ago, was something like two hundred grand, and that got slashed on appeal, according to our lawyer. Assholes like you, Mr. Wade, and the insurance companies you whore for and the politicians they buy with their big bucks make sure that greedy little people like us and the greedy lawyers we hire are kept in place. Our lawyer told us that askin' for a million bucks was dangerous because nobody else in Ford County has a million bucks, so why give it to us? We talked about this for hours before the trial and finally agreed that we should ask for somethin' less than a million. Nine hundred thousand, remember that, Lawyer Wade?"

Stanley nodded. He did in fact remember.

Cranwell took a step closer and pointed down at Stanley. "And you, you little sonofabitch, you told the jury that we didn't have the courage to ask for a million dollars, that we really wanted a million dollars because we were trying to profit from our little boy. What was your word, Mr. Wade? It wasn't 'greed.' You didn't call us greedy. What was it, Becky?"

"Opportunistic," she said.

"That's it. You pointed at us sittin' there with our lawyer, ten feet from you and the jurors, and you called us opportunistic. I never wanted to slap a man so hard in my life." And with that, Cranwell lunged forward and backhanded Stanley with a vicious slap across his right cheek. His eyeglasses flew toward the door.

"You rotten miserable piece of scum," Cranwell growled.

"Stop it, Jim," Becky said.

There was a long heavy pause as Stanley shook off the numbness and tried to focus his eyes. One of the four men reluctantly handed him his glasses. The sudden assault seemed to stun everybody, including Jim.

Jim walked back to the bed and patted Michael on the shoulder, then he turned and stared at the lawyer. "Lie number four,

Lawyer Wade, and right now I'm not sure I can remember all your lies. I've read the transcript a hundred times—over nineteen hundred pages in all—and ever' time I read it, I find another lie. Like, you told the jury that big verdicts are bad because they drive up the cost of health care and insurance, you remember that, Lawyer Wade?"

Stanley shrugged as if he wasn't sure. Stanley's neck and shoulders were aching now, and it hurt to even shrug. His face was burning, his ears were ringing, his crotch was still wet, and something told him that this was only round one and round one would be the easy part.

Jim looked at the four men and said, "You remember that, Steve?"

Steve said, "Yep."

"Steve's my brother, Michael's uncle. Heard every word of the trial, Lawyer Wade, and he learned to hate you as much as I did. Now, back to the lie. If juries return small verdicts, or no verdicts, then we're supposed to enjoy low-cost health care and low-cost insurance, right, Lawyer Wade? That was your brilliant argument. Jury bought it. Can't let those greedy lawyers and their greedy clients abuse our system and get rich. No, sir. Gotta protect the insurance companies." Jim looked at his own jury. "Now, fellas. Since Lawyer Wade got a zero verdict for his doctor and his insurance company, how many of ya'll have seen the cost of health care go down?"

No volunteers from his jury.

"Oh, by the way, Lawyer Wade. Did you know that Dr. Trane owned four Mercedes at the time of the trial? One for him, another for his wife, a couple for his two teenagers. Did you know that?"

"No."

"Well, what kinda lawyer are you? We knew that. My lawyer did his homework, knew ever'thang about Trane. But he couldn't bring it up in court. Too many rules. Four Mercedes. Guess a rich doctor deserves that many."

Cranwell walked to the file cabinet, opened the top drawer, and removed a three-inch stack of papers tightly compressed in a blue plastic binder. Stanley recognized it immediately because the floor of his office was littered with the blue binders. Trial transcripts. At some point, Cranwell had paid the court reporter a few hundred dollars for his own copy of every word uttered during Dr. Trane's trial for medical malpractice.

"Do you recall juror number six, Lawyer Wade?"

"No."

Cranwell flipped some pages, many of them tabbed and highlighted in yellow and green. "Just lookin' at the jury selection here, Lawyer Wade. At one point my lawyer asked the jury pool if any one of them worked for an insurance company. One lady said yes, and she was excused. One gentleman, a Mr. Rupert, said nothin' and got himself picked for the jury. Truth was, he didn't work for an insurance company because he'd just retired from an insurance company, after thirty years. Later, after the trial and after the appeal, we found out that Mr. Rupert was the biggest defender of Dr. Trane durin' deliberations. Said way too much. Raised hell if any of the other jurors as much as mentioned givin' Michael some money. Ring a bell, Lawyer Wade?"

"No."

"Are you sure?" Cranwell suddenly put down the transcript and took a step closer to Stanley. "Are you sure about that, Lawyer Wade?"

"I'm sure."

"How can that be? Mr. Rupert was an area claims man for Southern Delta Mutual for thirty years, worked all of north Mississippi. Your firm has represented a lot of insurance companies, including Southern Delta Mutual. Are you tellin' us you didn't know Mr. Rupert?" Another step closer. Another slap on the way.

"I did not."

Fingers thrust in the air. "Lie number five," Cranwell announced and waved his tally at his jury. "Or is it six? I've already lost count."

Stanley braced for a punch or a slap, but nothing came his way. Instead, Cranwell returned to the file cabinet and removed four other binders from the top drawer. "Almost two thousand pages of lies, Lawyer Wade," he said as he stacked the binders on top of each other. Stanley took a breath and exhaled in relief because he had momentarily escaped the violence. He stared at the cheap linoleum between his shoes and admitted to himself that once again he had fallen into the trap that often snared so many of the educated and upper-class locals when they convinced themselves that the rest of the population was stupid and ignorant. Cranwell was smarter than most lawyers in town, and infinitely more prepared.

Armed with a handful of lies, Cranwell was ready for more.

"And, of course, Lawyer Wade, we haven't even touched on the lies told by Dr. Trane. I suppose you're gonna say that's his problem, not yours."

"He testified. I did not," Stanley said, much too quickly.

Cranwell offered a fake laugh. "Nice try. He's your client. You called him to testify, right?"

"Yes."

"And before he testified, long before that, you helped him prepare for the jury, didn't you?"

"That's what lawyers are supposed to do."

"Thank you. So the lawyers are supposed to help prepare the lies." It was not a question, and Stanley was not about to argue. Cranwell flipped some pages and said, "Here's a sample of Dr. Trane's lies, at least according to our medical expert, a fine man who's still in the business and who didn't lose his license and who wasn't an alcoholic and drug addict and who didn't get run out of the state. Remember him, Lawyer Wade?"

"Yes."

"Dr. Parkin, a fine man. You attacked him like an animal, ripped him up in front of the jury, and when you sat down, you were one smug little bastard. Remember that, Becky?"

"Of course I do," Becky chimed in on cue.

"Here's what Dr. Parkin said about the good Dr. Trane. Said he failed to properly diagnose labor pains when Becky first arrived at the hospital, that he should not have sent her home, where she stayed for three hours before returnin' to the hospital while Dr. Trane went home and went to bed, that he sent her home because the fetal monitor strip was nonreactive when in fact he had misread the strip, that once Becky was in the hospital and once Dr. Trane finally got there he administered Pitocin over the course of several hours, that he failed to diagnose fetal distress, failed again to properly read the fetal monitorin' strips, which clearly showed Michael's condition was deterioratin' and that he was in acute distress, that he failed to diagnose that the Pitocin was creatin' hyperstimulation and excessive uterine activity, that he botched a vacuum delivery, that he finally performed a Cesarean some three hours after one should have been performed, that by performin' the Cesarean too late he allowed asphyxia and hypoxia to occur, and that the asphyxia and hypoxia could have been prevented with a timely and proper Cesarean. Any of this sound familiar, Lawyer Wade."

"Yes, I remember it."

"And do you remember telling the jury, as a fact because you as a brilliant lawyer are always accurate with your facts, that none of this was true, that Dr. Trane adhered to the highest standards of professional conduct, blah, blah, blah?"

"Is that a question, Mr. Cranwell?"

"No. But try this one. Did you tell the jury in your closin' arguments that Dr. Trane was one of the finest doctors you'd ever met, a real star in our community, a leader, a man you'd trust with your family, a great physician who must be protected by the fine folks of Ford County? Remember this, Lawyer Wade?"

"It's been eight years. I really can't remember."

"Well, let's look at page 1574, book five, shall we?" Cranwell was pulling on a binder, then flipping pages. "You wanna read your brilliant words, Lawyer Wade? They're right here. I read 'em all the time. Let's have a look and let the lies speak for them-selves." He thrust the binder at Stanley's face, but the lawyer shook his head and looked away.

It could have been the noise, the stifling tension in the room, or simply the broken circuits in his faulty wiring, but Michael suddenly came to life. The seizure gripped him from head to toe, and in an instant he was shaking rapidly and violently. Becky jumped to his side without a word and with a sense of purpose that came from experience. Jim forgot about Lawyer Wade for a moment and stepped to the bed, which was jerking and clicking, its metal joints and springs in need of lubrication. Doyle materi-alized from the back of the room, and all three of the Cranwells tended to Michael and his seizure. Becky cooed soothing words and gently clutched his wrists. Jim kept a soft rubber wedge in his mouth. Doyle wiped his brother's head with a wet towel and kept saying, "It's okay, bro, it's okay."

Stanley watched as long as he could, then leaned forward on his elbows, dropped his jaws into his hands, and studied his feet. The four men to his left stood like stone-faced sentries, and it oc-curred to Stanley that they had seen the seizures before. The room was growing hotter, and his neck was perspiring again. Not for the first time, he thought about his wife. His abduction was now well into its second hour, and he wondered what she was doing. She could be asleep on the sofa, where she'd spent the past four days, battling the flu with rest and juices and more pills than normal. There was an excellent chance she was out cold, unable to realize he was running late with dinner, if you could call it that.

If conscious, she had probably called his cell phone, but he'd left the damned thing in his briefcase, in his car, and besides he tried his best to ignore it when he wasn't at work. He spent hours each day on the phone and hated to be bothered after he left the office. There was a remote chance she was actually a bit worried. Twice a month he enjoyed a late drink at the country club with the boys, and this never bothered his wife. Once their children moved away to college, Stanley and his wife quickly fell out of the habit of being ruled by the clock. Being an hour late (never early) was perfectly fine with them.

So Stanley decided as the bed rattled and the Cranwells tended to Michael that the chances of a posse roaming the back roads searching for him were quite slim. Could the abduction in the Rite Price parking lot have been seen by someone, who then called the police, who were now in full alert? Possible, Stanley admitted, but a thousand cops with bloodhounds couldn't find him at this moment.

He thought about his will. It was up-to-date, thanks to a law partner. He thought about his two kids, but couldn't dwell there. He thought about the end and hoped it happened abruptly with no suffering. He fought the urge to argue with himself over whether or not this was a dream, because such an exercise was a waste of energy.

The bed was still. Jim and Doyle were backing away while Becky bent over the boy, humming softly and wiping his mouth.

"Sit up!" Jim suddenly barked. "Sit up and look at him!"

Stanley did as he was told. Jim opened the lower drawer of

the file cabinet and shuffled through another collection of paper-work. Becky silently crouched into her chair, one hand still on Michael's foot.

Jim removed another document, flipped pages while they all waited, then said, "There's one final question for you, Lawyer Wade. I'm holdin' here the brief you filed with the Supreme Court of Mississippi, a brief in which you fought like hell to up-hold the jury's verdict in favor of Dr. Trane. Lookin' back, I don't know what you were worried about. Accordin' to our lawyer, the supreme court sides with the doctors over 90 percent of the time. That's the biggest reason you didn't offer us a fair settle-ment before trial, right? You weren't worried about losin' a trial, because a verdict for Michael would be thrown out by the supreme court. In the end Trane and the insurance company would win. Michael was entitled to a fair settlement, but you knew the system wouldn't let you lose. Anyway, on the next-to-the-last page of your brief, here's what you wrote. These are your words, Lawyer Wade, and I quote: 'This trial was conducted fairly, fiercely, and with little give-and-take from either side. The jury was alert, engaged, curious, and fully informed. The verdict represents sound and deliberate consideration. The verdict is pure justice, a decision our system should be proud of.'"

With that, Cranwell flung the brief in the general direction of the file cabinet. "And guess what?" he asked. "Our good ol' supreme court agreed. Nothin' for poor little Michael. Nothin' to compensate. Nothin' to punish dear Dr. Trane. Nothin'."

He walked to the bed, rubbed Michael for a moment, then turned and glared at Stanley. "One last question, Lawyer Wade.

And you'd better think before you answer, because your answer could be real important. Look at this sad little boy, this damaged child whose injuries could've been prevented, and tell us, Lawyer Wade, is this justice, or is it just another courtroom victory? The two have little in common."

All eyes were on Stanley. He sat slumped in the awkward chair, his shoulders sagging, his lousy posture even more evident, his trousers still wet, his wing-tipped shoes touching each other, mud around the soles, and his unflinching stare straight ahead at the matted and unruly mop of black hair atop the hideous forehead of Michael Cranwell. Arrogance, stubbornness, denial—all would get him shot, though he had no illusions of seeing the morning sun. Nor was he inclined to stick with his old thoughts and training. Jim was right. Trane's insurance company had been willing to make a generous offer before the trial, but Stanley Wade would have no part of it. He rarely lost a jury trial in Ford County. His reputation was that of a hardball litigator, not one who capitulates and settles. Besides, his swagger was bolstered by a friendly supreme court.

"We don't have all night," Cranwell said.

Oh, why not? Stanley thought. Why should I hurry along to my execution? But he instead removed his glasses and wiped his eyes. They were moist not from fear but from the harsh reality of being confronted by one of his victims. How many others were out there? Why had he chosen to spend his career screwing these people?

He wiped his nose on a sleeve, readjusted his glasses, and said, "I'm sorry. I was so wrong."

"Let's try again," Cranwell said. "Justice, or a courtroom victory?"

"It's not justice, Mr. Cranwell. I'm sorry."

Jim carefully and neatly returned the binders and the brief to their proper places in the file cabinet drawers and closed them. He nodded at the four men, and they began to shuffle toward the door. The room was suddenly busy as Jim whispered to Becky. Doyle said something to the last man out. The door sprang back and forth. Jim grabbed Wade by the arm, yanked him up, and growled, "Let's go." It was much darker outside as they moved quickly away from the room, around the house. They passed the four men, who were busy near a utility shed, and as he looked at their shadows, Stanley heard, clearly, the word "shovels."

"Get in," Jim said as he pushed Stanley into the same Ford truck. The pistol was back, and Jim waved it near Stanley's nose and promised, "One funny move, and I'll use this." With that, he slammed the door and said something to the other men. There were several hushed voices as the mission was organized. The driver's door opened and Jim hopped in, waving the pistol. He pointed it at Stanley and said, "Put both hands on your knees, and if you move either hand, then I'll stick this in your kidney, pull the trigger. It'll blow a sizable hole out the other side. Do you understand me?"

"Yes," Stanley said, as his fingernails clawed into his knees.

"Don't move your hands. I really don't wanna make a mess in my truck, okay?"

"Okay, okay."

They backed along the gravel drive, and as they drove away from the house, Stanley saw another truck leaving, following them. Evidently, Cranwell had said enough because he had nothing to say now. They sped through the night, changing roads at every opportunity, gravel to asphalt, back to gravel, north then south, east, and west. Though Stanley didn't look, he knew the pistol was ready in the right hand while the left one handled the truck. He continued to clutch his knees, terrified any move would be considered a false one. His left kidney was aching anyway. He was sure the door was locked, and any clumsy effort to jerk it open would simply not work. That, plus Stanley was rigid with fear.

There were headlights in the right-hand mirror, low beams from the other truck, the one carrying his death squad and their shovels, he presumed. It disappeared around curves and over hills, but always returned.

"Where are we going?" Stanley finally asked.

"You're goin' to hell, I reckon."

That response took care of the follow-ups, and Stanley pondered what to say next. They turned onto a gravel lane, the narrowest yet, and Stanley said to himself, This is it. Deep woods on both sides. Not a house within miles. A quick execution. A quick burial. No one would ever know. They crossed a creek and the road widened.

Say something, man. "You're gonna do what you want, Mr. Cranwell, but I'm truly sorry about Michael's case," Stanley said, but he was certain his words sounded as lame as they felt. He could be sincerely drenched with remorse, and it would mean nothing to the Cranwells. But he had nothing left but words. He said, "I'm willing to help with some of his expenses."

"You're offering money?"

"Sort of. Yes, why not? I'm not rich, but I do okay. I could pitch in, maybe cover the cost of a nurse."

"So let me get this straight. I take you home, safe and sound, and tomorrow I stop by your office and have a chat about your sudden concern over Michael's support. Maybe we have some coffee, maybe a doughnut. Just a couple of old pals. Not one word about tonight. You draw up an agreement, we sign it, shake hands, I leave, and the checks start coming."

Stanley could not even respond to the absurd idea.

"You're a pathetic little creep, you know that, Wade? You'd tell any lie in the world right now to save your ass. If I stopped by your office tomorrow, you'd have ten cops waitin' with handcuffs. Shut up, Wade, you're just makin' things worse. I'm sick of your lies."

How, exactly, could things get worse? But Stanley said nothing. He glanced at the pistol. It was cocked. He wondered how many victims actually saw their own murder weapons in those last horrible seconds.

Suddenly the darkest road in the thickest woods crested on a small rise, and as the truck barreled forward, the trees thinned, and there were lights beyond. Many lights, the lights of a town. The road ended at a highway, and when they turned south, Stanley saw a marker for State Route 374, an old winding trail that connected Clanton with the smaller town of Karraway. Five minutes later they turned onto a city street, then zigzagged into the southern section of town. Stanley soaked up the familiar sights— a school to the right, a church to the left, a cheap strip mall owned by a man he'd once defended. Stanley was back in Clanton, back home, and he was almost elated. Confused, but thrilled to be alive and still in one piece.

The other truck did not follow them into town.

A block behind the Rite Price, Jim Cranwell turned in to the gravel lot of a small furniture store. He slammed the truck in park, turned off its lights, then pointed the gun and said, "Listen to me, Lawyer Wade. I don't blame you for what happened to Michael, but I blame you for what happened to us. You're scum, and you have no idea of the misery you've caused."

A car passed behind them, and Cranwell lowered the gun for a moment. Then he continued, "You can call the cops, have me arrested, thrown in jail, and all that, though I'm not sure how many witnesses you can find. You can cause trouble, but those guys back there'll be ready. A stupid move, and you'll regret it immediately."

"I'll do nothing, I promise. Just let me out of here."

"Your promises mean nothing. You go on now, Wade, go home, and then go back to the office tomorrow. Find some more little people to run over. We'll have us a truce, me and you, until Michael dies."

"Then what?"

He just smiled and waved the gun closer. "Go on, Wade. Open the door, get out, and leave us alone."

Stanley hesitated only briefly and was soon walking away

from the truck. He turned a corner, found a sidewalk in the darkness, and saw the sign for the Rite Price. He wanted to run, to sprint, but there were no sounds behind him. He glanced back once. Cranwell was gone.

As Stanley hustled toward his car, he began to think about the story he would tell his wife. Three hours late for dinner would require a story.

And it would be a lie, that was certain.

# Quiet Haven

⟩⊱ · · · · · · · · · · · · · · · · · · · ⊰⟨

*T*he Quiet Haven Retirement Home is a few miles outside the city limits of Clanton, off the main road north, tucked away in a shaded valley so that it cannot be seen by passing motorists. Such homes near such highways pose significant dangers. I know this from experience because I was employed at Heaven's Gate outside Vicksburg when Mr. Albert Watson wandered off and found his way onto a four-lane, where he got hit by a tanker truck. He was ninety-four and one of my favorites. I went to his funeral. Lawsuits followed, but I didn't stick around. These patients often wander. Some try to escape, but they're never successful. I don't really blame them for trying, though.

My first glimpse of Quiet Haven reveals a typical 1960s flat-roof, redbrick run-down building with several wings and the general appearance of a dressed-up little prison where people are sent to quietly spend their final days. These places were once generally called nursing homes, but now the names have been upgraded to retirement homes and retirement villages and assisted-living centers and other such misnomers. "Momma's at the retirement village" sounds more civilized than "We stuck her in a nursing home." Momma's at the same place; now it just sounds better, at least to everyone but Momma.

Whatever you call them, they're all depressing. But they are my turf, my mission, and every time I see a new one I'm excited by the challenges.

I park my ancient and battered Volkswagen Beetle in the small empty parking lot in front. I adjust my black-framed 1950s-style nerd glasses and my thickly knotted tie, no jacket, and get out of my car. At the front entrance, under the sheet-metal veranda, there are half a dozen of my new friends sitting in deep wicker rocking chairs, watching nothing. I smile and nod and say hello, but only a couple are able to respond. Inside, I'm hit by the same thick, putrid antiseptic smell that wafts through the halls and walls of every one of these places. I present myself to the receptionist, a robust young woman in a fake nurse's uniform. She's behind the front counter, going through a stack of paperwork, almost too busy to acknowledge me.

"I have a ten o'clock appointment with Ms. Wilma Drell," I say meekly.

She looks me over, doesn't like what she sees, and refuses to smile. "Your name?" Her name is Trudy, according to the cheap plastic badge pinned just above her massive left breast, and Trudy is precariously close to becoming the first name on my brand-new shit list.

"Gilbert Griffin," I say politely. "Ten a.m."

"Have a seat," she says, nodding at a row of plastic chairs in the open lobby.

"Thank you," I say and proceed to sit like a nervous ten-year-old. I study my feet, covered in old white sneakers and black socks. My pants are polyester. My belt is too long for my waist. I am, in a nutshell, unassuming, easily run over, the lowest of the low.

Trudy goes about her business of rearranging stacks of paper. The phone rings occasionally, and she's polite enough to the callers. Ten minutes after I arrive, on time, Ms. Wilma Drell swishes in from the hallway and presents herself. She, too, wears a white uniform, complete with white stockings and white shoes with thick soles that take a pounding because Wilma is even heavier than Trudy.

I stand, terrified, and say, "Gilbert Griffin."

"Wilma Drell." We shake hands only because we must, then she spins and begins to walk away, her thick white stockings grinding together and creating friction that can be heard at some distance. I follow like a frightened puppy, and as we turn the corner, I glance at Trudy, who's giving me a look of complete disdain and dismissal. At that moment, her name hits my list at number one.

There's no doubt in my mind that Wilma will be number two, with the potential of moving up.

We wedge into a small cinder-block office, walls painted government gray, cheap metal desk, cheap wooden credenza adorned with Wal-Mart photos of her chubby children and haggard husband. She settles herself behind the desk and into an executive swivel, as if she's the CEO of this exciting and prosperous outfit. I slide into a rickety chair that's at least twelve inches lower than the swivel. I look up. She looks down.

"You've applied for a job," she says as she picks up the application I mailed in last week.

"Yes." Why else would I be here?

"As an attendant. I see you've had experience in retirement homes."

"Yes, that's correct." On my application I listed three other such places. I left all three without controversy. There are about a dozen others, though, that I would never mention. The reference checking will go smoothly, if it happens at all. Usually there is a halfhearted effort to place a couple of calls. Nursing homes don't worry about hiring thieves or child molesters or even people like me, guys with a complicated past.

"We need an attendant for the late-night shift, from 9:00 p.m. to 7:00 a.m., four days a week. You'll be in charge of monitoring the halls, checking on the patients, caring for them in a general way."

"That's what I do," I say. And walking them to the bathroom, mopping floors after they've made a mess, bathing them, changing their clothes, reading them stories, listening to their life histories, writing letters, buying birthday cards, dealing with their families, refereeing their disputes, arranging and cleaning their bedpans. I know the routine.

"Do you enjoy working with people?" she asks, the same stupid question they always ask. As if all people were the same. The patients are usually delightful. It's the other employees who find their way onto my list.

"Oh yes," I say.

"Your age is—"

"Thirty-four," I say. You can't do the math? My date of birth is question number three on the application. What she really wants to say is, "Why does a thirty-four-year-old man choose to pursue such a demeaning career?" But they never have the guts to ask this.

"We're paying $6.00 an hour."

That was in the ad. She offers this as if it were a gift. The minimum wage is currently $5.15. The company that owns Quiet Haven hides behind the meaningless name of HVQH Group, a notoriously sleazy outfit out of Florida. HVQH owns some thirty retirement facilities in a dozen states and has a long history of nursing home abuse, lawsuits, lousy care, employment discrimination, and tax problems, but in spite of such adversity the company has managed to make a mint.

"That's fine," I say. And it's really not that bad. Most of the corporations that operate chains start their bedpan boys at minimum wage. But I'm not here for the money, at least not the modest wages offered by HVQH.

She's still reading the application. "High school graduate. No college?"

"Didn't have the opportunity."

"That's too bad," she offers, clucking her teeth and shaking her head in sympathy. "I got my degree from a community college," she says smugly, and with that Ms. Wilma Drell hits the list hard at number two. She'll move up. I finished college in three years, but since they expect me to be a moron, I never tell them this. It would make things far too complicated. Postgrad work was done in two years.

"No criminal record," she says with mock admiration.

"Not even a speeding ticket," I say. If she only knew. True, I've never been convicted, but there have been some close calls.

"No lawsuits, no bankruptcies," she muses. It's all there in black and white.

"I've never been sued," I say, clarifying a bit of language. I've been involved in a number of lawsuits, but none in which I was a named party.

"How long have you lived in Clanton?" she asks in an effort to drag out the interview and make it last more than seven minutes. She and I both know that I'll get the job because the ad has been running for two months.

"Couple of weeks. Came here from Tupelo."

"And what brings you to Clanton?" You gotta love the South. People seldom hesitate to ask personal questions. She really doesn't want the answer, but she's curious as to why someone like me would move to a new town to look for work at six bucks an hour.

"Bad romance in Tupelo," I say, lying. "Needed a change of scenery." The bad romance bit always works.

"I'm sorry," she says, but she's not, of course.

She drops my application on the desk. "When can you start work, Mr. Griffin?"

"Just call me Gill," I say. "When do you need me?"

"How about tomorrow?"

"Fine."

They usually need me right away, so the instant start date is never a surprise. I spend the next thirty minutes doing paperwork with Trudy. She goes about the routine with an air of importance, careful to convey the reality that her rank is far superior to mine. As I drive away, I glance at the forlorn windows of Quiet Haven and wonder, as always, how long I will work there. My average is about four months.

❦

My temporary home in Clanton is a two-room apartment in what was once a flophouse but is now a decaying apartment building one block off the town square. The ad described it as furnished, but during my initial walk-through I saw only an army-surplus cot in the bedroom, a pink vinyl sofa in the den, and a dinette set near the sofa with a round table about the size of a large pizza. There's also a tiny stove that doesn't work and a very old refrigerator that barely does. For such amenities I promised to pay to the owner, Miss Ruby, the sum of $20 a week, in cash.

Whatever. I've seen worse, but not by much.

"No parties," Miss Ruby said with a grin as we shook hands on the deal. She's seen her share of parties. Her age is somewhere between fifty and eighty. Her face is ravaged less by age than by hard living and an astounding consumption of cigarettes, but she fights back with layers of foundation, blush, rouge, mascara, eye-liner, lipstick, and a daily drenching of a perfume that, when mixed with the tobacco smoke, reminds me of the odor of dried, stale urine that's not uncommon in nursing homes.

Not to mention the bourbon. Just seconds after we shook hands, Miss Ruby said, "How about a little toddy?" We were in the den of her apartment on the first floor, and before I could an-swer, she was already headed for the liquor cabinet. She poured a few ounces of Jim Beam into two tumblers and deftly added soda water, and we clinked glasses. "A highball for breakfast is the best way to start the day," she said, taking a gulp. It was 9:00 a.m.

She fired up a Marlboro as we moved to the front porch. She lives alone, and it was soon obvious to me that she was a very lonely woman. She just wanted someone to talk to. I rarely drink alcohol, never bourbon, and after a few sips my tongue was numb. If the whiskey had any impact on her, it wasn't obvious as she went on and on about people in Clanton I would never meet. After thirty minutes, she rattled her ice and said, "How 'bout some more Jimmy?" I begged off and left soon thereafter.

❦

Orientation is led by Nurse Nancy, a pleasant old woman who's been here for thirty years. With me in tow, we move from door to door along the North Wing, stopping at each room and saying hello to the residents. Most rooms have two. I've seen all the faces before: the bright ones happy to meet someone new, the sad ones who couldn't care less, the bitter ones who are just suffering through another lonely day, the blank ones who've already checked out of this world. The same faces are on the South Wing. The Back Wing is a little different. A metal door keeps it secured, and Nurse Nancy enters a four-digit code on the wall to get us through.

"These are the more difficult ones," she says softly. "A few Alzheimer's, a few crazies. Really sad." There are ten rooms, with one patient each. I am introduced to all ten without incident. I follow her to the kitchen, the tiny pharmacy, the cafeteria where they eat and socialize. All in all, Quiet Haven is a typical nursing home, fairly clean and efficient. The patients appear to be as happy as you could expect.

I'll check the court dockets later to see if the place has ever been sued for abuse or neglect. I'll check with the agency in Jackson to see if complaints have been filed, citations issued. I have a lot of checking to do, my usual research.

Back at the front desk, Nurse Nancy is explaining visitation routines when I'm startled by the sound of a horn of some variety.

"Watch out," she says and takes a step closer to the desk. From the North Wing a wheelchair approaches at an impressive speed. In it is an old man, still in his pajamas, one hand waving us out of his way, the other squeezing the bladder of a bike horn mounted just above the right wheel. He is propelled by a crazed man who looks no older than sixty, with a large belly hanging out from under his T-shirt, dirty white socks, and no shoes.

"Quiet, Walter!" Nurse Nancy barks as they fly by, oblivious to us. They speed off into the South Wing, and I watch as other patients scurry to their rooms for safety.

"Walter loves his wheelchair," she says.

"Who's the pusher?"

"Donny Ray. They must do ten miles a day up and down the halls. Last week they hit Pearl Dunavant and near 'bout broke her leg. Walter said he forgot to honk his horn. We're still dealing with her family. It's a mess, but Pearl is thoroughly enjoying the attention."

I hear the honk again, then watch as they wheel around at the far end of the South Wing and head back to us. They roar by. Walter is eighty-five, give or take a year (with my experience I can usually get within three years of their age—Miss Ruby notwithstanding), and he's having far too much fun. His head is low, his eyes are squinted as if he were going a hundred miles an hour. Donny Ray is just as wild-eyed, with sweat dripping from his eyebrows and gathering under his arms. Neither acknowledges us as they go by.

"Can't you control them?" I ask.

"We tried, but Walter's grandson is a lawyer and he raised a ruckus. Threatened to sue us. Donny Ray flipped him over one time, no real injuries, but we think maybe a slight concussion. We certainly didn't tell the family. If there was more brain damage, it wasn't noticeable."

We finish orientation precisely at 5:00 p.m., quitting time for Nurse Nancy. My shift begins in four hours, and I have no place to go. My apartment is off-limits because Miss Ruby has already fallen into the habit of watching out for me, and when I'm caught,

I'm expected to have a little touch of Jimmy on the front porch. Regardless of the hour of the day, she's always ready for a drink. I really don't like bourbon.

So I hang around. I put on my white attendant's jacket and speak to people. I say hello to Ms. Wilma Drell, who's very busy running the place. I stroll down to the kitchen and introduce myself to the two black ladies who prepare the wretched food. The kitchen is not as clean as I would like, and I begin making mental notes. At 6:00 p.m., the diners begin their protracted arrivals. Some can walk with no assistance whatsoever, and these proud and lucky souls go to great lengths to make sure the rest of the seniors are reminded that they are much healthier. They arrive early, greet their friends, help arrange seating for those in wheelchairs, flit from table to table as quickly as possible. Some of those with canes and walking carts actually park them at the door of the cafeteria so their colleagues won't see them. The attendants help these to their tables. I join in, offering assistance and introducing myself along the way.

Quiet Haven currently has fifty-two residents. I count thirty-eight present for dinner, then Brother Don stands to say the blessing. All is suddenly quiet. He's a retired preacher, I'm told, and insists on delivering grace before every meal. He's about ninety, but his voice is still clear and remarkably strong. He goes on for a long time, and before he's finished, a few of the others begin rattling their knives and forks. The food is served on hard plastic trays, the kind we used in elementary school. Tonight they're having baked chicken breasts—no bones—with green beans, instant mashed potatoes, and, of course, Jell-O. Tonight it's red. Tomorrow it'll be yellow or green. It's in every nursing home. I don't know why. It's as if we spend our entire lives avoiding Jell-O but it is always there at the end, waiting. Brother Don finally fades and sits, and the feast begins.

For those too frail for the dining room, and for the unpredictable ones on the Back Wing, the food is rolled out on trays. I volunteer for this service. A couple of patients are not long for this world.

Tonight's after-dinner entertainment is provided by a den of Cub Scouts who arrive promptly at 7:00 and hand out brown bags they've decorated and filled with cookies and brownies and such. They then gather near the piano and sing "God Bless America" and a couple of campfire songs. Eight-year-old boys do not sing voluntarily, and the tunes are carried by their den mothers. At 7:30 the show is over, and the residents begin drifting back to their rooms. I push one in a wheelchair, then help with the cleanup. The hours drag by. I have been assigned to the South Wing—eleven rooms with two each, one room with a single occupant.

Pill time is 9:00 p.m., and it's one of the highlights of the day, at least for the residents. Most of us poked fun at our grandparents for their keen interest in their ailments, treatments, prognoses, and medications, and for their readiness to describe all of this to anyone who would listen. This strange desire to dwell on the details only increases with age, and is often the source of much behind-the-back humor that the old folks can't hear anyway. It's worse in a nursing home because the patients have been put away by their families and they've lost their audience. Therefore, they seize every opportunity to carry on about their afflictions whenever a staff member is within earshot. And when a staff member arrives with a tray of pills, their excitement is palpable. A few feign distrust, and reluctance, and fear, but they, too, soon swallow the meds and wash them down with water. Everyone gets the same little sleeping pill, one that I've taken on occasion and never felt a thing. And, everyone gets a few other pills because no one would be satisfied with just a single dose. Most of the drugs are legitimate, but many placebos are consumed during this nightly ritual.

After the pills, the place gets quieter as they settle into bed for the night. Lights are off at 10:00 p.m. As expected, I have the South Wing all to myself. There's one attendant for the North Wing and two on the Back Wing with the "sad ones." Well past midnight, when everyone is asleep, including the other attendants, and when I'm alone, I begin to snoop around the front desk, looking at records, logs, files, keys, anything I can find. Security in these places is always a joke. The computer system is predictably common, and I'll hack my way into it before long. I'm never on duty without a small camera in my pocket, one I use to document such things as dirty bathrooms, unlocked pharmacies, soiled and unwashed linens, doctored logbooks, expired food products, neglected patients, and so on. The list is long and sad, and I'm always on the prowl.

❦

The Ford County Courthouse sits in the middle of a lovely and well-kept lawn, in the center of the Clanton square. Around it are fountains, ancient oaks, park benches, war memorials, and two gazebos. Standing near one of them, I can almost hear the parade on the Fourth of July and the stump speeches during an election. A lonely Confederate soldier in bronze stands atop a granite statue, gazing north, looking for the enemy, holding his rifle, reminding us of a glorious and lost cause.

Inside, I find the land records in the office of the chancery clerk, the same place in every county courthouse in the state. For these occasions I wear a navy blazer with a tie, nice khakis, dress shoes, and in such a getup I can easily pass for just another out-of-town lawyer checking titles. They come and go. There is no requirement to sign in. I don't speak to anyone unless I'm spoken to. The records are open to the public, and the traffic is scarcely monitored by clerks who are too disinterested to notice. My first visit is to simply get acquainted with the records, the system, to find everything. Deeds, grants, liens, probated wills, all sorts of registries that I'll need to peruse in the near future. The tax rolls are down the hall in the assessor's office. The lawsuit filings and cases are in the circuit clerk's office on the first floor. After a couple of hours, I know my way around and I've spoken to no one. I'm just another out-of-town lawyer pursuing his mundane business.

⚜

At each new stop, my first challenge is to find the person who's been around for years and is willing to share the gossip. This person usually works in the kitchen, is often black, often a woman, and if indeed it's a black woman doing the cooking, then

I know how to get the gossip. Flattery doesn't work, because these women can smell bullshit a mile away. You can't brag on the food, because the food is slop and they know it. It's not their fault. They are handed the ingredients and told how to prepare them. At first, I simply stop by each day, say hello, ask how they're doing, and so on. The fact that one of the fellow employees, a white one, is willing to be so nice and to spend time on their turf is unusual. After three days of being nice, Rozelle, aged sixty, is flirting, and I'm giving it right back to her. I told her that I live alone, can't cook, and need a few extra calories on the side. Before long, Rozelle is scrambling eggs for me when she arrives at 7:00 a.m., and we are having our morning coffee together. I punch out at 7:00, but usually hang around for another hour. In my efforts to avoid Miss Ruby, I also arrive for work hours before I punch in, and I sign up for as much overtime as possible. Being the new guy, I am given the graveyard shift—9:00 p.m. to 7:00 a.m.—Friday through Monday, but I don't mind.

Rozelle and I agree that our boss, Ms. Wilma Drell, is a dim-witted, lazy slug who should be replaced but probably won't because it's highly unlikely anyone better would take the job. Rozelle has survived so many bosses she can't remember them all. Nurse Nancy gets passing grades. Trudy at the front desk does not. Before my first week is over, Rozelle and I have assessed all the other employees.

The fun begins when we get around to the patients. I say to Rozelle: "You know, every night at pill time, I give Lyle Spurlock a dose of saltpeter in a sugar cube. What's the deal, Rozelle?"

"Lawd have mercy," she says with a grin that reveals her enormous teeth. She throws up her hands in mock surprise. She rolls her eyes around as if I've really opened up a can of worms. "You are one curious white boy." But I've hit a nerve, and I can tell that she really wants to shovel the dirt.

"I didn't know they still used saltpeter," I say.

She's slowly unwrapping an industrial-size package of frozen waffles. "Look here, Gill, that man has chased ever' woman that ever stayed here. Caught a lot of 'em too. Back a few years ago they caught him in bed with a nurse."

"Lyle?"

"Lawd have mercy, son. That's the dirtiest ol' man in the world. Can't keep his hands off any woman, no matter how old. He's grabbed nurses, patients, attendants, ladies from the churches who come in to sing Christmas songs. They used to lock 'im up during visitation, else he'd be chasin' the girls from the families. Came in here one time, lookin' around. I picked up a butcher's knife and waved it at him. Ain't had no problem since."

"But he's eighty-four years old."

"He's slowed a little. Diabetes. Cut off a foot. But he's still got both his hands, and he'll grab any woman. Not me, mind you, but the nurses stay away from him."

The visual of old Lyle bedding a nurse was too good to ignore. "And they caught him with a nurse?"

"That's right. She wadn't no young thang, mind you, but he still had thirty years on her."

"Who caught them?"

"You met Andy?"

"Sure."

She glanced around before telling me something that had been a legend for years. "Well, Andy was workin' North Wing back then, now he's in the Back, and, you know that storage room at the far end of North Wing?"

"Sure." I didn't, but I wanted the rest of the story.

"Well, there used to be a bed in there, and Lyle and the nurse wadn't the first ones to use it."

"Do tell."

"That's right. You wouldn't believe the hanky-panky that's gone down round here, specially when Lyle Spurlock was in his prime."

"So Andy caught them in the storage room?"

"That's right. The nurse got fired. They threatened to send Lyle somewhere else, but his family got involved, talked 'em out of it. It was a mess. Lawd have mercy."

"And they started giving him saltpeter?"

"Not soon enough." She was scattering the waffles on a baking sheet to put in the oven. She glanced around again, obviously guilty of something, but no one was watching. Delores, the other cook, was wrestling with the coffee machine and too far away to hear us.

"You know Mr. Luke Malone, room 14?"

"Sure, he's on my wing." Mr. Malone was eighty-nine years old, bedridden, virtually blind and deaf, and spent hours each day staring at a small television hanging from the ceiling.

"Well, he and his wife were in room 14 forever. She died last year, cancer. 'Bout ten years ago, Mizz Malone and ol' Spurlock had a thang goin'."

"They had an affair?" Rozelle was willing to tell all, but she needed prodding.

"I don't know what you call it, but they's havin' a good time. Spurlock had two feet then, and he was quick. They'd roll Mr. Malone down here for bingo, and Spurlock'd duck into room 14, jam a chair under the doorknob, and hop in the sack with Mizz Malone."

"They get caught?"

"Several times, but not by Mr. Malone. He couldn't've caught 'em if he'd been in the room. Nobody ever told him, either. Poor man."

"That's terrible."

"That's Spurlock."

She shooed me away because she had to prepare breakfast.

❦

Two nights later, I give Lyle Spurlock a placebo instead of his sleeping pill. An hour later, I return to his room, make sure his roommate is fast asleep, and hand him two *Playboy* magazines. There is no express prohibition against such publications at Quiet Haven, but Ms. Wilma Drell and the other powers that be have certainly taken it upon themselves to eliminate all vices. There is no alcohol on the premises. Lots of card playing and bingo, but no gambling. The few surviving smokers must go outside. And the notion of pornography being consumed is virtually unthinkable.

"Don't let anyone see them," I whisper to Lyle, who grabs the magazines like a starving refugee goes for food.

"Thanks," he says eagerly. I turn on the light next to his bed, pat him on the shoulder, and say, "Have some fun." Go get 'em, old boy. Lyle Spurlock is now my newest admirer.

My file on him is getting thicker. He's been at Quiet Haven for eleven years. After the death of his third wife, his family evidently decided they could not care for him and placed him in the "retirement home," where, according to the visitors' logs, they pretty much forgot about him. In the past six months, a daughter from Jackson has dropped by twice. She's married to a shopping center developer who's quite wealthy. Mr. Spurlock has a son in Fort Worth who moves rail freight and never sees his father. Nor does he write or send cards, according to the mail register. Throughout most of his life, Mr. Spurlock ran a small electrical contracting business in Clanton, and he accumulated little in the way of assets. However, his third wife, a woman who'd had two previous marriages herself, inherited six hundred and forty acres of land in Tennessee when her father died at the age of ninety-eight. Her will was probated in Polk County ten years ago, and when her estate was closed, Mr. Lyle Spurlock inherited the land. There is a decent chance his two offspring know nothing about it.

It takes hours of tedious research in the county land records to find these little nuggets. Many of my searches go nowhere, but when I find such a secret, it makes things exciting.

⚜

I'm off tonight, and Miss Ruby insists that we go out for a cheeseburger. Her car is a 1972 Cadillac sedan, half a block long, bright red, and with enough square footage for eight passengers. As I chauffeur it, she talks and points and sips her Jimmy, all with a Marlboro hanging out the window. Going from my Beetle to the Cadillac gives me the impression of driving a bus. The car will barely fit into a slot at the Sonic Drive-In, a modern-day version of an earlier classic, and built with much smaller vehicles in mind. But I wedge it in, and we order burgers, fries, and colas. She insists that we eat on the spot, and I'm happy to make her happy.

After several late-afternoon toddies and early-morning highballs, I've come to learn that she never had children. Several husbands abandoned her over the years. She has yet to mention a brother, sister, cousin, niece, or nephew. She is incredibly lonely.

And according to Rozelle back in the kitchen, Miss Ruby ran, until twenty or so years ago, the last surviving brothel in Ford County. Rozelle was shocked when I told her where I was living, as if the place were infested with evil spirits. "Ain't no place for a young white boy," she said. Rozelle goes to church at least four times a week. "You'd better get outta there," she warned. "Satan's in the walls."

I don't think it's Satan, but three hours after dinner I'm almost asleep when the ceiling begins to shake. There are sounds— determined, steady, destined to end real soon in satisfaction. There is a clicking sound, much like the cheap metal frame of a bed inching across the floor. Then the mighty sigh of a conquering hero. Silence. The epic act is over.

An hour later, the clicking is back, and the bed is once again hopping across the floor. The hero this time must be either bigger or rougher because the noise is louder. She, whoever she is, is more vocal than before, and for a long and impressive while I listen with great curiosity and a growing eroticism as these two abandon all inhibitions and go at it regardless of who might be listening. They practically shout when it's over, and I'm tempted to applaud. They grow still. So do I. Sleep returns.

About an hour later, our working girl up there is turning her third trick of the night. It's a Friday, and I realize that this is my first Friday in my apartment. Because of my accumulation of overtime, Ms. Wilma Drell ordered me off the clock tonight. I will not make this mistake again. I can't wait to tell Rozelle that Miss Ruby has not retired from her role as a madam, that her old flophouse is still used for other purposes, and that Satan is indeed alive and well.

Late Saturday morning, I walk down to the square, to a coffee shop, and buy some sausage biscuits. I take them back to Miss Ruby's. She answers the door in her bathrobe, teased hair shooting in all directions, eyes puffy and red, and we sit at her kitchen table. She makes more coffee, a wretched brew of some brand she buys by mail, and I repeatedly refuse Jim Beam.

"Things were pretty noisy last night," I say.

"You don't say." She's nibbling around the edge of a biscuit.

"Who's in the apartment right above me?"

"It's empty."

"It wasn't empty last night. Folks were having sex and making a lot of noise."

"Oh, that was Tammy. She's just one of my girls."

"How many girls do you have?"

"Not many. Used to have a bunch."

"I heard this used to be a brothel."

"Oh yes," she says with a proud smile. "Back fifteen, twenty years ago, I had a dozen girls, and we took care of all the big boys in Clanton—the politicians, the sheriff, bankers, and lawyers. I let 'em play poker on the fourth floor. My girls worked the other rooms. Those were the good years." She was smiling at the wall, her thoughts far away to better days.

"How often does Tammy work now?"

"Fridays, sometimes on Saturdays. Her husband's a truck driver, gone on weekends, and she needs the extra money."

"Who are the clients?"

"She has a few. She's careful and selective. Interested?"

"No. Just curious. Can I expect the same noise every Friday and Saturday?"

"More than likely."

"You didn't tell me this when I rented the place."

"You didn't ask. Come on now, Gill, you're not really upset. If you'd like, I could put in a good word with Tammy. It'd be a short walk. She could even come to your room."

"How much does she charge?"

"It's negotiable. I'll fix it for you."

"I'll think about it."

⚜

After thirty days, I'm beckoned to the office of Ms. Drell for an evaluation. Big companies adopt these policies that fill up their various manuals and handbooks and make them all feel as though they're being superbly managed. HVQH wants each new employee evaluated at thirty, sixty, and ninety-day intervals, then once every six months. Most nursing homes have similar language on the books but rarely bother with actual meetings.

We dance through the usual crap about how I'm doing, what I think of the job, how I'm getting along with the other employees. So far, no complaints. She compliments me on my willingness to volunteer for overtime. I have to admit that she's not as bad as I first thought. I've been wrong before, but not often. She's still on my list, but down to number three.

"The patients seem to like you," she says.

"They're very sweet."

"Why do you spend so much time talking to the cooks in the kitchen?"

"Is that against the rules?"

"Well, no, just a bit unusual."

"I'll be happy to stop if it bothers you." I have no intention of stopping, regardless of what Ms. Drell says.

"Oh no. We found some *Playboy* magazines under Mr. Spurlock's mattress. Any idea where they came from?"

"Did you ask Mr. Spurlock?"

"Yes, and he's not saying."

Attaboy, Lyle. "I have no idea where they came from. Are they against the rules?"

"We frown on such filth. Are you sure you had nothing to do with them?"

"It seems to me that if Mr. Spurlock, who's eighty-four and paying full rent, wants to look at *Playboys*, then he should be allowed to do so. What's the harm?"

"You don't know Mr. Spurlock. We try to keep him in a state of non-arousal. Otherwise, well, he's a real handful."

"He's eighty-four."

"How do you know he's paying full rent?"

"That's what he told me."

She flipped a page as if there were many entries in my file. After a moment, she closed it and said, "So far so good, Gill. We are pleased with your performance. You may go."

Dismissed, I went straight to the kitchen and told Rozelle about the recent events at Miss Ruby's.

❦

After six weeks in Clanton, my research is complete. I've combed through all public records, and I've studied hundreds of old issues of the *Ford County Times*, which are also stored in the courthouse. No lawsuits have been filed against Quiet Haven. Only two minor complaints are on record with the agency in Jackson, and both were handled administratively.

Only two residents of Quiet Haven have any assets to speak of. Mr. Jesse Plankmore owns three hundred acres of scrub pine near Pidgeon Island, in the far northeastern section of Ford County. But Mr. Plankmore doesn't know it anymore. He checked out years ago and will succumb any day now. Plus, his wife died eleven years ago, and her will was probated by a local lawyer. I've read it twice. All assets were willed to Mr. Plankmore, then to the four children upon his death. It's safe to assume he has an identical will, the original of which is locked away in the lawyer's safe-deposit box.

The other property owner is my pal Lyle Spurlock. With six hundred and foty acres of unencumbered land in his neglected portfolio, he's one of the brightest prospects I've seen in years. Without him, I would begin my exit strategy.

Other research is revealing, and good for gossip, but not that valuable. Miss Ruby is actually sixty-eight years old, has three divorces on record, the most current one filed twenty-two years ago, has no children, no criminal record, and her building is appraised by the county at $52,000. Twenty years ago, when it was a full-fledged whorehouse, the appraisal was twice that. According to an old story in the *Ford County Times*, the police raided her eighteen years ago and arrested two of her girls and two of their customers, one of whom was a member of the state legislature, but from another county. Other stories followed. The legislator resigned in disgrace, then killed himself. The moral majority raised a ruckus, and Miss Ruby was effectively out of business.

Her only other asset, at least of interest to the county, is her 1972 Cadillac. Last year the license tags cost her $29.

It is the Cadillac I'm pondering when I allow her to catch me arriving home from work at 8:00 a.m. "Mornin', Gill," she rasps through her tar-laden lungs. "How 'bout a Jimmy?" She's on the narrow front porch, in some hideous ensemble of pink pajamas, lavender bathrobe, red rubber shower shoes, and a sweeping black hat that would deflect more rain than an umbrella. In other words, one of her usual outfits.

I glance at my watch, smile, say, "Sure."

She disappears inside and hurries back with two large tumblers of Jim Beam and soda water. There's a Marlboro stuck between her sticky red lips, and as she talks, it bounces rapidly up and down. "A good night at the nursing home, Gill?"

"The usual. Did you rest well?"

"Up all night."

"I'm sorry." She was up all night because she sleeps all day, a holdover from her previous life. She usually fights the whiskey until about 10:00 a.m., when she goes to bed and sleeps until dark.

We ramble about this and that, more gossip about people I'll never meet. I toy with the drink, but I'm afraid not to consume most of it. She's questioned my manhood on several occasions when I tried to slip by without fully enjoying the bourbon.

"Say, Miss Ruby, did you ever know a man by the name of Lyle Spurlock?" I ask during a lull.

It takes quite a while for her to recall all the men she's known, but Lyle eventually does not make the cut. "Afraid not, dear. Why?"

"He's one of my patients, my favorite, really, and I was thinking of taking him to the movies tonight."

"How sweet of you."

"There's a double feature at the drive-in."

She almost blows a mouthful of whiskey across the front yard, then laughs until she can't breathe. Finally, when she collects herself, she says, "You're taking an old man to the dirty movies?"

"Sure. Why not?"

"That's funny." She's still highly amused, her large yellow

teeth on full display. A pull of Jimmy, a drag of the cigarette, and she's now under control.

According to the archives of the *Ford County Times*, the Daisy Drive-In showed its outdoor version of *Deep Throat* in 1980, and the town of Clanton erupted. There were protests, marches, ordinances, lawsuits attacking ordinances, sermons and more sermons, speeches by politicians, and when the brouhaha was over and the dust settled, the drive-in was still in business, still showing dirty movies whenever it wanted, fully embraced by a federal court's interpretation of the First Amendment. As a compromise, though, the owner agreed to show the XXX stuff only on Wednesday nights, when the church folks were in church. The other nights were heavy on teenage horror flicks, but he promised as much Disney as he could get. Didn't matter. A boycott by the Christians had been in place for so long that the Daisy was generally regarded as a blight on the community.

"I don't suppose I could borrow your car?" I ask, apologetically.

"Why?"

"Well," I nodded at my sad little Beetle parked at the curb. "It's a bit small."

"Why don't you get something bigger?"

As small as it was, it was still worth more than her tank.

"I've been thinking about that. Anyway, it might be crowded. Just a thought, no big deal. I understand if you don't want to."

"Let me think about it." She rattles her ice and says, "Believe I'll have just a tad more. You?"

"No, thanks." My tongue is on fire and I'm suddenly groggy. I go to bed. She goes to bed. After a long sleep, we meet back on her porch at dusk, and she continues, "I think I'll have a little Jimmy. You?"

"No, thanks. I'm driving."

She mixes one, and we're off. I never expressly invited her to join me and Lyle for our boys' night out, but once I realized she had no intention of the Cadillac leaving without her, I said what the hell. Lyle Spurlock won't care. She confesses, as we sort of float through town in a vehicle that must feel similar to an oil barge going downriver, that she hopes the movies are not too raunchy. She says this with an exaggerated flapping of the eyelids, and I get the impression that Miss Ruby can take whatever filth the Daisy Drive-In can dish out.

I crack a window to allow fresh air a chance to dilute the fumes emanating from Miss Ruby. For the night out, she's chosen to give herself an extra dousing of her various perfumes. She lights a Marlboro but does not crack her window. For a second I fear that the flame might ignite the vapors engulfing the front seat and we could both be burned alive. The moment passes.

As we make our way to Quiet Haven, I regale Miss Ruby with all the gossip I've picked up in the kitchen on the subject of Mr. Lyle Spurlock and his roving eyes and hands. She claims to have heard the rumor, years back, about an elderly gent caught bedding a nurse, and seems genuinely excited about meeting such a character. Another nip of Jimmy, and she declares that she might just remember a Spurlock as a client after all, back in the glory days.

The second shift is run by Nurse Angel, a pious, hard woman who's currently number two on my shit list and may quite possibly become the first person I get fired here. She immediately informs me that she doesn't approve of my plans to take Lyle to the movies. (I've told no one but Lyle, and now Miss Ruby, which movies we're going to.) I fire back that it doesn't matter what she disapproves of because Ms. Wilma Drell, the number-one Queen Bee, has given approval, said approval not coming forth voluntarily until Mr. Spurlock and his daughter (by phone) had raised more hell than the Queen could take.

"It's in writing," I say. "Check the file. Approved by W. Drell."

She flings some paperwork, mumbles incoherently, frowns as if migraines were attacking. Within minutes, Lyle and I are shuffling out of the front door. He's wearing his nicest slacks and his only jacket, an old shiny navy blazer he's had for decades, and he walks with a determined limp. Outside the building, I grab his elbow and say, "Listen, Mr. Spurlock, we have an unexpected guest with us."

"Who?"

"She goes by Miss Ruby. She's my landlady. I borrowed her car and she came with it, sort of a package deal. Sorry."

"It's okay."

"She's nice. You'll like her."

"Thought we were going to watch dirty movies."

"That's right. Don't worry, they won't bother Miss Ruby. She's not much of a lady, if you know what I mean."

Lyle understands. With a gleam in his eyes, Lyle gets it completely. We stop at the front passenger's door and I introduce them, then Lyle crawls into the cavernous backseat. Before we're out of the parking lot, Miss Ruby is turning around, saying, "Lyle, dear, would you like a little Jim Beam?"

From her large red purse she's already pulling out a quart-size flask.

"I reckon not," Lyle says, and I relax. It's one thing to take Lyle out for a little porn, but if I brought him home sloshed, I could get into trouble.

She leans in my direction and says, "He's cute."

Away we go. I expect Miss Ruby to mention the Sonic, and within minutes she says, "Now, Gill, I'd like a cheeseburger and fries for dinner. How 'bout we run by the Sonic?"

With effort, I manage to fit the oil barge into a narrow slip at the Sonic. The place is packed, and I catch stares from some of the other customers, all sitting in vehicles that are noticeably smaller and newer. I don't know if they're amused by the bright red Cadillac that will barely fit, or by the sight of the odd trio inside it. Not that I care.

I've done this before, at other homes. One of the greatest gifts I can give to my favorite friends is freedom. I've taken old ladies to churches, to country clubs, to funerals and weddings, and, of course, to shopping centers. I've taken old men to Legion halls, ball games, bars, churches, and coffee shops. They are childishly grateful for these little excursions, these simple acts of kindness that get them out of their rooms. And, sadly, these forays into the real world always cause trouble. The other employees, my esteemed co-workers, resent the fact that I'm willing to spend extra time with our residents, and the other residents become very jeal-

ous of the ones lucky enough to escape for a few hours. But trouble doesn't bother me.

Lyle claims to be full, no doubt stuffed with rubber chicken
and green Jell-O. I order a hot dog and a root beer, and soon we're
floating down the street again, Miss Ruby nibbling on a fry and
Lyle way in the back somewhere relishing the open spaces.
Abruptly, he says, "I'd like a beer."

I turn in to the lot of a convenience store. "What brand?"

"Schlitz," he says, with no hesitation.

I purchase a six-pack of sixteen-ounce cans, hand them over,
and we're off again. I hear a top pop, then a slurp. "You want
one, Gill?" he asks.

"No, thanks." I hate the smell and taste of beer. Miss Ruby
pours some bourbon into her Dr Pepper and sips away. She's grinning now, I guess because she has someone to drink with.

At the Daisy, I buy three tickets at five bucks each, no offer
to pay from my pals here, and we ease through the gravel lot and
select a spot on the third row, far away from any other vehicle. I
count six others present. The movie is under way. I mount the
speaker on my window, adjust the volume so Lyle can hear all the
groaning, then settle low in my seat. Miss Ruby is still nibbling
at her cheeseburger. Lyle slides across the rear seat to a spot directly in the middle so his view is unobstructed.

The plot soon becomes evident. A door-to-door salesman is
trying to sell vacuum cleaners. You would expect a door-to-door
salesman to be somewhat well-groomed and to at least try to have
a pleasing personality. This guy is greased from head to toe, with
earrings, tattoos, a tight silk shirt with few buttons, and a lusty

sneer that would frighten any respectable housewife. Of course, in this film, there are no respectable housewives. Once our slimy salesman gets in the front door, dragging a useless vacuum cleaner behind him, the wife attacks him, clothes are removed, and all manner of frolicking ensues. The husband catches them on the sofa, and instead of beating the guy senseless with a vacuum cleaner hose, the hubby joins the fun. It's soon a family affair, with naked people rushing into the den from all directions. The family is one of those porn families where the children are the same age as the parents, but who cares? Neighbors arrive, and the scene becomes one of frenzied copulating in ways and positions few mortals can imagine.

I slide deeper into my seat, just barely able to see over the steering wheel. Miss Ruby nibbles away, chuckling at something on the screen, not the least bit embarrassed, and Lyle opens another beer, the only sound from back there.

Some redneck in a pickup two rows behind us lays on his horn every time a climactic moment is featured on film. Other than that, the Daisy is fairly quiet and deserted.

After the second orgy, I'm bored and I excuse myself to visit the men's room. I stroll across the gravel lot to a shabby little building where they sell snacks and have the toilets. The projection room is a wobbly appendage above it. The Daisy Drive-In has certainly seen better days. I pay for a bucket of stale popcorn and take my time returning to the red Cadillac. Along the way, I never consider glancing up at the screen.

Miss Ruby has disappeared! A split second after I realize her seat is empty, I hear her giggle in the backseat. Of course the dome light doesn't work, probably hasn't in twenty years or so. It's dark back there, and I do not turn around. "You guys okay?" I ask, much like a babysitter.

"You betcha," Lyle says.

"There's more room back here," Miss Ruby says. After ten minutes, I excuse myself again, and I go for a long walk, across the lot to the very back row and through an old fence, up an incline to the foot of an ancient tree where beer cans are scattered around a broken picnic table, evidence left behind by teenagers too young or too poor to buy tickets to the show. I sit on the rickety table and have a clear view of the screen in the distance. I count seven cars and two pickups, paying customers. The one nearest Miss Ruby's Cadillac still honks at just the right moments. Her car shines from the reflection on the screen. As far as I can tell, it is perfectly still.

My shift begins at 9:00 p.m., and I'm never late. Queen Wilma Drell confirmed in writing that Mr. Spurlock was to return promptly by 9:00, so with thirty minutes to go, I amble back to the car, break up whatever is happening in the backseat, if anything, and announce it's time to leave.

"I'll just stay back here," Miss Ruby says, giggling, her words a bit slurred, which is unusual since she's immune to the booze.

"You okay, Mr. Spurlock?" I ask as I crank the engine.

"You betcha."

"You guys enjoy the movies?"

Both roar with laughter, and I realize they are drunk. They

giggle all the way to Miss Ruby's house, and it's very amusing. She says good night as we transfer to my Beetle, and as Mr. Spurlock and I head toward Quiet Haven, I ask, "Did you have fun?"

"Great. Thanks." He's holding a Schlitz, number three as far as I can tell, and his eyes are half-closed.

"What'd ya'll do in the backseat?"

"Not much."

"She's nice, isn't she?"

"Yes, but she smells bad. All that perfume. Never thought I'd be in the backseat with Ruby Clements."

"You know her?"

"I figured out who she is. I've lived here for a long time, son, and I can't remember much. But there was a time when most everybody knew who she was. One of her husbands was a cousin to one of my wives. I think that's right. A long time ago."

You gotta love small towns.

❧

Our next excursion, two weeks later, is to the Civil War battlefield at Brice's Crossroads, about an hour from Clanton. Like most old Southerners, Mr. Spurlock claims to have ancestors who fought gallantly for the Confederacy. He still carries a grudge and can get downright bitter on the subject of Reconstruction ("never happened") and Yankee carpetbaggers ("thievin' bastards").

I check him out early one Tuesday, and under the watchful and disapproving eye of Queen Wilma Drell we escape in my little Beetle and leave Quiet Haven behind. I stop at a convenience store, buy two tall cups of stale coffee, some sandwiches and soft drinks, and we're off to refight the war.

I really couldn't care less about the Civil War, and I don't get all this lingering fascination with it. We, the South, lost and lost big. Get over it. But if Mr. Spurlock wants to spend his last days dreaming of Confederate glory and what might have been, then I'll give it my best. In the past month I've read a dozen war books from the Clanton library, and there are three more in my room at Miss Ruby's.

At times he's sharp with the details—battles, generals, troop movements—and at other times he draws blanks. I keep the conversation on my latest hot topic—the preservation of Civil War battlefields. I rant about the destruction of the sacred grounds, especially in Virginia, where Bull Run and Fredericksburg and Winchester have been decimated by development. This gets him worked up, then he nods off.

On the ground, we look at a few monuments and battlefield markers. He's convinced that his grandfather Joshua Spurlock was wounded in the course of some heroic maneuver during the battle at Brice's Crossroads. We sit on a split-rail fence and eat sandwiches for lunch, and he gazes into the distance in a forlorn trance, as if he's waiting for the sounds of cannon and horses. He talks about his grandfather, who died in either 1932 or 1934, somewhere around the age of ninety. When Lyle was a boy, his grandfather delighted him with stories of killing Yankees and getting shot and fighting with Nathan Bedford Forrest, the greatest of all Southern commanders. "They were at Shiloh together," he said. "My grandfather took me there once."

"Would you like to go again?" I ask.

He breaks into a grin, and it's obvious that he'd love to see the battlefield again. "It'd be a dream," he says, moisture in his eyes.

"I can arrange that."

"I want to go in April, when the battle was fought, so I can see the Peach Orchard and the Bloody Pond and the Hornet's Nest."

"You have my promise. We'll go next April." April was five months away, and given my track record, I doubted if I would still be employed at Quiet Haven. But if not, nothing would prevent me from visiting my friend Lyle and taking him on another road trip.

He sleeps most of the way back to Clanton. Between naps, I explain that I am involved with a national group working to preserve Civil War battlefields. The group is strictly private, no help from the government, and thus depends on donations. Since I obviously earn little, I send a small check each year, but my uncle, who's stout, sends large checks at my request.

Lyle is intrigued by this.

"You could always include them in your will," I say.

No reaction. Nothing. I leave it alone.

We return to Quiet Haven, and I walk him to his room. As he's taking off his sweater and his shoes, he thanks me for a "great day." I pat him on the back, tell him how much I enjoyed it too, and as I'm leaving, he says, "Gill, I don't have a will."

I act surprised, but then I'm not. The number of people, especially those in nursing homes, who have never bothered with

a will is astounding. I feign a look of shock, then disappoint-
ment, then I say, "Let's talk about it later, okay? I know what to
do."

"Sure," he says, relieved.

¥

At 5:30 the following morning, the halls deserted, the lights
still off, everyone asleep or supposed to be, I'm at the front desk
reading about General Grant's Southern campaign when I'm startled by the sudden appearance of Ms. Daphne Groat. She's eighty-
six, suffers from dementia, and is confined to the Back Wing. How
she managed to pass through the locked door is something I'll
never know.

"Come quick!" she hisses at me, teeth missing, voice hollow
and weak.

"What's the matter?" I ask as I jump up.

"It's Harriet. She's on the floor."

I sprint to the Back Wing, punch in the code, pass through
the thick locked door, and race down the hall to room 158, where
Ms. Harriet Markle has lived since I went through puberty. I flip
on the light to her room, and there she is, on the floor, obviously
unconscious, naked except for black socks, lying in a sickening
pool of vomit, urine, blood, and her own waste. The stench buckles my knees, and I've survived many jolting odors. Because I've
been in this situation before, I react instinctively. I quickly pull
out my little camera, take four photos, stick it back into my
pocket, and go for help. Ms. Daphne Groat is nowhere to be seen,
and no one else is awake on the wing.

There is no attendant on duty. Eight and a half hours earlier, when our shift began, a woman by the name of Rita had checked in at the front desk, where I was at the time, and then headed to the Back Wing. She was on duty, alone, which is against the rules because two attendants are required back there. Rita is now gone. I sprint to the North Wing, grab an attendant named Gary, and together we swing into action. We put on rubber gloves, sanitary masks, and boots and quickly get Ms. Harriet off the floor and back into her bed. She is breathing, but barely, and she has a gash just above her left ear. Gary scrubs her while I mop up the mess. When the situation is somewhat cleaner, I call an ambulance, and then I call Nurse Angel and Queen Wilma. By this time, others have been awakened and we've drawn a crowd.

Rita is nowhere to be seen. Two attendants, Gary and me, for fifty-two residents.

We bandage her wound, put on clean underwear and a gown, and while Gary guards her bed, I dash to the wing desk to check the paperwork. Ms. Harriet has not been fed since noon the day before—almost eighteen hours—and her meds have also been neglected. I quickly photocopy all the notes and entries because you can bet they'll be tampered with in a matter of hours. I fold the copies and stick them into a pocket.

The ambulance arrives, and Ms. Harriet is loaded up and taken away. Nurse Angel and Ms. Drell huddle nervously with each other and begin flipping through the paperwork. I return to the South Wing and lock the evidence in a drawer. I'll take it home in a few hours.

The following day, a man in a suit arrives from some regional office and wants to interview me about what happened. He's not a lawyer, those will show up later, and he's not particularly bright. He begins by explaining to Gary and me exactly what he thinks we saw and did during the crisis, and we let him ramble. He goes on to assure us that Ms. Harriet was properly fed and medicated—it's all right there in the notes—and that Rita had simply gone outside for a smoke and fell ill, which required her to dash home for a moment before returning, only to find the "unfortunate" situation relative to Ms. Harriet.

I play dumb, my speciality. Gary does too; it's more natural for him, but he's also worried about his job. I am not. The idiot finally leaves, and does so with the impression that he has eased into our little redneck town and skillfully put out yet another fire for good old HVQH Group.

Ms. Harriet spends a week in the hospital with a cracked skull. She lost a lot of blood, and there's probably some more brain damage, though how the hell can you measure it? Regardless, it's a beautiful lawsuit, in the hands of the right person.

Because of the popularity of these lawsuits, and the sheer number of vultures circling nursing homes, I have learned that one must move with haste. My lawyer is an old friend named Dexter Ridley, from Tupelo, a man I turn to on occasion. Dex is about fifty, with a couple of wives and lives under his belt, and he made the decision a few years ago that he could not survive in the business by drawing up deeds and filing no-fault divorces. Dex stepped up a notch and became a litigator, though he seldom actually goes to trial. His real talent is filing big lawsuits, then huffing and puffing until the other side settles. He's got billboards with his smiling face on them scattered around north Mississippi.

I drive to Tupelo on a day off, show him the color photos of Ms. Harriet naked and bleeding, show him the copies of the attendants' notes, both before the tampering and after, and we strike a deal. Dex kicks into high gear, contacts the family of Harriet Markle, and within a week of the incident notifies HVQH that they have a real problem. He won't mention me and my photos and my purloined records until he has to. With such inside information, the case will likely be settled quickly, and I'll be unemployed once again.

By order from the home office, Ms. Wilma Drell suddenly becomes very nice. She calls me in and tells me that my performance has improved so dramatically that I'm getting a raise. From six bucks an hour to seven, and I'm not to tell anyone else on the floor. I give her a load of sappy thanks, and she's convinced we're bonding now.

Late that night, I read Mr. Spurlock a magazine story about a developer in Tennessee who's trying to bulldoze a neglected Civil War battlefield so he can throw up another strip mall and some cheap condos. The locals and the preservation types are fighting, but the developer has the money and the politics on his side. Lyle is upset by this, and we talk at length about ways to help the good guys. He doesn't mention his last will and testament, and it's still too soon for me to make a move.

In retirement homes, birthdays are a big deal, and for obvious reasons. You'd better celebrate 'em while you can. There's always a party in the cafeteria, with cake and candles and ice cream, photos and songs and such. We, the staff, work hard at creating merriment and noise, and we try our best to drag out the festivities for at least thirty minutes. About half the time a few family members will be here, and this heightens the mood. If no family is present, we work even harder. Each birthday might be the last, but I guess that's true for all of us. Truer for some, though.

Lyle Spurlock turns eighty-five on December 2, and his loud-mouth daughter from Jackson shows up, along with two of her kids and three of her grandchildren, and along with her customary barrage of complaints, demands, and suggestions, all in a noisy and lame effort to convince her beloved father that she cares so deeply about him that she must raise hell with us. They bring balloons and silly hats, a store-bought coconut cake (his favorite), and several cheap gifts in gaudy boxes, things like socks and handkerchiefs and stale chocolates. A granddaughter rigs up a boom box and plays Hank Williams (his alleged favorite) in the background. Another mounts a display of enlarged black-and-white photos of young Lyle in the army, young Lyle walking down the aisle (the first time), young Lyle posing this way and that so many decades ago. Most of the residents are present, as are most of the employees, including Rozelle from the kitchen, though I know she's there for the cake and not out of any affection for the birthday boy. At one point Wilma Drell gets too close to Lyle, who, off his saltpeter, makes an awkward and obvious grab for her ample ass. He gets a handful. She yelps in horror, and almost everyone laughs as though it's just part of the celebration, but it's obvious to me that Queen Wilma is not amused. Then Lyle's daughter overreacts badly by squawking at him, slapping his arm, and scolding him, and for a few seconds the mood is tense. Wilma disappears and is not seen for the rest of the day. I doubt if she's had that much fun in years.

After an hour the party loses steam, and several of our friends begin to nod off. The daughter and her brood pack quickly and are soon gone. Hugs and kisses and all that, but it's a long way back to Jackson, Daddy. Lyle's eighty-fifth celebration is soon over. I escort him back to his room, carrying his gifts, talking about Gettysburg.

Just after bedtime, I ease into his room and deliver my gift. A few hours of research, and a few phone calls to the right people, and I learned that there was indeed a Captain Joshua Spurlock who fought in the Tenth Mississippi Infantry Regiment at the Battle of Shiloh. He was from Ripley, Mississippi, a town not far from where Lyle's father was born, according to my fact-checking. I found an outfit in Nashville that specializes in Civil War memorabilia, both real and fake, and paid them $80 for their work. My gift is a matted and framed Certificate of Valor, awarded to Captain Spurlock, and flanked on the right by a Confederate battle flag and on the left by the Tenth Regiment's official insignia. It's not meant to be anything other than what it is—a very handsome and very bogus re-creation of something that never existed in the first place—but for someone as consumed with past glory as Lyle, it is the greatest of all gifts. His eyes water as he holds it. The old man is now ready for heaven, but not so fast.

"This is beautiful," he says. "I don't know what to say. Thank you."

"My pleasure, Mr. Spurlock. He was a brave soldier."

"Yes, he was."

§

Promptly at midnight, I deliver my second gift.

Lyle's roommate is Mr. Hitchcock, a frail and fading gent who's a year older than Lyle but in much worse shape. I'm told he lived a pure life, free from alcohol, tobacco, and other vices, yet there's not much left. Lyle chased women his entire life, caught many of them, and at one time chain-smoked and hit the bottle hard. After years in this work I'm convinced that DNA is at least half the solution, or half the problem.

Anyway, at pill time I juiced Mr. Hitchcock with a stronger sleeping pill, and he's in another world. He won't hear a thing.

Miss Ruby, who I'm sure has been hitting the Jimmy with her usual fealty, follows my instructions perfectly and parks her massive Cadillac next to the Dumpster just outside the back entrance to the kitchen. She crawls out of the driver's side, already giggling, glass in hand. From the passenger's side I get my first glimpse of Mandy, one of Miss Ruby's "better" girls, but it's not the time for introductions. "Shhhh," I whisper, and they follow me through the darkness, into the kitchen, into the dimly lit cafeteria, where we stop for a second.

Miss Ruby says proudly, "Now, Gill, this is Mandy."

We shake hands. "A real pleasure," I say.

Mandy barely offers a smile. Her face says, "Let's just get this over with." She's about forty, a bit plump, heavily made up, but unable to hide the strains of a hard life. The next thirty minutes will cost me $200.

All lights are low at Quiet Haven, and I glance down the south hall to make sure no one is stirring. Then we, Mandy and I, walk quickly to room 18, where Mr. Hitchcock is comatose but Mr. Spurlock is walking the floor, waiting. He looks at her, she looks at him. I offer a quick "Happy Birthday," then close the door and backtrack.

Miss Ruby and I wait in the cafeteria, drinking. She has her toddy. I sip from her flask, and I have to admit that after three months the bourbon is not as bad as it was. "She's a sweetheart," Miss Ruby is saying, thoroughly delighted that she has once again managed to bring people together.

"A nice girl," I say, mindlessly.

"She started working for me when she dropped out of high school. Terrible family. Couple of bad marriages after that. Never had a break. I just wish I could keep her busier. It's so hard these days. Women are so loose they don't charge for it anymore."

Miss Ruby, a career and unrepentant madam, is bemoaning the fact that modern women are too loose. I think about this for a second, then take a sip and let it pass.

"How many girls do you have now?"

"Just three, all part-time. Used to have a dozen, and kept them very busy."

"Those were the days."

"Yes, they were. The best years of my life. You reckon we could find some more business here at Quiet Haven? I know in prison they set aside one day a week for conjugal visits. Ever thought about the same here? I could bring in a couple of girls one night a week, and I'm sure it would be easy work for them."

"That's probably the worst idea I've heard in the past five years."

Sitting in the shadows, I see her red eyes turn and glare at me. "I beg your pardon," she hisses.

"Take a drink. There are fifteen men confined to this place, Miss Ruby, average age of, oh, let's say eighty. Off the cuff, five are bedridden, three are brain-dead, three can't get out of their wheelchairs, and so that leaves maybe four who are ambulatory. Of the four, I'd wager serious money that only Lyle Spurlock is capable of performing at some level. You can't sell sex in a nursing home."

"I've done it before. This ain't my first rodeo." And with that she offers one of her patented smoke-choked cackles, then starts coughing. She eventually catches her breath, just long enough to settle things down with a jolt of Jim Beam.

"Sex in a nursing home," she says, chuckling. "Maybe that's where I'm headed."

I bite my tongue.

When the session is over, we quickly get through a round of awkward good-byes. I watch the Cadillac until it is safely off the premises and out of sight, then finally relax. I've actually arranged such a tryst once before. Ain't my first rodeo.

Lyle is sleeping like an infant when I check on him. Dentures out, mouth sagging, but lips turned up into a pleasant smile. If Mr. Hitchcock has moved in the past three hours, I can't tell.

He'll never know what he missed. I check the other rooms and go about my business, and when all is quiet, I settle into the front desk with some magazines.

⚓

Dex says the company has mentioned more than once the possibility of settling the Harriet Markle lawsuit before it's actually filed. Dex has hinted strongly to them that he has inside information regarding a cover-up—tampered-with paperwork and other pieces of evidence that Dex knows how to skillfully mention on the phone when talking to lawyers who represent such companies. HVQH says it would like to avoid the publicity of a nasty suit. Dex assures them it'll be nastier than they realize. Back and forth, the usual lawyer routines. But the upshot for me is that my days are numbered. If my affidavit and photos and filched records will hasten a nice settlement, then so be it. I'll happily produce the evidence, then move along.

Mr. Spurlock and I play checkers most nights at 8:00 in the cafeteria, long after dinner and an hour before I officially punch the clock. We are usually alone, though a knitting club meets on Mondays in one corner, a Bible club gathers on Tuesdays in another, and a small branch of the Ford County Historical Society meets occasionally wherever they can pull three or four chairs together. Even on my nights off, I usually stop by at 8:00 for a few games. It's either that or drink with Miss Ruby and gag on her secondhand smoke.

Lyle wins nine games out of ten, not that I really care. Since his encounter with Mandy his left arm has been bothering him. It

feels numb, and he's not as quick with his words. His blood pressure is up slightly, and he's complained of headaches. Since I have
the key to the pharmacy, I've put him on Nafred, a blood thinner,
and Silerall for stroke victims. I've seen dozens of strokes, and my
diagnosis is just that. A very slight stroke, one unnoticeable to
anyone else, not that anyone is paying attention. Lyle is a tough
old coot who does not complain and does not like doctors and
would take a bullet before he called his daughter and whined
about his health.

"You told me you never made a will," I say casually as I stare
at the board. There are four ladies playing cards forty feet away,
and believe me, they cannot hear us. They can barely hear each
other.

"I've been thinkin' about that," he says. His eyes are tired.
Lyle has aged since his birthday, since Mandy, since his stroke.

"What's in the estate?" I ask, as if I could not care less.

"Some land, that's about all."

"How much land?"

"Six hundred and forty acres, in Polk County." He smiles as
he pulls off a double jump.

"What's the value?"

"Don't know. But it's free and clear."

I haven't paid for an official appraisal, but according to two
agents who specialize in such matters, the land is worth around
$500 an acre.

"You mentioned putting some money aside to help preserve
Civil War battlefields."

This is exactly what Lyle wants to hear. He lights up, smiles

at me, and says, "That's a great idea. That's what I want to do."
For the moment, he's forgotten about the game.

"The best organization is an outfit in Virginia, the Confederate Defense Fund. You gotta be careful. Some of these nonprofits give at least half their money to build monuments to honor the Union forces. I don't think that's what you have in mind."

"Hell no."

His eyes flash hot for a second, and Lyle is once again ready for battle. "Not my money," he adds.

"I'll be happy to serve as your trustee," I say, and move a checker.

"What does that mean?"

"You name the Confederate Defense Fund as the recipient of your estate, and upon your death the money goes into a trust so that I, or whomever you choose, can watch the money carefully and make sure it's accounted for."

He's smiling. "That's what I want, Gill. That's it."

"It's the best way—"

"You don't mind, do you? You'd be in charge of everything when I die."

I clutch his right hand, squeeze it, look him firmly in the eyes, and say, "I'd be honored, Lyle."

We make a few moves in silence, then I wrap up some loose ends. "What about your family?"

"What about them?"

"Your daughter, your son, what do they get from your estate?"

His response is a cross between a sigh, a hiss, and a snort, and when they are combined with a rolling of the eyes, I know immediately that his dear children are about to get cut out. This is perfectly legal in Mississippi and in most states. When making a will, you can exclude everyone but your surviving spouse. And some folks still try.

"I haven't heard from my son in five years. My daughter has more money than I do. Nothing. They get nothing."

"Do they know about this land in Polk County?" I ask.

"I don't think so."

This is all I need.

Two days later, rumors race through Quiet Haven. "The lawyers are coming!" Thanks primarily to me, the gossip has been festering about a massive lawsuit under way in which the family of Ms. Harriet Markle will expose everything and collect millions. It's partially true, but Ms. Harriet knows nothing about it. She's back in her bed, a very clean bed, well fed and properly medicated, properly supervised, and basically dead to the world.

Her lawyer, the Honorable Dexter Ridley of Tupelo, Mississippi, arrives late one afternoon with a small entourage that consists of his faithful secretary and two paralegals, both wearing suits as dark as Dexter's and both scowling in the finest lawyerly tradition. It's an impressive team, and I've never seen such excitement at Quiet Haven. Nor have I seen the place as spiffed-up and shiny. Even the plastic flowers on the front desk have been replaced by real ones. Orders from the home office.

Dex and his team are met by a junior executive from the company who's all smiles. The official reason for this visit is to allow Dex the opportunity to inspect, examine, photograph, measure, and in general poke around Quiet Haven, and for an hour or so he does this with great skill. This is his specialty. He needs to "get the feel of the place" before he sues it. Anyway, it's all an act. Dex is certain the matter will be settled quietly, and generously, without the actual filing of a lawsuit.

Though my shift doesn't start until 9:00 p.m., I hang around as usual. By now the staff and the residents are accustomed to seeing me at all hours. It's as if I never leave. But I'm leaving, believe me.

Rozelle, working late, is busy preparing dinner, not cooking, she reminds me, just preparing. I stay in the kitchen, pestering her, gossiping, helping occasionally. She wants to know what the lawyers are up to, and as usual I can only speculate, but I do so with a lot of theories. Promptly at 6:00 p.m., the residents start drifting into the cafeteria, and I begin carrying trays of the vapid gruel we serve them. Tonight the Jell-O is yellow.

At precisely 6:30, I swing into action. I leave the cafeteria and walk to room 18, where I find Mr. Spurlock sitting on his bed, reading a copy of his last will and testament. Mr. Hitchcock is down the hall having dinner, so we can talk.

"Any questions?" I ask. It's only three pages long, at times written clearly and at times loaded with enough legalese to stump a law professor. Dex is a genius at drafting these things. He adds just enough clear language to convince the person signing that though he or she may not know exactly what he or she is signing, the overall gist of the document is just fine.

"I suppose so," Lyle says, uncertain.

"Lots of legal stuff," I explain helpfully. "But that's required.

The bottom line is that you're leaving everything to the Confederate Defense Fund, in trust, and I'll oversee it all. Is that what you want?"

"Yes, and thank you, Gill."

"I'm honored. Let's go."

We take our time—Lyle is moving much slower since the stroke—and eventually get to the reception area just inside the front door. Queen Wilma, Nurse Nancy, and Trudy the receptionist all left almost two hours ago. There is a lull as dinner is being served. Dex and his secretary are waiting. The two paralegals and the company man are gone. Introductions are made. Lyle takes a seat and I stand next to him, then Dex methodically goes through a rough summary of the document. Lyle loses interest almost immediately, and Dex notices this.

"Is this what you want, Mr. Spurlock?" he asks, the compassionate counselor.

"Yes," Lyle responds, nodding. He's already tired of this legal stuff.

Dex produces a pen, shows Lyle where to sign, then adds his signature as a witness and instructs his secretary to do the same. They are vouching for Lyle's "sound and disposing mind and memory." Dex then signs a required affidavit, and the secretary whips out her notary seal and stamp and gives it her official blessing. I've been in this situation several times, and believe me, this woman will notarize anything. Stick a Xerox copy of the Magna Carta under her nose, swear it's the original, and she'll notarize it.

Ten minutes after signing his last will and testament, Lyle Spurlock is in the cafeteria eating his dinner.

A week later, Dex calls with the news that he's about to meet with the big lawyers from the corporate office and engage in a serious settlement conference. He's decided he will show them the greatly enlarged photos I took of Ms. Harriet Markle lying in a pool of her own body fluids, naked. And he will describe the bogus record entries, but not hand over copies. All of this will lead to a settlement, but it will also reveal to the company my complicity in the matter. I'm the mole, the leaker, the traitor, and though the company won't fire me outright—Dex will threaten them—I've learned from experience that it's best to move on.

In all likelihood, the company will fire Queen Wilma, and probably Nurse Angel too. So be it. I've seldom left a project without getting someone fired.

The following day, Dex calls with the news that the case settled, confidentially of course, for $400,000. This may sound low, given the company's malfeasance and exposure, but it's not a bad settlement. Damages can be difficult to prove in these cases. It's not as if Ms. Harriet was earning money and therefore facing a huge financial loss. She won't see a dime of the money, but you can bet her dear ones are already bickering. My reward is a 10 percent finder's fee, paid off the top.

The following day, two men in dark suits arrive, and fear grips Quiet Haven. Long meetings are held in Queen Wilma's office. The place is tense. I love these situations, and I spend most of the afternoon hiding in the kitchen with Rozelle as the rumors fly. I'm full of wild theories, and most of the rumors seem to originate from the kitchen. Ms. Drell is eventually fired and escorted out of the building. Nurse Angel is fired, and escorted out of the building. Late in the day we hear the rumor that they're looking for me, so I ease out a side door and disappear.

I'll go back in a week or so, to say good-bye to Lyle Spurlock and a few other friends. I'll finish up the gossip with Rozelle, give her a hug, promise to drop in from time to time. I'll stop by Miss Ruby's, settle up on the rent, gather my belongings, and indulge in a final toddy on the porch. It will be difficult to say good-bye, but then I do it so often.

So I leave Clanton after four months, and as I head toward Memphis, I can't help but succumb to smugness. This is one of my more successful projects. The finder's fee alone makes for a good year. Mr. Spurlock's will effectively gives everything to me, though he doesn't realize it. (The Confederate Defense Fund folded years ago.) He probably won't touch the document again before he dies, and I'll pop in often enough to make sure the damned thing stays buried in the drawer. (I'm still checking on several of my more generous friends.) After he dies, and we'll know this immediately because Dex's secretary checks the obitu-aries daily, his daughter will rush in, find the will, and freak out, and soon enough she'll hire lawyers who'll file a nasty lawsuit to contest the will. They'll allege all manner of vile claims against me, and you can't blame them.

Will contests are tried before juries in Mississippi, and I'm not about to subject myself to the scrutiny of twelve average cit-izens and try to deny that I sucked up to an old man during his last days in a nursing home. No, sir. We never go to trial. We, Dex and I, settle these cases long before trial. The family usually buys us off for about 25 percent of the estate. It's cheaper than paying their lawyers for a trial, plus the family does not really want the embarrassment of a full-blown bare-knuckle trial in which they're grilled about how much time they didn't spend with their dearly departed.

After four months of hard work, I'm exhausted. I'll spend a day or two in Memphis, my home base, then catch a flight to Miami, where I have a condo on South Beach. I'll work on my tan for a few days, rest up, then start thinking about my next project.

# Funny Boy

━━ · · · · · · · · · · · · · · · · · · ━━

*L*ike most of the rumors that swept through Clanton, this one originated at either the barbershop, a coffee shop, or the clerk's office in the courthouse, and once it hit the street, it was off and running. A hot rumor would roar around the square with a speed that defied technology and often return to its source in a form so modified and distorted as to baffle its originator. Such is the nature of rumors, but occasionally, at least in Clanton, one turned out to be true.

At the barbershop, on the north side of the square, where Mr. Felix Upchurch had been cutting hair and giving advice for almost fifty years, the rumor was brought up early one morning by a man who usually had his facts straight. "I hear Isaac Keane's least boy is comin' back home," he said.

There was a pause in the haircutting, the newspaper reading, the cigarette smoking, the squabbling over the Cardinals game the night before. Then someone said, "Ain't he that funny boy?"

Silence. Then the clicking of scissors, the turning of pages, a cough over there, and the clearing of a throat over here. When delicate issues were first brought to the surface at the barbershop, they were met with a momentary caution. No one wanted to charge in, lest he be accused of trading in gossip. No one wanted to confirm or deny, because an incorrect fact or an erroneous assumption could quickly spread and do harm, especially in matters dealing with sex. In other places around town, folks were far less hesitant. There was little doubt, however, that the return of the least Keane boy was about to be dissected from a dozen directions, but, as always, the gentlemen proceeded cautiously.

"Well, I've always heard he didn't go for the girls."

"You heard right. My cousin's daughter was in school with that boy, said he was always on the queer side, a regular sissy, and soon as he could, he got outta here and went off to the big city. I think it was San Francisco, but don't quote me on that."

("Don't quote me on that" was a defensive ploy aimed at disclaiming what had just been said. Once properly disclaimed, others were then free to go ahead and repeat what had just been said, but if the information turned out to be false, the original gossiper could not be held liable.)

"How old is he?"

A pause as calculations were made. "Maybe thirty-one, thirty-two."

"Why's he comin' back here?"

"Well, now, I don't know for sure, but they say he's real sick, on his last leg, and ain't nobody in the big city to take care of him."

"He's comin' home to die?"

"That's what they say."

"Isaac would roll over in his grave."

"They say the family's been sendin' him money for years to keep him away from Clanton."

"I thought they'd gone through all of Isaac's money."

Whereupon a digression was begun on the topic of Isaac's money, and his estate, his assets and liabilities, his wives and children and relatives, the mysterious circumstances surrounding his death, and it was concluded with the general agreement that Isaac had died just in time because the family he left behind was nothing but a bunch of idiots.

"What's the boy sick from?"

Rasco, one of the bigger talkers in town and known to embelish, said, "They say it's that queer disease. No way to cure it."

Bickers, at forty the youngest present that morning, said, "You're not talkin' about AIDS, are you?"

"That's what they say."

"The boy's got AIDS and he's comin' to Clanton."

"That's what they say."

"This can't be."

The rumor was confirmed minutes later at the coffee shop on the east side of the square, where a sassy waitress named Dell had been serving breakfast for many years. The early-morning crowd was the usual collection of off-duty deputies and factory workers, with a white collar or two mixed in. One of them said, "Say, Dell, you heard anythang about that youngest Keane boy movin' back home?"

Dell, who often started benign rumors out of boredom but generally maintained good sources, said, "He's already here."

"And he's got AIDS?"

"He's got something. All pale, wasted away, looks like death already."

"When did you see him?"

"Didn't. But his aunt's housekeeper told me all about it yesterday afternoon." Dell was behind the counter, waiting on more food from the cook, and every customer in her café was listening. "He's a sick boy, all right. There's no cure, nothin' nobody can do. Won't nobody take care of him in San Francisco, so he's come home to die. Very sad."

"Where's he livin'?"

"Well, he won't be livin' in the big house, that's for sure. The family got together and decided he couldn't stay there. What he's got is contagious as hell, and deadly, and so they're puttin' him in one of Isaac's old houses in Lowtown."

"He's livin' with the coloreds?"

"That's what they say."

This took a while to sink in, but it began to make sense. The thought of a Keane living across the railroad tracks in the black section was hard to accept, but then it seemed logical that anyone with AIDS should not be allowed on the white side of town.

Dell continued, "God knows how many shacks and houses old man Keane bought and built in Lowtown. I think he still owns a few dozen."

"Reckon who the boy'll live with?"

"I don't really care. I just don't want him comin' in here."

"Now, Dell. What would you do if he walked in right now and wanted breakfast?"

She wiped her hands on a dishcloth, stared at the man who asked the question, tightened her jaws, and said, "Look, I can refuse service to anyone. Believe me, with my customers, I think about this all the time. But if he comes in here, I'll ask him to leave. You gotta remember, this boy is highly contagious, and we're not talkin' about the common cold. If I serve him, then one of you might get his plate or glass next time around. Think about that."

They thought about it for a long time.

Finally, someone said, "Reckon how long he'll live?"

That question was being discussed across the street on the second floor of the courthouse in the offices of the chancery clerk, where the early-morning coffee crowd was nibbling on pastries and catching up with the latest news. Myra, who was in charge of filing land deeds, had finished high school one year before Adrian Keane, and of course they knew even back then that he was different. She had the floor.

Ten years after graduation, Myra and her husband were vacationing in California when she gave Adrian a call. They met for lunch at Fisherman's Wharf and, with Alcatraz and the Golden Gate Bridge in the background, had a delightful time talking about their Clanton days. Myra assured Adrian nothing had changed in their hometown. Adrian talked freely about his lifestyle. The year was 1984, he was happily out of the closet, though not attached to anyone in particular. He was worried about AIDS, a disease Myra had never heard of in 1984. The first wave of the epidemic had roared through the gay community out there, and the casualties were heartbreaking, and frightening. Changes in lifestyles were being advocated. Some die within six months, Adrian had explained to Myra and her husband. Others hang on for years. He had already lost some friends.

Myra described the lunch again in great detail before a rapt audience of a dozen other clerks. The fact that she'd actually been to San Francisco and driven across that bridge made her special. They had seen the photographs, and more than once.

"They say he's already here," another clerk said.

"How long's he got?"

But Myra didn't know. Since the lunch five years earlier, she'd had no contact with Adrian, and it was obvious she wanted none now.

The first sighting was confirmed minutes later when a Mr. Rutledge entered the barbershop for his weekly trim. His nephew threw the Tupelo daily each morning at sunrise, and every house in downtown Clanton received one. The nephew had heard the rumors and was on the lookout. He rode his bike slowly down Harrison Street, even slower when he approached the old Keane place, and sure enough, that very morning, not two hours earlier, he came face-to-face with a stranger he would not soon forget.

Mr. Rutledge described the encounter. "Joey said he's never seen a sicker man, frail and gaunt, skin pale as a corpse, with splotches on his arm, sunken cheekbones, thin hair. Said it was like lookin' at a cadaver." Rutledge seldom encountered a fact he couldn't improve upon, and this was well-known to the others. But he had their attention. No one dared to question whether Joey, a limited thirteen-year-old, would use a word like "cadaver."

"What'd he say?"

"Joey said, 'Good morning,' and this fella said, 'Good morning,' and Joey handed over the newspaper, but he was careful to keep his distance."

"Smart boy."

"And then he got on his bike and hurried off. You can't catch that stuff just from the air, can you?"

No one ventured a guess.

By 8:30 Dell had heard of the sighting, and there was already some speculation about Joey's health. By 8:45, Myra and the clerks were chattering excitedly about the ghostlike figure who'd frightened the paperboy in front of the old Keane place.

An hour later, a police car made a run down Harrison Street, the two officers in it straining mightily to catch a glimpse of the ghost. By noon, all of Clanton knew that a man dying of AIDS was now in their midst.

❦

The deal was cut with little negotiation. Bickering back and forth was futile under the circumstances. The parties were not on level ground, and so it was no surprise that the white woman got what she wanted.

The white woman was Leona Keane, Aunt Leona to some, Leona the Lion to the rest, the ancient matriarch of a family long in decline. The black woman was Miss Emporia, one of only two black spinsters in Lowtown. Emporia was up in years too, about seventy-five, she thought, though there had never been a record of her birth. The Keane family owned the house Emporia had been renting forever, and it was because of the privilege of ownership that the deal was done so quickly.

Emporia would care for the nephew, and upon his death she would be given a full warranty deed. The little pink house on Roosevelt Street would become hers, free and clear. The transfer would mean little to the Keane family since they had been depleting Isaac's assets for many years. But to Emporia, the transfer meant everything. The thought of owning her beloved home far outweighed her reservations about taking care of a dying white boy.

Since Aunt Leona would never think of being seen on the other side of the tracks, she arranged for her gardener to drive the boy over and deliver him to his final destination. When Aunt Leona's old Buick stopped in front of Miss Emporia's, Adrian Keane looked at the pink house with its white porch, its hanging ferns, its flower boxes brimming with pansies and geraniums, its tiny front lawn lined with a picket fence, and he looked next door to a small house, painted a pale yellow and just as neat and pretty. He looked farther down the street, to a row of narrow, happy homes adorned with flowers and rocking chairs and welcoming doors. Then he looked back at the pink house, and he decided that he'd rather die there than in the miserable mansion he'd just left, less than a mile away.

The gardener, still wearing pruning gloves to ward off any

chance of infection, quickly unloaded the two expensive leather suitcases that held all of Adrian's things and hurried away without a farewell and without a handshake. He was under strict orders from Miss Leona to bring the Buick home and scrub the interior with a disinfectant.

Adrian looked up and down the street, noticed a few porch sitters hiding from the sun, then picked up his luggage and walked through the front yard, along the brick walkway to the steps. The front door opened and Miss Emporia presented herself, with a smile. "Welcome, Mr. Keane," she said.

Adrian said, "Please, none of this 'Mister' stuff. Nice to meet you." At this point in the pleasantries a handshake was in order, but Adrian understood the problem. He quickly added, "Look, it's safe to shake hands, but let's just skip it."

That was fine with Emporia. She'd been warned by Leona that his appearance was startling. She quickly took in the hollow cheeks and eyes and the whitest skin she'd ever seen, and she pretended to ignore the bony frame draped with clothing much too large now. Without hesitation, she waved at a small table on the porch and asked, "Would you like some sweet tea?"

"That would be nice, thank you."

His words were crisp, his southern accent abandoned years ago. Emporia wondered what else the young man had lost along the way. They settled around the wicker table, and she poured the sugary tea. There was a saucer with gingersnaps. She took one; he did not.

"How's your appetite?" she asked.

"It's gone. When I left here years ago, I lost a lot of weight. Got away from all the fried stuff and never really became much of an eater. Now, with this, there's not much of an appetite."

"So I won't be cookin' much?"

"I guess not. Are you okay with this, this arrangement here? I mean, it seems like my family forced this down your throat, which is exactly what they do. If you're not happy, I can find an-other place."

"The arrangement is fine, Mr. Keane."

"Please call me Adrian. And what should I call you?"

"Emporia. Let's just go with the first names."

"Deal."

"Where would you find another place?" she asked.

"I don't know. It's all so temporary now." His voice was hoarse, and his words were slow, as if talking required exertion. He wore a blue cotton shirt, jeans, and sandals.

Emporia once worked in the hospital, and she had seen many cancer patients in their final days. Her new friend reminded her of those poor folks. Sick as he was, though, there was no doubt that he had once been a fine-looking young man.

"Are you happy with this arrangement?" she asked.

"Why wouldn't I be?"

"A white gentleman from a prominent family living here in Lowtown with an old black spinster."

"Might be fun," he said, and managed his first smile.

"I'm sure we'll get along."

He stirred his tea. His smile vanished as the moment of levity passed. Emporia stirred hers too and thought: This poor man. He has little to smile about.

"I left Clanton for a lot of reasons," he said. "It's a bad place for people like me, homosexuals. And it's not so wonderful for people like you. I loathe the way I was raised. I'm ashamed of the way my family treated blacks. I hated the bigotry in this town. I couldn't wait to get out of here. Plus, I wanted the big city."

"San Francisco?"

"I went to New York first, lived there a few years, then got a job on the West Coast. I eventually moved to San Francisco. Then I got sick."

"Why'd you come back if you have such strong feelings against the town?"

Adrian exhaled as if the answer might take an hour, or as if he really didn't know the answer. He wiped some sweat from his forehead, sweat caused not by the humidity but by the sickness. He sipped from his glass. And he finally said, "I'm not sure. I've seen a lot of death recently, been to more than my share of memorials. I couldn't stand the thought of being buried in a cold mausoleum in a faraway city. Maybe it's just the Southern thing. We all come home eventually."

"That makes sense."

"And, I ran out of money, to be honest. The drugs are very expensive. I needed my family, or at least its resources. There are other reasons. It's complicated. I didn't want to burden my friends with another agonizing death."

"And you planned to stay over there, not here in Lowtown?"

"Believe me, Emporia, I'd much rather be here. They didn't want me back in Clanton. For years they paid me to stay away. They disowned me, cut me out of their wills, refused to speak my name. So, I figured I'd upset their lives one last time. Make them suffer a little. Make them spend some money."

A police car drove slowly down the street. Neither mentioned it. When it was gone, Adrian took another sip and said, "You need some background, some of the basics. I've had AIDS for about three years, and I won't live much longer. I'm basically safe to be around. The only way to catch the disease is through the exchange of body fluids, so let's agree right now that we will not have sex."

Emporia howled with laughter, and she was soon joined by Adrian. They laughed until their eyes were wet, until the porch shook, until they were laughing at themselves for laughing so hard. A few of the neighbors perked up and looked from far away. When things were finally under control, she said, "I haven't had sex in so long I've forgotten about it."

"Well, Miss Emporia, let me assure you that I've had enough for me, you, and half of Clanton. But those days are over."

"Mine too."

"Good. Keep your hands to yourself and I'll do the same. Other than that, it's wise if we take some precautions."

"The nurse lady came out yesterday and explained thangs."

"Good. Laundry, dishes, food, medicine, rules of the bathroom. All that?"

"Yes."

He rolled up his left sleeve and pointed to a dark bruise.

"Sometimes these things open up, and when they do, I'll put on a bandage. I'll tell you when this happens."

"I thought we weren't gonna touch."

"Right, but just in case you can't control yourself."

She laughed again, but briefly.

"Seriously, Emporia, I'm pretty safe."

"I understand."

"I'm sure you do, but I don't want you living in fear of me. I just spent four days with what's left of my family, and they treated me like I'm radioactive. All these folks around here will do the same. I'm grateful that you agreed to care for me, and I don't want you to worry. It won't be pretty from now on. I look like I'm already dead, and things will get worse."

"You've seen it before, haven't you?"

"Oh yes. Many times. I've lost a dozen friends in the last five years. It's horrible."

She had so many questions, about the disease and the lifestyle, about his friends, and so on, but she put them aside for later. He seemed tired all of a sudden. "Let me show you around," she said.

The police car drove by again, slowly. Adrian watched and asked, "So how often do the cops patrol this street?"

Almost never, she wanted to say. There were other sections of Lowtown where the houses were not as nice, the neighbors not as reliable. There were honky-tonks, a pool hall, a liquor store, groups of young unemployed men hanging around the corners, and there you would see a police car several times a day. She said, "Oh, they come by occasionally."

They stepped inside, into the den. "It's a little house," she said, almost in defense. He, after all, had been raised in a fine home on a shady street. Now he was standing in a cottage built by his father and owned by his family.

"It's twice as large as my apartment in New York was," he said.

"You don't say."

"I'm serious, Emporia. It's lovely. I'll be happy here."

The wooden floors shined with polish. The furniture was per-fectly centered along the walls. The windows were bright and clear. Nothing was out of order, and everything had the look of constant care. There were two small bedrooms behind the den and kitchen. Adrian's had a double bed with an iron frame that covered half the floor. There was a tiny closet, a dresser too small for a child, and a compact air conditioner in the window.

"It's perfect, Emporia. How long have you lived here?"

"Hmmm, maybe twenty-five years."

"I'm so happy it'll be yours, and soon."

"So am I, but let's not get in a hurry. Are you tired?"

"Yes."

"Would you like a nap? The nurse said you need a lot of sleep."

"A nap would be great."

She closed the door, and the room was silent.

While he was sleeping, a neighbor from across the street strolled over and sat with Emporia on the porch. His name was Herman Grant, and he tended to be on the curious side.

"What's that white boy doin' here?" he asked.

Emporia was ready with the answer, one she had been planning for a few days now. The questions and confrontations would come and go, she hoped. "His name is Adrian Keane, Mr. Isaac Keane's youngest, and he's very sick. I have agreed to take care of him."

"If he's sick, why ain't he at the hospital?"

"He's not that kind of sick. There's nothin' they can do at the hospital. He has to rest and take a sackful of pills every day."

"Is he a dead man?"

"Probably so, Herman. He will only get worse, then he'll die. It's very sad."

"Has he caught cancer?"

"No, it's not cancer."

"What is it?"

"It's a different disease, Herman. Something they have out in California."

"That don't make any sense."

"A lot of things don't."

"I don't understand why he's livin' with you, here in our side of town."

"As I said, Herman, I'm takin' care of him."

"They makin' you do it 'cause they own the house?"

"No."

"You gettin' paid?"

"Mind your own business, Herman."

Herman left and headed down the street. Before long, word had spread.

⚱

The chief stopped by the coffee shop for pancakes, and before long Dell had him cornered. "I just don't understand why you can't quarantine the boy," she said loudly, for the benefit of all, and all were listening.

"That takes a court order, Dell," the chief said.

"So he's free to just walk around town, spreadin' germs everywhere?"

The chief was a patient man who'd handled many crises over the years. "We're all free to walk around, Dell. It's somewhere in the Constitution."

"What if he infects somebody else? Then what'll you say?"

"We checked with the state health department. AIDS killed seventy-three people last year in Mississippi, so those folks have seen it before. AIDS ain't like the flu. The only way to catch it is through body fluids."

Silence, as Dell and the rest of the customers thought hard about all the different fluids the human body can produce. During the pause the chief worked on a mouthful of pancakes, and after he swallowed, he said, "Look, no need to get excited. We're watchin' thangs closely. He's not botherin' anybody. Just sits on the porch mainly, him and Emporia."

"I hear folks're already upset down there."

"That's what they say."

At the barbershop, a regular said, "I hear the coloreds ain't too happy down there. Word's out they got this funny boy hidin' in one of his dead daddy's old rental houses. Folks're angry."

"Can't blame them. What if he moved in next to you?"

"I'd get my shotgun and keep his ass on his side of the fence, for sure."

"He's not hurtin' anybody. What's all the fuss?"

"I read an article last night. They're predictin' AIDS will become the deadliest disease in the history of the world. It'll kill millions, mainly in Africa, where evidently ever'body just screws ever'body."

"Thought that was Hollywood."

"There too. California has more AIDS cases than any other state."

"Ain't that where the Keane boy picked it up?"

"That's what they say."

"It's hard to believe we got AIDS here in Clanton in 1989."

In the clerk's office, a young lady named Beth had center stage over doughnuts because her husband was a city police officer and yesterday he'd been sent to check on things in Lowtown. He drove past the little pink house of Emporia Nester, and sure enough, as rumored, sitting there on the front porch was a pale, emaciated young white man. Neither the policeman nor his wife had ever met Adrian Keane, but since half the town had been scrambling to find old yearbooks from Clanton High, there were class photos circulating. Since the policeman had been trained to quickly identify suspects, he was fairly certain that he had seen Adrian Keane.

"Why are the police watchin' him?" Myra asked, somewhat irritated.

"Well, my husband was there because that's what he was told to do," Beth answered sharply.

"It's not a crime to have a disease, is it?" Myra shot back.

"No, but the police are supposed to protect the public, aren't they?"

"So, by watchin' Adrian Keane and makin' sure he stays on the porch, the rest of us will be safer, is that what you're sayin', Beth?"

"I didn't say that, so don't put words in my mouth. I can speak for myself."

And so it went.

He slept late and stayed in the bed for a long time, staring at the white board ceiling and wondering how many days were left. Then he again asked himself why he was where he was, but he knew the answer. He had watched so many of his friends waste away. Months earlier he had made the decision that those friends still living would not be burdened with watching him. It was easier to say good-bye with a quick kiss and a strong embrace, while he was still able.

His first night in the pink house had been the usual series of chills and sweats, memories and nightmares, brief naps and long periods of staring into the darkness. He was tired when he awoke, and he knew the fatigue would never leave. Eventually, he eased out of bed, got dressed, then faced the chemicals. There were over a dozen bottles of pills, all lined up in a neat row, all in an order that the doctors had decreed. The first barrage included eight medications, and he washed them down with a glass of water. He would return several times during the day for more combinations, and as he screwed the caps back on, he thought about how futile it was. The pills were not advanced enough to save his life—that cure was so far away—but designed only to prolong it. Maybe. Why bother? The cost was $1,000 a month, money his family grudgingly supplied. Two friends had committed suicide, and that thought was never far away.

The house was already warm, and he remembered the long humid days of his childhood, the hot, sticky summers he had not missed in his other life.

He heard Emporia in the kitchen and went to say hello.

He didn't eat meat or dairy products, so they eventually settled on a plate of sliced tomatoes from her garden. A strange breakfast, she thought, but Aunt Leona had said to feed him whatever he wanted. "He's been gone for a long time," she'd said. Afterward, they fixed cups of instant chicory coffee with sugar and moved to the front porch.

Emporia wanted to know all about New York City, a place she'd only read about and seen on television. Adrian described it, talked about his years there, college, his first job, the crowded streets, endless stores and shops, ethnic neighborhoods, masses of people, and wild nightlife. A lady at least as old as Emporia stopped in front of the house and called out, "Hello, Emporia."

"Mornin', Doris. Come sit with us."

Doris did not hesitate. Introductions were made, without handshakes. Doris was the wife of Herman Grant, from across the street, a very close friend of Emporia's. If she was nervous around Adrian, it was not evident. Within minutes the two women were talking about their new preacher, a man they were not sure they liked, and from there they launched into church gossip. For some time they forgot about Adrian, who was content to listen with amusement. When they finished with church business, they moved on to the families. Emporia, of course, had no children, but Doris had enough for both. Eight, most of them scattered up north, with thirty-some-odd grandchildren and younger ones after that. All sorts of adventures and conflicts were discussed.

After an hour of listening, Adrian jumped in during a pause. "Say, Emporia, I need to go to the library and check out some books. It's probably too far to walk."

Emporia and Doris looked at him oddly, but held their tongues. Even a casual glance at Adrian revealed a man too frail to make it to the end of the street. In this heat the poor boy would collapse within a rock's throw of the pink house.

Clanton had one library, near the square, and had never considered a branch in Lowtown.

"How do you get around?" he asked. It was obvious Emporia did not own a car.

"Just call the Black and White."

"The what?"

"Black and White Taxi," Doris said. "Use 'em all the time."

"You don't know the Black and White?" Emporia asked.

"I've been gone for fourteen years."

"Yes, you have. It's a long story," Emporia said as she shifted her weight and settled in for the tale.

"Yes, it is," Doris added.

"There are two brothers, both named Hershel. One black, one white, about the same age. I'd say forty, wouldn't you, Doris?"

"Forty's 'bout right."

"Same father, different mothers. One over here. One over there. Father ran off long ago, and the Hershels knew the truth but couldn't come to grips with it. Eventually, they got together and accepted what the whole town knew anyway. They sorta look alike, don't you thank, Doris?"

"White one's taller, but the colored one's even got green eyes."

"So they start a taxi company. Got a couple of old Fords with a million miles. Painted 'em black and white, and that's the name of the company. They pick up folks here and haul 'em over there to clean houses and shop, and they sometimes pick up folks over there and bring 'em here."

"For what?" Adrian asked.

Emporia looked at Doris, who met her gaze, then looked away. Adrian smelled some wonderful small-town dirt and wasn't about to back off. "So, tell me ladies. Why do the taxis bring white folks across the tracks?"

"They have some poker games over here," Emporia admitted. "From what I hear."

"And some women," Doris added quietly.

"And illegal whiskey."

"I see," Adrian said.

Now that the truth was out, the three of them watched a

young mother walk down the street with a brown sack of groceries.

"So, I can just call one of the Hershels and catch a ride to the library?" Adrian asked.

"I'm happy to call for you. They know me well."

"They're nice boys," Doris added. Emporia left the porch and went inside. Adrian smiled to himself and tried to believe the story of two brothers named Hershel.

"She's a sweet woman," Doris said, fanning herself.

"She certainly is," he said.

"Just never found the right man."

"How long have you known her?"

"Not long. Thirty years, maybe."

"Thirty years is not long?"

A chuckle. "Maybe to you, but some of these folks along here I grew up with, and I grew up a long time ago. How old you thank I am?"

"Forty-five."

"You're full of baloney. I'll be eighty in three months."

"No."

"God's truth."

"How old is Herman?"

"Says he's eighty-two, but you can't believe him."

"How long you been married?"

"Got married when I was fifteen. Long time ago."

"And you have eight children?"

"Got eight. Herman, he's got eleven."

"Herman has more children than you do?"

"He's got three outside children."

Adrian decided not to explore the concept of outside children. Maybe he understood this when he lived in Clanton, maybe not. Emporia returned with a tray of glasses and a pitcher of ice water. To ease her mind, Adrian had insisted, gently, that he use the same glass, plate, bowl, cup, knife, fork, and spoon every time. She poured ice water, with lemon, into his designated glass, an odd souvenir from the county fair, 1977.

"Got the white Hershel. He'll be here in a minute," Emporia said.

They sipped the ice water, fanned themselves, discussed the heat. Doris said, "He thanks I'm forty-five years old, Emporia. Whatta you say 'bout that?"

"White folks can't tell. There's the cab."

Evidently, business was slow for a Tuesday morning because the car arrived less than five minutes after Emporia called. It was indeed an old Ford Fairlane, black with white doors and a white hood, clean with shiny wheels, phone numbers on the fenders.

Adrian stood and slowly stretched, as if every movement had to be contemplated. "Well, I'll be back in an hour or so. I'm just going to the library to get a few books."

"You gonna be all right now?" Emporia asked with great concern.

"Sure. I'll be fine. Nice to meet you, Miss Doris," he said, almost like a real Southerner.

"I'll be seein' you," Doris said with a huge smile.

Adrian stepped off the porch, down the steps, and was halfway to the street when the white Hershel scrambled out of the car and yelled, "Oh no! No way in hell you're gettin' in my taxi!" He walked to the front of the car and pointed angrily at Adrian. "I've heard about you!"

Adrian froze, stunned, unable to respond.

Hershel kept on. "You ain't ruinin' my business!"

Emporia was at the steps. She said, "It's okay, now, Hershel. You have my word."

"That's enough, Miss Nester. This ain't about you. He ain't gettin' in my car. You shoulda told me it was him."

"Now, Hershel."

"Ever'body in town knows about him. No way. No way in hell." Hershel stomped back to the open driver's door, got in, slammed it, and sped away. Adrian watched the car as it disap-peared down the street, then slowly turned and walked up the steps, past the women, and into the house. He was tired and needed a nap.

❦

The books arrived late in the afternoon. Doris had a niece who taught in the elementary school, and she agreed to check out whatever Adrian wanted. He had decided to finally con-front the fictional world of William Faulkner, an author who'd been forced upon him in high school. Back then, Adrian be-lieved, as did all students in Mississippi, that there was a state law requiring English teachers to include Faulkner. He had struggled through *A Fable, Requiem for a Nun, The Unvan-quished,* and others he'd tried to forget, and he'd finally sur-rendered in bewildering defeat halfway through *The Sound and* the *Fury*. Now, in his last days, he was determined to understand Faulkner.

After dinner, or "supper," as it was called, he sat on the porch while Emporia washed the dishes and started at the beginning, with *Soldiers' Pay*, published in 1926, when Faulkner was just twenty-nine. He read a few pages and stopped for a break. He listened to the sounds around him: the soft laughter from the other porches, the squeals of children playing in the distance, a television three doors down, the shrill voice of a woman angry at her husband. He watched the languid foot traffic on Roosevelt, and was quite aware of the curious looks when anyone walked past the pink house. He always smiled and nodded when there was eye contact, and there were a few reluctant hellos in return.

At dusk, Emporia came to the porch and settled herself into her favorite rocker. Nothing was said for a while. Nothing needed to be said because by now they were old friends.

Finally, she said, "I feel real bad about Hershel and his taxi."

"Don't worry yourself with it. I understand."

"He's just ignorant."

"I've seen far worse, Emporia, and so have you."

"I suppose. But that don't make it right."

"No, it doesn't."

"Can I get you some iced tea?"

"No. I'd like something stronger."

She thought about this for a second and didn't respond.

"Look, Emporia, I know you don't drink, but I do. I'm not a big boozer, but I'd really like a drink."

"I've never had alcohol in my house."

"Then I'll drink on the porch. Right here."

"I'm a Christian woman, Adrian."

"I know a lot of Christians who drink. Look at First Timothy, chapter 5, verse 23, where Paul tells Timothy to have a little wine to settle his stomach."

"You got problems with your stomach?"

"I got problems everywhere. I need some wine to make me feel better."

"I don't know about this."

"It would make you feel better too."

"My stomach's good."

"Fine. You drink tea and I'll drink wine."

"Where you gonna find wine. Liquor stores are closed."

"They close at ten o'clock. State law. I'll bet there's one not far from here."

"Look here, I can't tell you what not to do, but it'd be a big mistake for you to go to the whiskey store at this hour of the day. You might not make it back." She couldn't imagine a white man, especially one in his condition, walking four blocks to Willie Ray's whiskey store, where the young toughs loitered in the parking lot, buying his liquor, then making it back to her house. "It's a bad idea, let me tell you."

A few minutes passed without a word. A man approached on foot in the middle of the street. "Who's that guy?" Adrian asked.

"Carver Sneed."

"Nice fella?"

"He's all right."

Adrian suddenly called out, "Mr. Sneed!"

Carver was in his late twenties and currently living with his parents at the far end of Roosevelt Street. He was going nowhere, in fact was walking by for the sole purpose of catching a glimpse of the "ghost" who was dying on Emporia Nester's porch. He had not planned to come face-to-face with the man. He veered over to the picket fence and said, "Evenin', Miss Emporia."

Adrian was standing at the top step.

"This here is Adrian," Emporia said, not happy with the encounter.

"Nice to meet you, Carver," Adrian said.

"And you."

No sense wasting time, Adrian thought. "Don't suppose you'd make a run to the liquor store, would you?" he said. "I'd like something to drink, and Miss Emporia here doesn't keep much in the way of liquor."

"Ain't no whiskey in my house," she said. "Never has been."

"I'll buy you a six-pack of beer for your trouble," Adrian added quickly.

Carver walked to the steps and looked up at Adrian, then he looked at Emporia, who sat with her arms folded across her chest and her jaws clenched. "He for real?" he asked Emporia.

"He ain't lied yet," she said. "Not sayin' he won't."

"Whatta you want from the store?" Carver asked Adrian.

"I'd like some wine, preferably a chardonnay."

"A what?"

"Any kind of white wine will do."

"Willie Ray don't carry much wine. Not much of a demand for it."

Adrian was suddenly worried about the definition of wine on this side of the tracks. The selection on the other side was paltry enough. He could almost see a bottle of spiked fruit juice with a screw-on cap. "Does Willie Ray have any wine with corks in the bottles?"

Carver pondered this for a moment, then said, "What's the cork for?"

"How do you open the wine bottles at Willie Ray's?"

"Screw off the top."

"I see. And about how much is a bottle of wine at Willie Ray's?"

Carver shrugged and said, "I don't buy much. I prefer beer."

"Just guess. How much?"

"Boone's Farm'll run you 'bout four bucks a bottle."

Adrian took some cash out of the right pocket of his dungarees. "Let's forget the wine. I want you to buy the most expensive bottle of tequila you can find in the store. Got it?"

"Whatever you say."

"Buy a six-pack for you, and bring me the change." Adrian held out the cash, but Carver froze. He looked at the money, looked at Adrian, then looked at Emporia for help.

"It's okay," Adrian said. "You can't get sick from handling money."

Carver still couldn't move, couldn't force himself to reach up and take the cash.

"No need to worry, Carver," Emporia said, suddenly anxious to help with the transaction. "Trust me."

"I swear you'll be fine," Adrian said.

Carver began shaking his head, then began backing away. "I'm sorry," he mumbled, almost to himself.

Adrian returned the cash to his pocket as he watched Carver disappear into the night. His legs were weak, and he needed to sit, maybe to sleep. He slowly squatted, then came to rest on the top step, where he leaned his head on the rail and for a long time said nothing. Emporia moved behind him and went into the house.

When she returned to the porch, she asked, "Does 'tequila' have a *q* or a *c* in it?"

"Forget it, Emporia."

"A *q* or a *c*?" She brushed by him and went down the steps onto the walkway.

"No, Emporia. Please. I'm not thirsty anymore."

"I think it's a 'q,' am I right?" She was in the street, wearing an old pair of white sneakers and moving away at an impressive gait.

"It's *q*," Adrian yelled.

"I knew it," came the reply, two doors down.

⚓

And often the rumors were completely false, outright fabrications created by those who either enjoyed watching their little lies sweep around the town or found pleasure in causing trouble.

The latest one began in the courthouse, on the second floor, in the office of the chancery clerk, where the lawyers came and went at all hours of the day. When a group of lawyers gathered to do title work, there was no shortage of gossip. Since the Keane family was getting more than its share of attention at the moment, it was only natural that the lawyers played an active role in the discussions. Even more natural that one of them would start trouble.

Though variations of it cropped up immediately, the basic rumor was: Adrian had more money than most people thought because his grandfather had set up some complicated trusts before Adrian was even born, and upon his fortieth birthday he would inherit an impressive sum, but since he wouldn't see his fortieth birthday, the inheritance could be transferred by him through a last will and testament to any beneficiary he wanted. And the good part: an unnamed lawyer had been hired by Adrian to draft his last will and testament, with directions that this mysterious future inheritance would be given to (a) Emporia Nester, or (b) a new gay rights advocacy group that was struggling to get started over in Tupelo, or (c) a boyfriend back in San Francisco, or (d) a college scholarship fund for black students only. Take your pick.

Because of its complexity, the rumor got little traction and almost sank under its own weight. When people whispered about, say, who's seeing someone else's wife, the issue was fairly straightforward and easily grasped. But most folks had no experience with generation-skipping trusts and inheritances and other lawyerly creations, and the details became far more muddled than usual. By the time Dell finished with it at the coffee shop, the boy was due a fortune, of which Emporia would get the most, and his family was threatening to sue.

Only at the barbershop did a voice of reason ask the obvious. "If he's got money, why is he dyin' away in an old shack down in Lowtown?"

Whereupon an argument ensued about how much money he actually had. The majority view was that he had little, but was counting on the inheritance from the trusts. One brave soul mocked the others, claiming it was all nonsense, claiming to know for a fact that the entire Keane clan was "as poor as Job's turkey."

"Look at the old house," he said. "They're too poor to paint and too proud to whitewash."

†

In late June, the heat rose to a new level, and Adrian kept to himself in his room, near the noisy air conditioner that barely worked. The fevers arrived with greater frequency, and he simply could not survive the heavy, suffocating air on the front porch. In his room, he wore nothing but his underwear, which was often soaked with sweat. He read Faulkner and wrote dozens of letters to friends from his other life. And he slept, off and on, throughout the day. A nurse stopped by every third day for a quick exam and another supply of pills, all of which he was now flushing down the toilet.

Emporia worked hard to put some fat on him, but he had no appetite. Since she had never cooked for a family, she had limited experience in the kitchen. Her small garden produced enough tomatoes, squashes, peas, butter beans, and cantaloupes to keep her fed throughout the year, and Adrian gamely tried to enjoy the generous meals she prepared. She convinced him to eat corn bread—though it contained butter, milk, and eggs. She had never met a person who refused meat, fish, chicken, and dairy products, and more than once she asked, "All them folks in California eat like that?"

"No, but there are a lot of vegetarians."

"You was raised better."

"Let's not talk about the way I was raised, Emporia. My entire childhood was a nightmare."

She set the table three times a day, at the hours he chose, and they worked at prolonging the meals. Adrian knew it was important for her to make sure he was properly fed, and he ate as much as he could. It was obvious, though, that after two weeks he was still losing weight.

It was during lunch that the preacher called. Emporia, as always, answered the phone, which hung on a wall in the kitchen. Adrian was certainly permitted to use the phone, but he rarely did. There was no one to talk to in Clanton. He did not call anyone in his family, and they did not call him. There were friends in San Francisco, but they were almost all gone now, and he did not want to hear their voices.

"Good afternoon, Reverend," she said, then turned away and stretched the cord as far as possible. They talked briefly, and she hung up with a pleasant "I'll see you at three o'clock." She sat down and immediately took a bite of corn bread.

"So how's the reverend?" Adrian asked.

"Fine, I reckon."

"He's coming by at three this afternoon?"

"No. I'll run by the church. Said he wants to talk about somethin'."

"Any idea what?"

"You're right curious these days."

"Well, Emporia, I've lived in Lowtown for two weeks now, and I've realized that everybody's business belongs to everybody else. It's almost impolite not to pry a little. Plus, gay people are nosier than straight people. Did you know that?"

"Ain't never heard such."

"It's true. It's a proven fact. So why won't the reverend stop by and see you? Isn't that part of his job, making house calls, checking on his flock, welcoming newcomers like me? I saw him three days ago over on the porch chatting with Doris and Herman. Kept looking over here like he might catch a fever. You don't like him, do you?"

"I liked the other man better."

"Me too. I'm not going to church with you, Emporia, so please don't ask me again."

"I've only asked you twice."

"Yes, and I've said thanks. It's very nice of you, but I have no interest in going to your church or any other. Not sure I'd be too welcome anywhere these days."

She had no comment.

"I had this dream the other night. There was a revival service at a church, white church, here in Clanton, one of those rowdy hell-fire-and-brimstone affairs with people rolling in the aisles and fainting and the choir singing 'Shall We Gather at the River' at full throttle, and the preacher was at the altar begging and pleading for all sinners to come on down and surrender all. You get the picture."

"Ever' Sunday."

"And I walked through the door, dressed in white, looking

worse than I look now, and I started down the aisle toward the preacher. He had this look of terror on his face, couldn't say a word. The choir stopped mid-stanza. Everyone froze as I kept walking down the aisle, which took a long time. Finally, someone yelled, 'It's him! The guy with AIDS!' Somebody else yelled, 'Run!' And all hell broke loose. There was a stampede. Mothers grabbed their children. I kept walking down the aisle. Men jumped out of windows. I kept walking. These really large women in gold choir robes were falling all over their fat asses trying to get out of the sanctuary. I kept walking toward the preacher, and finally, just as I got to him, I reached out my hand. He didn't move. He couldn't speak. The church was empty, not a sound." Adrian took a sip of tea and wiped his forehead.

"Go on. What happened then?"

"Don't know, I woke up, and I had a good laugh. Dreams can be very real. I guess some sinners are too far gone."

"That's not what the Bible says."

"Thank you, Emporia. And thank you for lunch. I need to lie down now."

At 3:00 p.m., Emporia met with Reverend Biler in his office at the church. Such a meeting in such a place could only mean trouble, and not long after the initial pleasantries the reverend got to the point, or at least to one of them. "I hear you've been seen in Willie Ray's whiskey store."

This was no surprise whatsoever, and Emporia was ready. "I'm seventy-five years old, at least thirty years older than you, and if I choose to buy medication for a friend, then I'll do so."

"Medication?"

"That's what he calls it, and I told his family he'd be properly medicated."

"Call it whatever you want, Emporia, but the elders are upset over this. One of our senior ladies seen in a whiskey store. What kind of example is that for our youth?"

"It's my job, and this job won't last much longer."

"There's a rumor you've invited him to worship with us."

Thank you, Doris, Emporia thought but didn't say. Doris was the only person she'd told about inviting Adrian to church. "I invite everyone to worship with us, Reverend. That's what you want. That's what the Bible says."

"Well, this is a little different."

"Don't worry. He ain't comin'."

"Praise the Lord. The wages of sin is death, Emporia, and this young man is paying for his sins."

"Yes, he is."

"And how safe are you, Emporia? This disease is sweeping across our country, across the world. It's highly contagious, and, to be honest with you, there are grave concerns in our community over your safety. Why are you running this risk? Why take this chance? It seems so unlike you."

"The nurse tells me I'm safe. I keep him clean and fed, and medicated, and I wear rubber gloves when I do his laundry. The virus is spread through intercourse and blood, both of which are being avoided." She smiled. He did not.

He folded his hands together and set them on the desk, very piouslike. His face was hard when he said, "Some of our members are uneasy around you."

She had anticipated everything but that, and when she realized the meaning of it, she was speechless.

"You touch what he touches. You breathe the same air, eat the same food, drink the same water and tea, and God knows what else these days. You clean his clothes and laundry and bedsheets, and you wear rubber gloves because of the virus. Shouldn't that tell you how great the danger is, Emporia? Then you bring the germs here, to the house of the Lord."

"I'm safe, Reverend. I know I'm safe."

"Maybe so, but perception is everything. Some of your brothers and sisters here think you're crazy for doing this, and they are afraid."

"Someone has to care for him."

"These are wealthy white people, Emporia."

"He has no one else."

"We'll not argue that. My concern is my church."

"It's my church too. I was here long before you came, and now you're askin' me to stay away?"

"I want you to consider a leave of absence, until he passes."

Minutes dragged by without a word. Emporia, her eyes wet but her head high, stared through a window and watched the leaves of a tree. Biler remained motionless and studied his hands. When she finally stood, she said, "Then let's call it a leave of absence, Reverend. It'll start now, and it'll be over when I decide it's over. And while I'm absent, I'll walk in the whiskey store anytime I choose, and you and your little spies can gossip all you want."

He was following her to the door. "Don't overreact, Emporia. We all love you."

"I feel the love."

"And we'll be prayin' for you, and for him."

"I'm sure he'll be pleased to hear that."

⚜

The lawyer's name was Fred Mays, and his was the only name in the yellow pages that Adrian recognized. Adrian spoke briefly with him on the phone, then wrote him a long letter. At four o'clock on a Friday afternoon Mays and a secretary parked in front of the pink house. Mays unloaded his briefcase. He also unloaded a case of wine from the nicer liquor store on the other side of the tracks. Emporia walked across the street to visit Doris so the legal matters could be tended to in private.

Contrary to the varied rumors floating around, Adrian had nothing in the way of assets. There was no mysterious trust created by long-dead relatives. The will prepared by Mays required all of one page, with the remnants of Adrian's dwindling supply of cash going to Emporia. The second document, and the more important one, set forth the burial arrangements. When everything was signed and notarized, Mays hung around for a glass of wine and some idle talk about Clanton. The glass of wine didn't last long. Mays and his secretary seemed anxious to conclude the meeting. They left, good-byes and nods but no handshakes, and as soon as they were back in the office on the square, they were describing the boy's dreadful condition.

The following Sunday, Emporia complained of a headache and announced she would not go to church. It was raining, and the weather gave her another excuse to stay home. They ate biscuits on the porch and watched the storm.

"How's your headache?" Adrian asked.

"It's better. Thank you."

"You told me once you haven't missed church in over forty years. Why are you staying home today?"

"I don't feel too good, Adrian. It's that simple."

"You and the preacher have a falling-out?"

"No."

"Are you sure?"

"I said no."

"You haven't been yourself since you met with him the other day. I think he said something to offend you, and I think it was something to do with me. Doris comes over less and less. Herman, never. Isabelle hasn't stopped by in a week. The phone doesn't ring as much. Now you're staying away from church. If you ask me, I'd say Lowtown is giving you the cold shoulder, and it's all because of me."

She didn't argue. How could she? He was telling the truth, and any objection from her would ring false.

Thunder rattled the windows and the wind turned, blowing rain onto the porch. They went inside, Emporia to the kitchen, Adrian to his room, with the door closed. He stripped to his underwear and reclined on the bed. He was almost finished with *As I Lay Dying*, Faulkner's fifth novel and one Adrian had seriously considered skipping, for obvious reasons. But he found it much more accessible than the others, and unexpectedly humorous. He finished it in an hour, and fell asleep.

By late afternoon the rain was gone; the air was clear and pleasant. After a light supper of peas and corn bread, they drifted back to the porch, where Adrian soon announced that his stomach was in disarray and he need some wine, per First Timothy, chapter 5, verse 23. His designated wineglass was a cracked coffee mug with permanent chicory stains. He'd taken a few sips when Emporia announced, "You know, my stomach is a bit unsettled too. I might try some of that."

Adrian smiled and said, "Wonderful. I'll get it."

"No. You sit tight. I know where the bottle is."

She returned with a similar mug and settled into her rocking chair. "Cheers," Adrian said, happy to have a drinking buddy.

Emporia took a swallow, smacked her lips, and said, "Not bad."

"It's a chardonnay. Good, but not great. The best they had in the store."

"It'll do," she said, still cautious.

After the second cup she started giggling. It was dark and the street was quiet.

"Somethin' I've wanted to ask you," she said.

"Anything."

"When did you realize that you were, you know, different? How old were you?"

A pause, a long sip of wine, a story he'd told before but only to those who understood. "Things were pretty normal until I was about twelve. Cub Scouts, baseball and soccer, camping and fishing, the usual boy stuff, but as puberty loomed down the road, I began to realize I wasn't interested in girls. The other boys talked about girls and girls, but I just didn't care. I lost interest in sports and began to read about art and design and fashion. As I got older, the boys got more involved with girls, but not me. I knew something was wrong. I had a friend, Matt Mason, a great-looking guy who drove the girls crazy. One day I realized I had a crush on him too, but, of course, I never told anyone. I fantasized about the guy. It drove me nuts; then I started looking at other boys and thinking about them. When I was fifteen, I finally admitted to myself that I was gay. By then, the other kids were beginning to whisper. I couldn't wait to get out of here and live the way I wanted."

"Do you have any regrets?"

"Regrets? No, I don't regret being what I am. Wish I wasn't sick, but then so does everybody else with a terminal illness."

She set her empty cup on the wicker table and gazed into the darkness. The porch light was off. They sat in the shadows, rocking slowly. "Can I tell you somethin' private?" she said.

"Of course. I'll take it to my grave."

"Well, I was sorta like you, except I never liked boys. I never thought about bein' different, you know, and I never thought somethin' was wrong with me. But I never wanted to be with no man."

"You never had a boyfriend?"

"Maybe, one time. There was a boy hangin' around the house, and I felt like I needed to have a boy, you know. My family was gettin' worried 'cause I was almost twenty and still single. We went to bed a few times, but I didn't like it. In fact, it made me sick. I couldn't stand bein' touched like that. You promise you won't tell, now."

"I promise. And who would I tell?"

"I trust you."

"Your secret is safe. Have you ever told anyone else?"

"Lord, no. I wouldn't dare."

"Did you ever fool around with a girl?"

"Son, you just didn't do thangs like that back then. They'd ship you off to the nuthouse."

"And now?"

She shook her head and thought about this. "Ever' now and then, there's some gossip 'bout a boy over here who won't fit in, but it's kept real quiet. You hear rumors, you know, but no one ever comes out and lives openly, know what I mean?"

"I do indeed."

"But I've never heard of a woman over here who goes for other women. I suspect they keep it hidden and get married and never tell a soul. Or they do like me—they just play along and say they never found the right man."

"That's sad."

"I'm not sad, Adrian. I've had a happy life. How 'bout just a touch more wine?"

"Good idea."

She hurried away, anxious to leave the conversation behind.

✿

The fevers returned and did not go away. His skin leaked sweat, then he began to cough, a painful hacking cough that gripped him like a seizure and left him too weak to move. Emporia washed and ironed sheets throughout the day, and at night she could only listen to the painful sounds from his room. She prepared meals he could not eat. She put on gloves and bathed him with cold water, neither bothered by his nakedness. His arms and legs were like broom handles now, and he was not strong enough to walk to the front porch. He no longer wanted to be seen by the neighbors, so he stayed in bed, waiting. The nurse came every day now, but did nothing but check his temperature, rearrange his pill bottles, and shake her head gravely at Emporia.

On the last night, Adrian managed to dress himself in a pair of twill slacks and a white cotton shirt. He neatly packed his shoes and clothing in his two leather suitcases, and when everything was in order, he took the black pill and washed it down with wine. He stretched out on the bed, looked around the room, placed an envelope on his chest, managed a smile, and closed his eyes for the last time.

By ten the next morning, Emporia realized she had not heard a sound from him. She pecked on the door to his bedroom, and when she stepped in, there was Adrian, neatly dressed, still smiling, eternally at rest.

The letter read:

Dear Emporia:

Please destroy this letter after you read it. I'm sorry you found me like this, but this moment was, after all, inevitable. The disease had run its course and my time was up. I simply decided to speed things up a bit.

Fred Mays, the lawyer, has taken care of the final arrangements. Please call him first. He will call the coroner, who will come here and pronounce me legally dead. Since neither of the funeral homes in town would handle my body, a rescue-squad ambulance will take me to a crematorium in Tupelo. There, they will happily incinerate me and place my ashes in a container made for the occasion. Standard container, nothing fancy. Fred will then bring my ashes back to Clanton and deliver them to Mr. Franklin Walker at the funeral home here in Lowtown. Mr. Walker has agreed, reluctantly, to bury me in the black section of the cemetery, as far away from my family's plot as possible.

All of this will be done quickly, and, I hope, without the knowledge of my family. I do not want those people getting involved, not that they will want to be. Fred has my written instructions and plans to deal with them, if necessary.

When my ashes are buried, I'd be honored if you would offer a silent word or two. And feel free to stop by my little spot occasionally and leave some flowers. Again, nothing fancy.

There are four bottles of wine left in the fridge. Please drink in remembrance of me.

Thank you so much for your kindness. You've made my last

days bearable, even enjoyable at times. You're a wonderful human being, and you deserve to be what you are.

Love, Adrian

Emporia sat on the edge of the bed for a long time, wiping her eyes and even patting his knee. Then she collected herself and went to the kitchen, where she threw the letter in the trash and picked up the phone.